VALLEY OF THE KINGS

Center Point
Large Print

Also by Arthur Henry Gooden and available from Center Point Large Print:

Call of the Range
Death Rides the Range

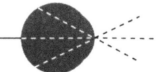
This Large Print Book carries the Seal of Approval of N.A.V.H.

VALLEY
OF THE
KINGS

ARTHUR HENRY GOODEN

CENTER POINT LARGE PRINT
THORNDIKE, MAINE

This Center Point Large Print edition
is published in the year 2024 by arrangement with
Golden West Inc.

Copyright © 1935 by Arthur Henry Gooden.

All rights reserved.

First published in the US by
H. C. Kinsey & Company, Inc.

The text of this Large Print edition is unabridged.
In other aspects, this book may vary
from the original edition.
Printed in the United States of America
on permanent paper sourced using
environmentally responsible foresting methods.
Set in 16-point Times New Roman type.

ISBN 979-8-89164-106-8 (hardcover)
ISBN 979-8-89164-110-5 (paperback)

The Library of Congress has cataloged this record
under Library of Congress Control Number: 2023952075

To
Marian Postlethwaite Greene

CONTENTS

CHAPTER		PAGE
I.	OMENS	11
II.	IN THE VALLEY OF THE KINGS	23
III.	DEATH IN THE DESERT	40
IV.	THE SECRET TOKEN	52
V.	MARIA AND MIGUEL	62
VI.	BILL BRANT'S GRANDSON	68
VII.	SAM HALLY SINGS AN OLD SONG	82
VIII.	COUNCIL FIRES	100
IX.	POP DALY WANTS TO KNOW	116
X.	SANDELL SMELLS DANGER	137
XI.	GUNSMOKE	161
XII.	DARK HOURS	176

XIII.	THE PAINTED VALLEY	192
XIV.	THE DEVIL'S PITCHFORK	205
XV.	CHICO LOPEZ TALKS	223
XVI.	A MESSAGE FROM SAM	235
XVII.	NEWS FOR SHIRLEY	241
XVIII.	A MAN DIES	254
XIX.	MOONLIGHT—AND A KISS	260
XX.	SHIRLEY RIDES ALONE	279
XXI.	BEFORE THE DAWN	288
XXII.	THE BOTTLE NECK	295
XXIII.	MIDNIGHT LOOKS THE OTHER WAY	304
XXIV.	TRAMPLING HOOVES	315
XXV.	THE DAY'S WORK DONE	317

VALLEY
OF THE
KINGS

CHAPTER I
OMENS

They rode stirrup to stirrup, spurs jingling soft music, eyes wary under wide-brimmed hats pulled low against the glare of the desert sunrise.

Grizzled veterans of the western cattle country, these two bronzed-faced hardy riders; perhaps in their early sixties—still lean of waist and lance-straight; strong stalwart men, whom years of clean living in the open had toughened and seasoned and ripened with the wisdom that experience alone can give.

The man on the big roan was tall and lanky, considerably over six feet; he had deep-set, horizon-blue eyes, and drooping mustaches that framed an out-flung square jaw. He swayed easily to the roan's rhythmic running-walk, a wide-shouldered giant whose kindly, tolerant expression did much to soften a somewhat stern face.

His companion was shorter by several inches, a sturdy little man with twinkling bright black eyes. Despite the almost cherubic look of him there was something formidable about the rider of the chunky bay horse—a bleakness when the twinkle left the eyes.

He broke the silence, spoke softly, reflectively.

"Supposing Clay Brant don't show up today, Sam? What you aim to do if he don't show up at the Injun Head today?"

"We ain't got to *that* ford, yet, Seth," answered his big companion, placidly.

"This makes three times we done rode out here to meet him," worried the little man. "Looks kind of bad, Sam."

"Long ways from Cimarron, Seth. The day ain't done, yet—"

"You make me sick!" declared his friend irritably; "don't you ever worry none—you dang old longhorn?"

The roan's tall rider chuckled reminiscently. "You and me is both a pair of old mossy horns, Seth. We done pushed a heap of 'em up the old Chisolm Trail in our time."

"Sure took plenty dust doing the same," grunted the bay's rider.

"Dust—hard knocks—didn't fuss us none, feller. We was young—sort o' reckless—ready for any trouble that come on the prod." The big man chuckled.

His partner snorted. "Speak for your own self, mister! I ain't laid away on a shelf yet by a dang sight. Mebbe we're a pair of mossy horns—but I figger our horns is still plenty sharp."

They rode on, in silence, memories leaping down the long lane of the years, to the wild, roaring saga of Cattle, when the southwest was one vast free range. Memories of countless herds on the march from Texas to faraway northern markets—the Pecos—the Red River; the Canadian, the Cimarron; treacherous quicksands, Indians, rustlers—the dread stampede. Memories of the stirring, history-building days of their lusty youth; memories of turbulent frontier towns—far-flung outposts of a virile young nation—Dodge, Abilene, Tascosa—memories of old friends long since gone.

Suddenly the taller rider straightened his lank frame.

"Somebody heading this way," he said softly.

"A gal!" exclaimed his companion in a surprised voice; "what you s'pose a female's doing way out here in the rimrock this time of day?"

They slowed their horses to a walk, watched with lively interest as the newcomer emerged from the coulée.

Glimpsing the approaching riders the girl reined her horse, then with a wave of recognition came loping toward them.

"*Buenos dias*!" she greeted brightly; "what brings Sam Hally and Seth McGee so far from home? I thought your range was over in the Spanish Sinks country!"

"You ain't thinking wrong, Miss Shirley," chuckled the tall Sam Hally; "Seth and me has a mighty nice place over in the Sinks. The HM outfit mebbe ain't so big, but we figger she'll keep us from the poor-house in our old age."

"Oh, I'm so glad, Sam! You and Seth both deserve success."

A touch of sadness crept into the girl's voice. "Dad never quite got over you two leaving the old Box B. Somehow, things never seemed to go just right—after you two old darlings left the ranch."

Stirrup leathers squeaked as the two cowmen shifted uneasily in their saddles; a strained, far-away look was in Seth McGee's black eyes, a deep red stained the weathered face of Sam Hally. The latter spoke in a husky voice.

"How's things at the old ranch, Miss Shirley?"

"Not so good, Sam," answered the girl. She was suddenly pale, they saw. "You—you haven't heard about—about what's happened, then?"

They nodded, faces hard grim masks.

"You—you know that Dad was—killed by rustlers?"

Again the two cowmen nodded, exchanged brief looks.

"Ed Benson was one fine hombre, and a good cowman," Seth McGee said in his cold, thin voice.

"One fine hombre!" echoed Sam Hally's deep growl. "Seth and me knowed Ed Benson afore you was born and we know they don't come better than him—"

"It left things in an awful mess," confided the

girl. She smiled wistfully. "It's good to see you two old darlings again," she added.

They looked at her with admiring, approving eyes. Five years had transformed Ed Benson's girl into a comely young woman, straight and supple, with bright fair hair tucked under a jaunty black sombrero—an eager, lovely face.

"How do you mean—things is in an awful mess, Miss Shirley?" queried Sam Hally in his deep, gentle voice.

"Oh—" she shrugged slim shoulders, "maybe you can guess. You know the ranch has been carrying a mortgage for years, and, well—the old mortgage has been growing and growing—and now . . ."

"You mean you're due to lose the ranch?" The pleasant twinkle was gone from Seth McGee's eyes, leaving them bleak and mirthless.

"The ranch is already lost," Shirley told her attentive listeners. "At least," she amended, "the old Box B *will* be forever lost, when I sign the quit-claim deed."

"Quit-claim deed, huh!" Sam's voice was thoughtful. "Seems like you're being sort of hurried along."

"It really doesn't matter, under the circumstances," she explained; "there's no possible chance of saving the ranch now; and Mr. Sandell has been as kind about it all as anybody could be"—she shrugged her shoulders—"you two

15

dears know that Ed Benson's daughter can't accept charity, and that is what it would mean—if I allowed Mr. Sandell to do a thing more for me."

"You mean Mort Sandell of the San Luis Stockman's Bank?"

Sam Hally's voice was a low growl, the menacing rumble of a huge mastiff suddenly scenting a hated enemy. Again he exchanged looks with his partner. There was cold fury in the latter's eyes.

"He weren't in San Luis when Seth and me worked for your pa," Sam explained. "Was wondering if he was the same feller we run across in San Antone one time—"

"Oh, no!" Shirley shook her head. "He couldn't be the same man. Mr. Sandell is from New York—"

Sam looked doubtful.

"Well—no matter where he come from it kind of seems to me this Sandell hombre ain't giving you a fair chance to git the old Box B on her feet." He shook his grizzled head sorrowfully. "Sure is awful bad news, Miss Shirley. Ain't thinking much of this here Sandell feller."

"You misjudge him," she interrupted almost impatiently; "that last raid was worse than you know. I doubt if there are more than three or four hundred cows left on the range. I can't pay interest—nor buy more cows."

Seth McGee scowled. "Don't seem right to let the old Box B die on her legs thataways," he declared. "It sure got me and Sam on the prod when we heard how things was with you, Shirley gal."

The girl eyed the two old HM partners shrewdly. "Is *that* the reason you're riding around here like lost souls?" Affection was in her voice.

"Seth and me helped your pa mark the fust cows that wore the Box B on their hides," reminded Sam gently. "We don't aim to set round twiddling our thumbs."

She smiled sadly. "I know how you feel, but—I'm afraid it's the finish. I can't pay up—keep the ranch going—so I have agreed to give Mr. Sandell's bank a quit-claim deed—sort of cut the Gordian knot, if you know what I mean. It's the only fair thing for me to do," she added a bit defensively, "and you two old darlings needn't glower at me—"

"Ain't you we're glowering at," Seth said grimly. "If I'd my way 'bout thisahere business I'd tie a knot *no* hombre could cut—tie it plenty tight round that there Sandell feller's onery neck."

"Please!" she begged, "you mustn't talk so dreadfully of him," her voice trembled, "I—I suppose if Father were here he would have done something; but it's all too much for me."

"Yes," agreed Sam in his gentle voice, "Ed

Benson would have done a heap o' fighting to keep the old ranch on her legs—"

"Things might be a lot worse for me," Shirley interrupted with a lift of her chin; "at least I've a good job in prospect. Mr. Sandell has promised me the school! I'm going to teach— earn money—pay my own way! I think it is wonderful—and splendid of Mr. Sandell to be so kind."

Seth McGee's bright black eyes twinkled. "Sam and me, now, we sure need plenty more schooling," he insinuated.

"Old sillies!" jeered the girl in a fond voice. She tightened her reins. "It's been nice to see you both—"

Sam Hally's rumbling tones interrupted her. "Sure been one big s'prise—running into you out here in the rimrock, Miss Shirley. Seems to me you're a long way from home—so early in the morning," he added bluntly.

There was a sudden droop to the girl's slender shoulders; her eyes wavered, avoided their questioning looks; gauntleted fingers nervously fumbled the reins.

"I—I couldn't sleep," she confided in a faint voice; "it was yesterday that Mr. Sandell told me about the quit-claim deed—and last night I tossed and tossed! Oh!" she cried desperately, "I can't bear the thought of losing the dear old ranch! It breaks my heart! So I was up before sunrise and have been riding and riding, just anywhere, trying to make myself face what has to be—"

"Seth and me know how you feel about it," Sam told her gently; "you're a brave lass—you couldn't be else but a brave lass. Your folks was pioneers out here in the west, and to be brave is your inheritance," the big cowman nodded, "the brave ain't never been really licked," he reminded.

She gave them a misty-eyed smile, straightened in her saddle. "You blessed encouraging old darling," she told him; "both of you! And now I *must* be on my way—"

"One thing more I'm wanting to say to you," Sam broke in hurriedly, "don't you sign that fool quit-claim paper too quick. Figger out some way to put that Sandell feller off a few days."

"But I—I promised to sign tomorrow—"

"You can tell Mort Sandell you've got writer's cramp in all your fingers," suggested Seth McGee acidly.

Shirley hesitated, impressed by their earnestness. "Mr. Sandell is coming out to the ranch in the morning," she explained. "It's a long way, more than ten miles from San Luis." She shook her head. "He'd be dreadfully annoyed, I'm afraid—"

"Tell him you've got the smallpox and can't see nobody," growled Sam. "Tell him anything you've a mind to tell him, only don't you sign any quit-claim paper nor nothing—leastways not till Seth and me come to see you at the ranch."

"I'll promise," finally decided the girl. "I'll think up some way to—to put him off."

In silence the two veterans watched until Shirley vanished into the chaparral; in silence they went on their own way.

Sam was the first to break the silence.

"Worse than we figgered, Seth."

The chubby-faced Seth nodded glumly, finally gave voice to his own thoughts.

"If this Clay Brant feller ain't meeting us at Indian Head today, I'm sure riding pronto for San Luis and talk plenty to a buzzard that wears the name o' Mort Sandell," he announced in his chill, deadly voice.

His tall partner eyed down at him, drooping grizzled mustaches stiffening in a grim smile.

"I'll be riding with you, Seth."

Again silence, broken only by the clink of spurs, the squeak of saddle-leathers—the grind of shod hoofs; and suddenly they were at the edge of the rimrock, the vast panorama of the desert spread below. Heat waves rose to meet their eager, searching gaze, shimmered crazily—tortured their eyes.

To the left of them towered the jagged pinnacle known as Indian Head, a landmark for miles. They rode to its shadow and dismounted. Sam produced binoculars.

"See anything?" presently demanded the impatient Seth. "What are you looking at so hard, Sam? D'you see him down there?"

Sam's face was troubled. "Don't see nothing, 'cept buzzards, Seth." He lowered the glasses and gave his dour little partner a grim look. "Plenty buzzards over Poison Springs way." He held out the glasses. "You take a squint, feller. Your eyes is some smarter than mine these days."

Seth snatched the surrendered glasses, stared intently down at the blistering floor of the desert.

"Buzzards," he muttered; "sure plenty buzzards—and buzzards mean dead things—*dead men*—sometimes—" In turn he lowered the glasses and eyed his tall partner worriedly. "Don't look good to me, Sam!"

"Climb your saddle!" There was panic, dismay, in the big HM man's voice. "We're riding down there and we're riding fast!"

High-heeled boots clattered on flinty rocks; horses' hoofs went hammering down a trail that plunged steeply to the sun-baked desert floor.

Sam Hally's fast roan gelding moved quickly into the lead. High above the pale fringe of green that marked Poison Springs, three black dots swam in a pale turquoise sea, and to the northeast, low against the molten dawn, floated other dark specks—sinister winged heralds of death.

The old cowman's craggy face was a grim mask. The story written in the sky by those soaring buzzards was all too plain to his desert-wise eyes. A man lay dying, or dead, at Poison Springs; and where the vultures sailed low in the golden glare of the lifting sun would be found the lifeless clay of what was once a horse.

Sam muttered words the Recording Angel would forgive and write down as a prayer. His letter to the grandson of old Bill Brant had proved young Clay's death warrant, it seemed . . .

He had under-estimated the cunning of Mort Sandell. And now the young daughter of Bill Brant's one-time partner would be at the mercy of Mort Sandell and his fellow human buzzards, gathering in San Luis to feast upon the corpse of the old Box B ranch.

Sam's hairy, calloused hand went to the worn black butt of the ancient six-gun clamped to his thigh. There were reasons why young Clay Brant could have done so much to save the Box B ranch for Shirley Benson. There was so little Seth McGee and himself could do for the daughter of their former boss, save die in San Luis with their guns smoking.

The roan horse slid to a snorting standstill. Sam swung from his saddle, hastened with dragging spurs to the limp form sprawled under a giant bristling cactus.

22

CHAPTER II
IN THE VALLEY OF THE KINGS

When Ed Benson and Bill Brant first rode into the valley they knew a dream had come true. It was Spring, the grass still green in the meadows and on the foothill slopes. Wild flowers smiled at them, a magic symphony of color from the hands of a master weaver. It was a long valley, reaching north to distant towering cliffs that flung back misty lavender to the setting sun. It was a wide valley, perhaps some five or six miles between wooded foothills that undulated to lofty snow-capped mountain ridges. An ideal home ranch for an ambitious young cattle outfit. Good grass and plenty of water in the arroyo streams.

Brant, the elder by some half score years, smiled contentedly at his slim, red-headed companion. He was well above the average height, a strongly-built, brown-faced man with thoughtful gray eyes and dark hair touched with gray at the temples.

"No need for us to look further, Ed," he said softly. "This place was made for cattle."

"You've said it, Bill," declared the red-headed youth. "Here is where you and me go into the cow business in a big way, sure as I'm a born Texan!"

The pride of discovery glistened in his blue eyes. "What'll we call her—this here valley? You've been to college, back there in Virginia where you come from and know more'n I do about names."

Brant's gaze went to the loftiest of the snow-capped peaks.

"That's San Luis Rey," he said; "I reckon, Ed, we couldn't do better than call this place *El Valle de los Reyes*—the Valley of the Kings—"

"The Valley of the Kings!" echoed young Benson. "That means you and me, huh, Bill? We'll be kings—*cattle kings!*"

A few months later a herd of Texas longhorns bellowed up from the Rio Grande, their hides freshly scarred with the brand of Benson and Brant. Such was the modest beginning of the Box B ranch, forty odd years before the time Sam Hally and Seth McGee kept their three-day vigil at Indian Head.

Sam and Seth had seen that first herd swell into thousands, and the original range expand far beyond the confines of the Valley of the Kings.

Busy years, and hard years, that first decade of the Box B's existence. Rustlers, and border desperadoes, and drought, with now and then an occasional Apache war party taking the scalp of a luckless cowboy. The frosting in Bill Brant's dark hair grew more pronounced, his fine gray eyes more thoughtful—gentle. Sam Hally, alone among the Box B outfit came to know of the tragedy that had caused him to leave his native Virginia. The two men were curiously alike, despite the fact that one was an illiterate cowboy, the other, the product of a great university. Sam was innately an intellectual, an idealist; and in the giant Texan the Virginian found one whose mind was in harmony with his own. The same quiet reserve, the ability to ignore the petty things, marked both. Tolerant of weaknesses in others, they were on guard against their own. One sensed the same quiet self-control, the same iron strain, resolute courage.

"She died, Sam—died the hour the boy was born—"

They were riding in from an out-lying cattle camp the night Bill Brant told Sam of the sorrow that had come near to breaking him.

"—I couldn't bear to look at him, Sam . . . his life had taken her from me—"

"He was her baby, Bill," the big cowboy told him gently. "Mebbe if you'd looked at things right you'd have knowed she wasn't really dead. This here little Steve laddie was part of her; she'd want you to love him for her sake."

"I know it now, Sam. I was a fool—kicking against the pricks—"

"Where's the little tad these days, Bill?"

"He's back in Richmond—with her people. He's not so little, though . . . Steve is going on twenty this year."

"You should send for him," advised Sam. "We'll make a cowman out of him, Bill."

"Maybe I'll do just that," mused Brant. "Steve would make good company for Paula. Lonesome for Paula—here on the ranch."

"I figger Paula won't be lonesome, long," surmised Sam Hally; "ain't you noticed how that gal has growed up, Bill? She's most a woman—a mighty pretty woman if you ask me."

"A girl isn't a woman at sixteen."

"Some of 'em are," declared Sam, "and Paula is one of 'em." He darted a quizzical look at his boss. "She'd make a mighty sweet little wife for some decent hombre, Bill. Why don't you let loose of the past and kind of see Paula the way she is—a woman? You ain't so old but what a gal would smile at you."

Brant flung the Box B foreman a startled look. "I'm past forty," he said in a curt tone. "Don't be a fool, Sam Hally!"

"What if you *is* forty," persisted Sam, "you're ten years younger than your age, and Paula is ten years older than hers. She'd be a bright candle, lightin' up a new world for you, Bill."

"May and December don't mate," reminded the Virginian gruffly.

At which remark the big Box B foreman shrugged wide shoulders skeptically.

The subject of the discussion had been a member of the Benson and Brant bachelor household for some six years, the sole survivor of an Apache raid on an Oregon-bound wagon train. Sam and Seth had found her, a sobbing, terrified child of ten, hiding in the chaparral near the smoldering embers of the prairie schooner. They had taken her to the ranch-house—sent men to bury the dead.

There was little the child could tell them save that her name was Paula Wynne and that her mother and father had set out from Kentucky some months earlier. The massacre had left her with no living relative to whom she could be sent and so she had been turned over to the care of Maria Cota, who, with her husband, Miguel, attended to the domestic needs of the Box B ranch-house.

Motherly Maria Cota was soon Paula's devoted slave, as in truth was every man of the outfit. The swiftly-passing years miraculously transformed a thin, frightened little child into a lovely bud of womanhood; a fact that Sam Hally was not the only one to realize. Ed Benson had known it for some months.

Ed was past thirty, the nine years as co-lord of the Valley of the Kings had matured him—increased his good looks. The ruddy-haired Texan was tall, almost as tall as Bill Brant; wide-shouldered, lean and hard of body. It was not unnatural that Paula should read the growing challenge in his handsome blue eyes—allow her own lovely dark eyes to return the challenge. Half child, half woman, though she was, Paula already instinctively sensed the mysterious alchemy of love. She knew that Ed Benson loved her—knew that she *loved* him. To realize suddenly that Bill Brant also loved her profoundly disturbed Paula.

If he had but known it there was no need for Sam Hally to blame himself so bitterly for the tragedy that split asunder the friendship between Bill Brant and Ed Benson. The Virginian had already fallen under the spell of the girl so long regarded as a foster-child. He had delighted in teaching her from his own well-filled storehouse of knowledge. Paula had proved an apt pupil, had eagerly absorbed the fundamentals of a sound classical education. His small library was always in great demand. Intrigued by an illustrated copy of *Les Miserables* in the French, Paula declared she wanted to read the book; and read it she did, a year later; and his dog-eared copy of Don Quixote, the last with the help of the soft-voiced Maria Cota.

Ed Benson might love Paula for her fresh young beauty—Bill Brant loved her for reasons beyond the comprehension of an Ed Benson.

Perhaps Sam Hally alone understood, which was why the faithful Sam grieved.

"He ain't got a chance with her," mourned the big Box B foreman to his top-hand rider and friend, Seth McGee, "that gal don't see nothin' but Ed Benson—him and his red hair and smilin' blue eyes."

The Box B's premier cowboy and gunman shrugged his deceptively plump shoulders.

"Ain't none of our business, Sam." He scowled. "Gals is p'isen, when they come 'tween old friends. Seems like a hombre goes clean out of his senses when the love bug bites him." Seth shook his head dolefully. "Wouldn't s'prise me none to see guns smokin' afore long. I tell you, feller, gals can sure make a lot of hell. Don't want none of 'em in *my* life—in *our* life, Sam. Me and you won't never let some pretty face start *our* guns smokin' at each other."

A long speech for the dour little cowboy, and one that brought no comfort to the troubled mind of Sam Hally.

The crisis came on Paula's seventeenth birthday, precipitated by a sudden flame of jealousy on the part of the fiery-haired Ed Benson.

Bill Brant's gift was a simple coral necklace, for which the delighted girl gave him a hug and a kiss, a favor she did not bestow upon the glowering Benson.

The young Texan was inexperienced in the way of a maid. He could not know that Paula's affection for Bill Brant was the innocent affection of a daughter for a father. He only knew that the woman he loved was in the arms of another man.

Too late, the girl sensed she had made a fatal

mistake. Brant also was misunderstanding the impulsive caress. She felt his arms tighten around her waist, saw the usually calm gray eyes grow hot with a sudden fierce exultation. Frightened, dismayed, she glanced apprehensively at the younger man. Mounting fury convulsed the latter's handsome face.

"Let loose of her, Bill—" The violence of his jealous rage seemed to strangle the Texan's voice. "No call to hug the girl because she give you a kiss—"

Steely gray eyes clashed savagely with angry blue eyes. Brant spoke softly:

"Maybe I don't want to let loose of her, Ed. I love her—"

"Take your paws off her!" shouted the younger man. His hand darted down to gun-butt.

Paula herself solved the situation by suddenly twisting free from the embrace.

"No!" she gasped, "if you start fighting over me I'll—I'll die for shame!"

Benson stared at her sullenly. "It's time for a showdown," he said in a quieter voice; "things can't go on this way for another day."

Her distressed gaze went from one to the other. Brant's face was expressionless, save for the hot light lurking in his eyes. She knew that the younger man was right—that the time had come for her to choose between them.

Paula's breath quickened. It was Ed Benson

she wanted, but she could not force herself to say the words that would so hurt Bill Brant. Good, faithful, always gentle Bill Brant. He had been so patient with her—had taught her all the things she knew. She loved him dearly . . . not in the way she loved Ed Benson . . . she knew that. She wondered miserably why Bill had been so stupid, so foolish as to fall in love with her. He was more than old enough to be her father! Men were strange creatures, deliberately doing things that could only hurt them. She felt their eyes upon her; they were waiting for her to choose—and she couldn't choose—now!

"Oh!" she cried piteously, "I can't—today! I can't choose! I won't!" She forced herself to anger. "It's cruel of you to act this way on my birthday—" Her eyes flashed. "I love you both—"

Paula broke off, struck suddenly dumb by the anguish in Benson's eyes.

He shook his head. "No," he told her stubbornly. "It's the showdown, Paula. You can't love but one of us, girl. It's Bill—or me."

She was silent, unable to cope further with the situation. Brant suddenly broke the silence.

"Don't plague the girl, Ed. It's her birthday . . . We should be ashamed of ourselves."

The fiery Texan's expression was unpleasant to see. "You're afraid," he challenged. "You're afraid to face it—afraid she won't choose you!"

31

"I withdraw," Brant said in a chill tone. "The field is yours, Ed."

"You'll not withdraw," declared his partner relentlessly. "Paula's got to say here and now which one of us she wants—you—or me—"

"I told you I won't!" flared the girl. "I—I hate you, Ed Benson—" She began to cry.

Brant took a step toward her; she waved him back.

"We'll settle it in another way, then," muttered the Texan. He stared at his partner. "The Box B ain't big enough for the two of us, Bill Brant. One of us is leaving tonight—for good."

"What do you mean?"

"Paula won't choose . . . we'll let the cards choose for her . . . the loser clears out . . . the winner takes the girl—and the ranch. Paula will deal the hands."

She started to protest, was suddenly silent, gaze questioning Brant. The tall Virginian hesitated, plainly disliking such a method of settling the fate of the girl he loved. Benson's grin was diabolic.

"It's cards—or guns," he said thinly. "I'm goin' through with this business, Brant. You and me have been partners a long time—but tonight we break for keeps."

"It's cards," decided the girl hurriedly for Brant. "I'll get a fresh deck—" She ran from the room.

The two men took seats at the table, battle-ground of many a friendly bout of poker between them but never such a game as this one proposed by Ed Benson. They made and lighted cigarettes.

"Ed," said Brant contemptuously, "if I didn't know you so well, I'd say you're a skunk."

"I'm in love," muttered his partner. "That's all I know."

Paula reappeared, a deck of cards in her hand. She was very pale.

"What is it to be," she asked in a low voice.

"Straight draw," Benson told her curtly. He looked at his opponent.

"One hand?"

Brant nodded. He was eyeing the girl intently. She kept her gaze lowered.

She dealt them their five cards each. Brant saw that her hands were trembling. He picked up his cards, flung the girl an odd look; she kept her face averted, dark lashes lowered. Benson was studying his own hand with frowning intentness. A great fear was in his face—and indecision. Brant made a lone discard and again glanced at Paula. Her face was very white, frightened, her gaze intent on Benson. The latter threw down two cards with a muttered exclamation. He, too, was as white as a sunburned man can be.

"I'm takin' two, girl," he said hoarsely.

She gave him his two cards, dealt the one Brant needed to fill his hand. There was a triumphant exclamation from Benson.

"What you got, Bill?" he demanded.

Brant silently upturned his cards—a full house.

There was a contented chuckle from the red-haired Texan.

"You lose, mister!" He showed four queens.

Bill Brant seemed not to hear him. He was looking steadily at Paula. The story he read in her averted face was a story Ed Benson would never know. His glance went indifferently to the out-spread four queens.

"No, Ed," he said, softly, "a man can't lose what he never possessed—"

"Huh?" The cryptic comment was above the younger man's head. "Seems to me you've lost plenty, Bill," now that the cards had fallen in his favor Benson was disposed to feel generous, "how about the ranch?" He stumbled a moment, "The—the ranch—reckon we can—can forget about the ranch part of it—"

"I can get another ranch." Brant smiled, pushed back from his chair. "Good luck, Ed . . . No hard feelings." He offered his hand.

There was a worried look in young Benson's blue eyes. "Sure, Bill, no hard feelings"—he frowned—"reckon we got some excited . . . no sense in us gettin' upset, old timer; let's ease up some on that fool bet. No call for you to step out of the old Box B. Won't seem like the same place—if you go. You've done more to make a cow ranch out of the place than I ever did," he added honestly.

"A bet is a bet, Ed," reminded the older man. "You wouldn't want me to do—what you *couldn't* do—"

The Texan looked at him dumbly. He knew that Brant spoke the truth. Their breed did not renege. Ed Benson then and there proved himself a gallant and generous victor. He rose slowly from his chair, wrung his partner's hand.

"*Adios*, Bill, I'm riding over to the Willow Creek camp. Sam says we should have a drift fence—"

Brant smiled. "One moment, Ed, before you rush away. I've something I want to fix up for you—" He strode into the ranch office. Benson followed, and when Bill Brant rode away, his partner possessed a paper giving him full ownership of the Box B ranch.

It was in the ranch office that Paula saw Bill Brant for the last time. She came in timidly, pausing in the doorway as he rose from the crudely-made rawhide chair.

"Don't cry, dear child—"

"I—I won't—Bill Brant—"

She did cry, her young arms clinging to him.

"You—you know—what I did, Bill? I—I cheated—"

He smiled.

"There was nothing else you could do, my dear child." He held her back gently. "I've been rather stupid—not to understand—"

"I do love you, Bill! I do—I *do*—only—"

35

"I understand, Paula . . . The fault has been entirely mine—"

Her arms clung to him desperately.

"—I've a son, older than you, Paula . . . in college . . . I'm sending for him—soon. I won't be alone—"

"You've always been so wonderful to me, Bill!" Paula lifted her dark head. "I—I don't know—understand—why I love Ed Benson the way I do. He's not the man you are, Bill Brant—"

"Ed Benson is one of the finest—"

"I know nothing about men," she confessed, "I only know that I do truly love him—"

"Ed Benson is one of the finest," Brant repeated gently. "It's all for the best, Paula. We'll not talk about it ever again." His gaze traveled around the little room. He had helped rear the rough-hewn timbers of the Box B ranch-house—the house his eyes would never again see. "I told Ed I'd not be here when he returned from Willow Creek," he informed the girl. "*Adios*, dear child—"

"*Vaya con Dios*, Bill Brant," she told him in the liquid Spanish of Maria Cota. Her arms went around him: "Go with God, my dear Bill Brant," she repeated, "I—I never can forget you, Bill Brant!" For a fleeting moment he felt the tender press of her fresh young lips. . . .

Bill Brant was seen no more in the Valley of the Kings. And with the passing of the years men forgot that Ed Benson once had a partner. Sam Hally alone came to know the story of that fateful birthday, and of the existence of the document giving Ed Benson full ownership of the Box B ranch.

Paula liked to believe that remorse was the reason why her husband had failed, or neglected, to put the bill of sale on record. It was years later that she found the paper Bill Brant had signed that tragic afternoon, hidden deep in a drawer of the ranch-office desk.

Paula had never ceased to reproach herself, nor to forget that Bill Brant had a son. She felt that her moment of madness had robbed Bill Brant's boy of his inheritance.

She told Sam the story.

"I cheated," she confessed to the man who had loved Bill Brant like a brother. "I didn't know what to do. Ed said it was cards—or guns. I was terrified—desperate—I decided for Bill Brant—chose the cards . . . And then I cheated—I wanted Ed to win—made certain he would have those four queens against Bill's full house—"

"Nothing we kin do 'bout it now," Sam told her a bit gruffly, "Bill is dead—"

"He has a son, Sam . . . Bill told me . . . that afternoon—"

"Steve is dead, too, Paula. He left old Bill a grandson, up there on the Cimarron. Clay is all of eight years old by now."

"I didn't know!" Mrs. Benson mused for a moment. "Oh, Sam—if we could arrange to have him up here on the ranch!"

Sam was dubious. "Bill wouldn't have had it that way, Paula—"

Paula persisted, "I think it would be wonderful . . . And after all, Sam, the boy really is half owner of the ranch—"

"Bill Brant wouldn't think he is—"

"I wish he would think the way I do," she sighed; "you know, Sam, I never shall forgive myself . . . what I did that day. I want Clay Brant to have his rights. He is just as much an heir to the ranch as my Shirley"—her smile was wistful— "and it would be so *wonderful* if Clay Brant— and Shirley some day—made it all come right. It's not an impossibility," she added musingly. "Shirley is two years old—Clay is eight. Oh, Sam Hally, we must get Bill's grandson up here!"

Sam shook his head. "Bill Brant wouldn't have had him come, Paula, and if Ed ever learned the truth 'bout them four queens—he'd never forgive you."

Paula was silenced. She knew that her husband must never know.

It was weeks later that she showed Sam the unrecorded bill-of-sale.

"I want you to keep it for me, Sam," she begged him. "I found it in Ed's desk; he'll never miss it. I'm sure that he never intends to use it—"

Sam nodded.

"I'd stake my last chip on Ed," he assured her. "Ed never aimed to cash in on that there fool bet."

Paula gave him a grateful smile.

"You always are so comforting, Sam. Now—listen to me—I want you to keep this paper, and if anything happens to me, or Ed, I want your solemn promise to do what seems right by Bill Brant's little grandson"—her voice faltered—"please, Sam, I'd rest easier in my grave. As you love me—love my little Shirley—promise me. I want to right the wrong that I did—that day—"

Sam took the paper, tucked it away in his pocket.

"You're a good man, Sam Hally!"

A year later, Paula Benson slept in a grave Sam and Seth prepared for her near the Box B ranchhouse, a grave that in time Shirley and her father came to call the "rose garden."

Seventeen more years were to pass before Sam Hally knew the time had come for him to keep his promise to Shirley's mother.

CHAPTER III
DEATH IN THE DESERT

Sam's hurried examination told him that the man was not dead. He glanced up at his partner as the latter rode up.

"Dead, Sam? Is he—dead?"

Seth's voice crackled with apprehension.

Sam shook his head, reached for the canteen Seth thrust at him.

"Should be a sign posted, warning folks," complained his partner. "He'd have been one dead hombre if he'd lapped a few mouthfuls of that arsenic water."

"Used to be a sign," Sam reminded him. "Reckon she was blowed down—or—"

"—or knocked down a-purpose!" Seth scowled.

Drop by drop they fed the canteen's cool water to the fevered swollen lips.

"Must have been laying here since yesterday," Sam muttered.

"We been looking for a man riding his bronc," Seth pointed out; "ain't so easy to spot a hombre crawling through the chaparral." He gestured toward the southeast. "Don't them buzzards tell you the story, feller? His bronc's laying out there, dead. I'd figger this poor jasper's been afoot since night afore last."

40

"Wouldn't take him so long to come less'n five miles," demurred Sam. "Not unless—" He broke off, hastily lifted the semi-conscious man to a sitting position.

"Huh, gun wound," he muttered, "that explains a lot. Been bushwhacked—"

With expert, gentle fingers the HM men cut away the blood-encrusted sleeve and explored the wound.

"No bone touched," diagnosed Sam, "the bullet went clean through."

"He's bled a-plenty," Seth grumbled; "lucky for him he passed out at that." He stared over at the green-fringed pool. "Sure lucky for him," he repeated. His gaze returned to the young man pillowed against his big partner's knee, and when he spoke again there was doubt, disappointment, in his cold voice.

"He don't look like I figgered he would, Sam? Are you plumb certain this hombre is Bill Brant's grandson? We ain't never seen young Clay—and this feller don't look like I figgered he would."

Sam worriedly eyed the swarthy face in the crook of his arm.

"Reckon he's Clay right enough, Seth. He's wearing that U. S. deputy marshal badge I sent him—the one I got for him special, and he's got that letter I wrote to Clay," Sam's voice was uneasy, "seems like he must be Clay Brant— when you figger that badge—and the letter—"

"You told him to burn the letter," reminded Seth; "didn't you tell me you said for him to burn the letter afore he headed down from Cimarron?"

"I sure did," Sam reluctantly admitted. "What you driving at, feller?"

"What you think I'm driving at?" Seth scowled at his partner. "I'm thinking that this here half-breed don't own the name of Clay Brant; even if he does carry that deputy marshal badge and has your letter in his pocket."

"He ain't claimed the name, yet, Seth. If he does, I know how to make him prove it. No call for you to git on the prod, mister."

Sam's dour little partner shrugged his shoulders, shifted his bleak gaze to the thin spread of green grass that marked the brief meanderings of Poison Springs.

"I'll be taking a look for that signpost, Sam—" He hurried away, high bootheels cutting deep into a crackleware of sun-baked mud.

Sam studied the wounded man with grave, thoughtful eyes. No question but what Seth was right about the mixed blood. The old cowman was conscious of bitter disappointment as he gazed at the swarthy, rather vicious face. It was something of a shock to learn that the mother of Bill Brant's grandson must have been a half-breed Indian woman. Not that Sam objected to a touch of Indian in a man. He had known too many decent men of like descent on the maternal side. It was the viciousness so plainly evident in the swarthy face that disturbed Sam. It seemed incredible that this young man could be the grandson of Bill Brant—could be the famed Clay Brant of Cimarron. And yet his brief search had discovered the special deputy marshal badge—and the letter he had written. The letter was another cause for speculation. He had warned Clay to destroy the letter.

Sam's face was grim. Was it possible that Seth's always wary mind had leaped to the proper answer—that this evil-eyed man was not the grandson of Bill Brant? If so, what had become of Clay Brant, for whom they had kept the three-day vigil at Indian Head? And who was this man carrying Clay's credentials?

The old cattleman tugged worriedly at his grizzled mustache. There were ways of settling the question of identity. There was another certain token this stranger must produce at the right time—and place. It was a more sinister angle that filled Sam with dire forebodings—the possible fate of Bill Brant's grandson—in the event that this half-breed proved not to be Clay.

The man stirred, muttered incoherently, was suddenly staring up at him. Sam's dislike and doubts grew as he met the shifty look of the hard black eyes.

"How you feel, son?"

For all his inward turmoil the old cowman managed a kindly solicitude.

"Mighty narrow squeak, young feller," he said. "Here—let's make you a mite more easy—" He propped the youth gently against the side of a big boulder. "Where you from, son?" he queried genially.

"That's my business," muttered the young man ungraciously, "and where I'm headed for is my business, too."

"Now—that was right careless of me, poking my nose where I hadn't ought to," chuckled Sam. "I sure must have left my manners home this morning."

The shifty eyes regarded him suspiciously. "You the feller that dry-gulched me an' my bronc?" he asked surlily.

"Now, what would I want to go and do a onery thing like that for?" Sam's voice was reproachful. "No, young feller, me and my pardner found you lying here—lucky for you."

Seth returned from his search for the missing signpost.

"Found it," he told Sam. "Wasn't blowed down, nuther. Some hombre snaked it out with his rope. Sure crave to meet up with the coyote that done it," he added grimly. His bleak gaze fastened on the swarthy young stranger. "Looks like there's folks got it in for you, mister—framing for you to drink that there poison water. Got any notion who shot you—and why?"

The youth shook his head, his gaze fixed on the slimy stream. His face had turned a sickly green.

"He ain't feeling very chatty," Sam commented dryly. "You warm up some coffee for him, Seth. I reckon he won't object none to them bacon sandwiches you fixed for our lunch." Sam moved toward his horse. "I'll mosey over and git your saddle gear," he told the youth. "By the looks of them buzzards yonder I figger your bronc is laying over there." He rode away.

Sam had a good reason for wanting to have a look at the stranger's dead horse. Horses usually wore brands of ownership. Clay Brant's horse should be marked with a Circle Dot, the brand Bill Brant had adopted for his new ranch on the Cimarron after leaving the Valley of the Kings.

The buzzards winged away lazily, reluctant to abandon their prospective feast. Sam scowled at them. He had small liking for buzzards, despite their usefulness as scavengers. He reined up, stared with growing dismay at the dead horse. The brand was unmistakable.

"A Circle Dot, sure 'nough," he muttered disconsolately.

He swung down and gloomily stripped off saddle and bridle. The entwined initials on the silver-mounted horn increased his gloom. CB— stood for Clay Brant. It began to seem that the shifty-eyed stranger was likely Clay Brant, after all.

Carrying the saddle in front of him, Sam rode in an easterly direction, toward a deep barranca, surmising that it was in the gully the ambushed killer had lain in wait. Also he was curious to learn the reason for the buzzards' obvious interest in the place.

"Something dead, down in there," he muttered.

Fear gripped him. Something that perhaps was once a man—known as Clay Brant!

The roan's head lifted suddenly, ears pricked up in a manner that Sam was quick to understand. There was also something alive down in the unseen depths of the barranca. A shrill nicker almost immediately confirmed the surmise. A tethered horse, waiting for a rider who never more would ride. Sam's fears grew to a ghastly certainty. Clay Brant was down in that gully— lying there—dead!

His first glance told Sam that he was wrong. The man lying with pain-contorted face in the boulder-strewn floor of the gully was assuredly not young Clay Brant. He was not a young man and Sam had seen the weazened rat-like face before. Whitey Joe—a hanger-on at Frenchy Larue's Red Front saloon in San Luis. Sam had long suspected Whitey Joe for a rustler and hired assassin. The sight of the twisted form

46

sprawled among the rocks was not displeasing to the old cowman.

Tied to a clump of tough mesquite further down the barranca was a speedy-looking bay mare, obviously overjoyed to see the newcomers. She nickered again, pawed impatiently. Sam threw her a commiserating look.

"Reckon you're plenty thirsty, old lady," he rumbled sympathetically. "Don't blame you for acting peevish." He lowered the salvaged saddle and swung down.

Although consumed with curiosity as to the cause of Whitey Joe's demise he first attended to the mare. Sam was that way when it came to the sufferings of the helpless. Canteen in hand he scrambled down the steep bank. The mare's gaunt flanks told his experienced eyes that she had been some two days without water or food. She nickered again as he approached.

Sam pulled off his wide-brimmed, deep-crowned hat and poured in the contents of the canteen. It was not the first time he had watered a horse from his battered old Stetson.

"That should keep you going, old lady," he told her when she lifted wet muzzle from the improvised bucket. He untied the short rope and led the animal up the bank to the roan horse and shook out the latter's feed of crushed barley.

"Kind of tough on you, old timer," he told the roan with a chuckle, "but when a gal's in trouble you and me can't stand by and do nothing."

Satisfied that he had done all he could for the moment, Sam went down to the mortal remains of Whitey Joe.

For a minute he was puzzled. Examination showed no sign of a bullet wound, or blow; and yet stark horror still looked from the staring agate eyes—distorted the thin ferret face. The old cowman straightened up, keen gaze searching for some clue that would unfold this story of violent death.

The .45 six-shooter had not been fired, nor drawn from its holster, Sam decided.

His searching eyes scrutinized the steep bank of the barranca, suddenly fastened on something that glinted against the morning sun. He climbed up the bank to the narrow crevice formed by the splitting of a huge boulder, and knew that he had found the ambush used by the dead Whitey Joe. He knew, too, that it was here the killer had taken his own death wound.

Sam stared thoughtfully at the broken rifle barrel lying across the battered body of an enormous rattlesnake. He could accurately visualize the scene—Whitey Joe, crouched in the cleft of the boulder, lying in wait for his unsuspecting victim. Two brass shells near the splintered gun-stock were mute evidence that the assassin had fired twice, one bullet dropping the horse, the second wounding the man. And then swift retribution from the poison-laden fangs of the unnoticed rattler. It was not difficult to reconstruct the story—Whitey Joe's horror, the violence of his fury as he battered the life from his fellow-reptile with clubbed rifle, his frantic attempt to reach his horse left tied in the barranca.

The old cowman nodded grimly.

"Of the two of 'em, the human snake was the meanest," he reflected as he scrambled down the steep bank, back to the dead man.

He was curious to see just where Whitey Joe had been bitten. Death had been unusually swift, even for a bite from so huge a snake. As he suspected, fang marks in the dead killer's throat, completed the story.

"The rattler was sunning on that flat ledge, just opposite Joe's head," Sam decided; "Joe never had a chance—with all that poison shot into the juglar vein—"

He made his way up the barranca slope and put the salvaged saddle and bridle on the mare. She carried the brand of the Bar 7 outfit, he observed.

Sam's face hardened. What was Whitey Joe doing with a Bar 7 horse?

It was not a difficult question to answer. The Bar 7 ranch had recently been acquired by San Luis' leading citizen and banker, Mort Sandell. It was an answer that brought small comfort to the troubled mind of Sam Hally. He understood fully, now, the reason for that ambush in the barranca.

Mort Sandell had heard of his message to young Clay Brant—had sent his hired killer to make certain that Clay Brant would never reach San Luis.

Leading the mare he rode thoughtfully toward Poison Springs.

Warm drink and food had done much for the swarthy stranger. He was ready to continue his journey, he informed his benefactors.

"I wouldn't keep that Bar 7 mare any longer than it'll take you to git another bronc," advised Sam. "Folks might be asking you how come you're forking a Bar 7 critter."

The youth's sneering lips parted in a contemptuous grin.

"Thanks, grandpop! Wasn't born yesterday." He gave them a glimpse of the deputy marshal badge pinned inside his coat. "Folks don't bother a man that wears one of these—"

"Mighty nice saddle you've got there, son," added Sam, choosing to ignore the ungracious retort.

"What of it, mister?" The swarthy stranger scowled. "Got to be on my way—no time to stay gabbin' all day." With a curt nod he spurred away.

"One sweet hombre," muttered Seth McGee disgustedly. "Sure grateful for us saving his onery life—couldn't thank us enough!" The little HM man shrugged his shoulders. "Sam, if that onery pup is Bill Brant's grandson, I'm a Chinaman!"

"Climb your saddle," answered his partner. "We got to be waiting up there at Indian Head. The hand ain't played out, yet, Seth. If he ain't Clay Brant he's sure going to tell us how come he's using Clay's saddle—and tell us some other things we want to know."

"He'll see us trailing him," worried Seth.

"Not if we take that short cut up the dry wash," Sam pointed out. "We kin beat him by a mile—if we hurry."

They mounted and rode into the deep wash, pressed their horses into a dead run up the hard-packed sandy floor.

CHAPTER IV
THE SECRET TOKEN

They reached the rendezvous at Indian Head and dismounted. Sam gave his partner a brief account of what he had discovered at the scene of the ambush.

Seth scowled.

"Mort Sandell is wise to us, Sam. He must have knowed about that letter or he wouldn't have sent Whitey Joe to dry-gulch Clay Brant. Not that I'm believing this here snaky-eyed feller *is* Clay; but Whitey Joe thought he was."

"We got to have more than suspicions afore we kin openly make charges ag'in Sandell," mused Sam. "We got to have proof—plenty proof."

Seth shook his head glumly.

"And there's that young gal—trusting Sandell for a honest hombre! Seems like we should tell her what we think, Sam. I figger we sure should. 'Tain't right for Shirley not to know what his game is."

"We'll see, we'll see," Sam said thoughtfully. "We'll know more when we done had a talk with this young feller. Here he comes," he added.

Seth eased the .45 in his right-hand holster.

52

He was frankly distrustful of their approaching visitor.

The bay mare swung around the granite face of the big butte, was reined to a quick halt as her rider recognized his recent benefactors. For a moment he stared at them suspicious and undecided, then with a grin he swung from his saddle and began to nonchalantly make a cigarette, gaze shifting from one to the other.

"Kind of s'prised you, huh, son?" Sam said mildly. "Wasn't expecting to run into us ag'in."

"Your name Sam Hally?" demanded the young man.

"That's me, mister."

"This the butte they call Injun Head?"

"Right ag'in, son."

"Well, here I am, like you said in your letter," the youth said confidently.

Sam regarded him for a moment.

"Just what was it I said in the letter?" he asked gently.

The dark young stranger touched a match to his cigarette, blew out a cloud of smoke. "You said you'd know I was Clay Brant if I met you here at the Injun Head rock and was wearin' this deputy marshal badge—" He unpinned the badge and held it out for their inspection.

Sam nodded.

"Sure, sure—wrote them very words, son, and that's the same badge you got there." Sam's voice was a low soft purr, which, had the confident young stranger known it, boded him no good. Seth McGee, familiar with the storm signals, grinned expectantly.

"Did you burn the letter, like I said to do?" The old cowman chuckled. "No sense my asking you a fool question like that, huh? You wouldn't be toting that letter round after me telling you to burn it—"

"Sure, I burned it," assured the swarthy youth with a grin. There was contempt in the hard black eyes for this graying old dodderer. "Any more questions you aim to ask me, mister?"

"Seems like there is, son," Sam said very gently; "if you was Clay Brant you'd have something else to show me—something I sent in that there letter," his voice took on a grim rumbling note, "or did you burn it, too—when you burned the letter?"

The young man gave him a startled look, hesitated. Sam continued in the same menacing voice.

"You lied—when you said you burned that there letter, mister. It's in your pocket, which means you sure ain't Clay Brant. Don't need no more proof to know that—"

An oath snarled from the man's lips and his hand went with the speed of a striking snake down to the holstered gun. Seth McGee's .45 roared; there was a yell of pain and the youth's

54

six-shooter spun from his hand to the rocks.

Seth's smoking gun menaced him.

"Coyotes like you are my meat, mister," he warned in his chill voice.

The man stared dumbly at his hand. Blood oozed from the gash across his knuckles—spread a crimson stain over stiffly curved fingers. His face was ashen.

"Looks like you done horned into plenty trouble, son," Sam told him grimly. "How come you're wearing the name of Clay Brant?"

The youth's black eyes cursed them.

"I'll bleed to death," he mumbled.

"Sit on that rock," ordered Sam. "I'll fix your scratch up. 'Tain't much. Lucky for you Seth didn't send his lead plumb through your heart."

"Mebbe I'll do that same thing yet," promised his partner bleakly.

Using the man's own bandanna Sam quickly bound the bleeding knuckles. "Didn't damage you so bad," he repeated. "Now, talk up, mister . . . where is Clay Brant?"

A low, amused chuckle came to them, spun them round on their heels.

"Clay Brant present, gentlemen—and what can I do for you?"

The newcomer smiled at them from the corner of the butte. He was young, perhaps in his late twenties; his hair was darkly red, his eyes the sort of gray that seems black under stress of excitement. They were singularly fearless eyes, set wide apart in a somewhat haughty, finely chiseled face. Like the other man he wore the garb of the country, travel-stained and gray with dust. Two guns hung in low-slung holsters. One sensed cool efficiency in this tall, lean-waisted, nonchalant stranger.

For a long moment the two old cowmen silently appraised him. There was a curious gleam in Sam Hally's blue eyes. He spoke softly:

"So your name is Clay Brant, huh?"

"The only name I ever owned," smiled the young man.

Sam nodded at the sullen prisoner.

"This feller claims the same name—just been telling us he's Clay Brant—"

"Where I'm from he's known as Chico Lopez—"

"He was riding a Circle Dot bronc—"

The new claimant to the name of Clay Brant eyed the speedy-looking bay mare.

"That's my saddle, but the mare never saw the Circle Dot."

"The Circle Dot horse he was ridin' is down there," Sam gestured at the desert floor, "where you see them buzzards."

The newcomer nodded thoughtfully, stared at the prisoner's bandaged shoulder, grinned at the freshly dressed knuckles.

"I gather that our friend Chico Lopez took a

bullet intended for me." His smile was ironic. "I've an idea you saved my life, Chico, when you made this fool play."

The swarthy youth shrugged his shoulders, gave him a sickly grin.

"He's got some other things belonging to Clay Brant," Sam went on leisurely, "a letter, and a U. S. deputy marshal badge, but there's something he ain't got—something what the real Clay Brant *would* have—" Sam paused, a question in his keen old eyes. "Mebbe you've got what he ain't able to show me," he added significantly, "a sort of secret token—"

The young cowboy grinned, seated himself on a boulder and tugged off a boot. Using the point of a knife blade he lifted out the insole and extracted a thin piece of ragged-edged calf skin.

"One thing you didn't know was in that letter you stole from me," he told the sulky-faced Chico with an amused chuckle. He tossed the fragment into the hands of Sam Hally. "Got the mate to it, mister?"

Sam eyed it for a moment. Burned into the hairy strip of red hide was the letter H. He nodded, fumbled in the pocket of his dusty flannel shirt and produced a similar fragment, into which was burned an M. Placed together the torn edges of the strips of skin fitted perfectly, the two pieces forming the HM brand of the Hally and McGee cattle outfit. The big senior partner of the HM ranch looked up with twinkling eyes.

"Wasn't needing this token to know who you was, Clay," he said placidly, "you're the image of Bill Brant when he was your age," his smile broadened, "I knowed you was Bill Brant's grandson the minute I laid eyes on you." He looked at his partner. "Reckon Seth knowed you, too, by the grin on his face."

Seth nodded, his wary gaze on the swarthy Chico Lopez.

"What I want to know is, how come Bill Brant's grandson let this coyote pull off the play he done," he grumbled.

Clay Brant tugged on his boot and got to his feet.

"Chico," he said softly, "I ought to kill you for what you did—"

"The only way to treat his kind is to string 'em up—let 'em dance on air," broke in Seth's chill voice. His fierce gaze swept the bleak surroundings. "Ain't no tree handy," he mourned.

"You put poison in my coffee," continued Clay, "you thought you'd left me to die, back there at the Circle Dot. Would have died, too, but for old Ah Wong. You thought Ah Wong had gone into Cimarron for his weekly game of fan tan, but luckily for me he got to worrying about the strychnine he'd bought to use on the rats. Somebody had run off with the can and he was

58

worried. He told me later he'd noticed you in the kitchen; and what that old Chinaman thinks of you, Chico, wouldn't be fit to print. So he hightailed it back to the ranch—just in time. He knows a thing or two, that cook, and he got that poison out of me."

The young cattleman's gray eyes were dark with suppressed fury, his voice suddenly brittle. "I didn't die, you murderous rat, but I was one sick man for the next two days. It wasn't until I learned you had gone off with Mingo and my best saddle that I put two and two together and knew who had sneaked Sam Hally's letter from my coat pocket. But you didn't know about the secret token, Chico. I'd already hidden it in my boot. Sam had said enough in his letter to make you think there'd be good pickings down in this country where you could pass yourself off as Clay Brant."

"I'm in favor of feeding the coyote a dose o' lead poison pronto," broke in Seth's cold voice.

Chico's shifty, terrified gaze went to him, read the promise of death in the little HM man's narrow-slitted stare.

"*Dios!*" he gasped, "Senor—do not let him kill me!" he cowered close to the side of the man whose own murder he had attempted.

Clay shook his head at the scowling Seth. "He's not worth wasting your good lead on, old timer," he drawled. "No gunplay, you fighting old longhorn." His eyes twinkled. "Been hearing about Seth McGee and Sam Hally ever since I was a yearling," he added affectionately. "Grandfather talked a lot about you two . . . said you were always ready to go on the prod for a friend."

Seth's bleak eyes softened. "Bill Brant was one square hombre, Clay," he assured the young Cimarron cattleman. "Never was a finer man than Bill Brant." The menacing gun lowered, slid into holster.

Sam nodded approval.

"Clay's right, Seth," he told his partner. "Reckon about all we kin do is give the skunk a swift kick and turn him loose—hightail it away from these parts and never come back."

"If he ever does come back and runs into me, he'll run into plenty hot lead," promised Seth.

Clay looked at his renegade cowhand. "You've heard the sentence, Chico," he said quietly; "hand over that letter—and the badge—and make plenty dust away from here."

With a gasping sigh of relief the swarthy man dropped letter and badge into Clay's outstretched hand and went on shaky legs to the bay mare.

"Don't forget he's got your saddle on that mare, Clay," reminded Sam.

Chico caught the words.

"I will not take the Senor's fine saddle," he muttered, and feverishly set to work, stripping off the silver-mounted saddle and bridle.

Clay sent out a shrill whistle. A horse nickered softly, came trotting from behind the butte, a magnificent animal, coal black, save for the star between intelligent lustrous eyes.

"Some bronc!" admired Seth.

"Midnight's no bronc, old timer," laughed Clay. "Midnight was sired by a thoroughbred."

In a few minutes the exchange of saddles was effected and Chico Lopez sending the bay mare at top speed down the trail dropping to the desert floor.

Seth McGee's bleak gaze followed the renegade regretfully.

"We ain't seen the last of that coyote," he prophesied gloomily. "We should have left him up here for the buzzards."

Clay shrugged his shoulders, grinned at the mildly amused Sam, thoughtfully holding a lighted match to the letter recovered from Chico. For a moment the three men watched the flame lick the paper into ashes that suddenly scattered before the lifting breeze.

Clay spoke softly:

"Well—and what comes next, my friends?"

"We got no time to lose, Clay," Sam told him soberly; "while we ride, I'll tell you about a promise I made seventeen years ago."

CHAPTER V
MARIA AND MIGUEL

Some forty odd years had whitened the once raven hair of Maria Cota. She was no longer the supple young woman Miguel had brought from the distant Rio Grande to take charge of the domestic welfare of Benson and Brant's new Box B ranch in *El Valle de los Reyes*. If her tongue was sharp at times, her heart was no less kindly than when long ago she had loved and mothered the little Paula, who later was to become the girl-bride of Ed Benson.

That almost fierce devotion had been transferred to Paula's motherless daughter.

Shirley Benson was a reincarnated Paula in Maria Cota's fond mind; save that her hair was a pale bright gold she was her mother over again. Maria loved her as she had loved Paula.

Her own numerous brood had long since scattered, save for her eldest son, Juan, and her youngest daughter, Carmel, who had been engaged to marry Ed Benson's ranch foreman, Clem Collins. The raid that left Shirley fatherless had also ended Carmel's romance, and made Juan Cota foreman of the Box B outfit; although it was rumored that the latter's capable old mother was the actual power on the ranch. When such talk came to the still shapely ears of Maria Cota she would lift a scornful plump shoulder. Only the Senorita was the boss of the Box B ranch, was invariably her tart rejoinder. As for herself, Maria Cota, she was, what she had been these past forty years, the ranch housekeeper, and the Senorita's devoted servant.

The old ranch-house had grown to a large rambling dwelling since the night Bill Brant had ridden away to make a new home for himself in the remote wilds of the Cimarron country. The original log and adobe structure now formed one of the wings enclosing the patio and was the undisputed domain of Maria Cota. It was here the Mexican servants had their quarters, and what had formerly been the living room was now a huge kitchen, a place floored with worn red adobe bricks and always redolent with savory smells of good things concocted under the watchful eyes of the capable Maria.

It was in a dim corner of the old kitchen, under colorful strings of dangling chili peppers that Maria's husband, Miguel, spent most of his hours, nodding drowsily, or rolling endless little brown paper cigarettes.

Old Miguel's active days were done. His thick hair and drooping mustaches were white, his once smooth face like withered brown leather. Perhaps Miguel was not always drowsing when he seemed to be. There were times when his sunken brown eyes showed a singular stealthy alertness since the night his daughter's sweetheart and Don Eduardo Benson had been slain by rustlers; especially when certain members of the Box B outfit held low-voiced conversation in his vicinity. Possibly old Miguel was not so deaf or senile as generally supposed. In fact, his wife, and Carmel, and the burly Juan, secretly held the aged ex-vaquero in vast respect. They knew that Miguel had vowed to live for the day that would see vengeance done on the men who had slain his beloved patron and robbed pretty Carmel of her husband-to-be.

Maria and Miguel were the last remaining links binding the old ranch to the dim past when two young men drove their bawling longhorns into the Valley of the Kings. Shirley had found herself unable to tell her father's faithful retainers of the disaster soon to overwhelm the Box B ranch. It was Maria herself who broached the matter, the morning of Shirley's chance meeting with Sam and Seth.

"You try to hide the truth from me," she accused. "I know why always you are not hungry, why you are so silent and sad." She spoke in the liquid tongue of her native Mexico.

"It's lonesome—without him, Maria," parried the girl. "You know how he always liked me to have breakfast with him—"

"It is not of Don Eduardo, I speak," persisted

the old housekeeper. "You grieve for him—*si*—as we all do, Miguel and Juan—my poor Carmel. It is another trouble that is on your mind—that keeps you awake these long nights," Maria nodded, "you go riding into the darkness that comes before the dawn—trying to forget—"

Shirley toyed listlessly with her coffee spoon. She was still in her riding clothes, fearing that Maria would worry if she were late for breakfast. It seemed that Maria was aware of her early-morning rides.

"I am worried," she admitted; "we can't run a cattle ranch without cattle, Maria. Juan must have told you how matters are. He's combed every canyon for miles and the best he can show for his work is a bunch of mangy old outlaw strays that even a cattle thief won't bother to steal."

"There are ways of procuring more cows," said the old woman, "the Box B has many acres—and banks lend money on good land." Her keen black eyes probed the girl—"what they call the mortgage," she added innocently.

Shirley shrugged her shoulders. "There is no more land to mortgage, Maria," she confessed a bit wearily.

"Ah, it is what I thought!" Maria nodded; "it is why the Senor Sandell comes here so many times these past months. It is he who plans to take our ranch from us. I do not trust the Senor Sandell," she added with a gloomy shake of her head; "he is a bad man, that one!"

"You must not say such things," reproved the girl. "Mr. Sandell was most kind to Father, and has been more than kind to me—generous and patient."

"There are tales about him," insisted the woman. "It is said he practically stole the Bar 7 from that poor sick Senor O'Flynn—"

"Mr. O'Flynn drank too much and gambled too much," Shirley retorted. "He has himself to blame!"

"The Senor O'Flynn has also lost many fat cattle to the rustlers," Maria reminded her; "and where did he lose his money with the cards but at the Red Front saloon which men say is really owned by the Senor Sandell?"

"Gossip!" flared the girl, "I don't believe a word of it."

"I have lived many years," grumbled the old woman. "I know a bad man when I see him, Senorita." Shaking her head dolefully, she went back to her kitchen.

"The child will not listen to the truth," she told Miguel, drowsing in his corner. Tears welled in her still splendid black eyes. "Ah, *Madre de Dios*! What shall we do, my husband? It is true, as we suspected! This beautiful *rancho* is fallen into the hands of a wicked man . . . our *Valle de los Reyes*—where we have been so happy these many years—where all our children were born—the graves of Felipe and our little Mercedes—and Don Eduardo, lie under the same earth made sacred by our beloved Senora Paula!"

The distraught woman wept softly into her apron.

"What shall we do, my Miguel?"

Miguel's bony fingers were busy with cigarette paper and tobacco, sunken brown eyes seemingly absorbed in the task. Finally he struck a match against the hand-hewn arm of his big chair, touched the flame to the cigarette and looked at his wife, spirals of smoke curling from his nostrils.

"Has the word yet come from the Senor Hally?" he asked in a surprisingly sonorous voice.

Maria shook her head despondently, dabbed at her wet eyes with the apron.

"It will come," Miguel tranquilly assured her. "Many years ago he made a promise to our Senora Paula. He will keep that promise. Do not abandon hope, my Maria."

His wife dried her eyes, smiled at him.

"You are so wise, Miguel," she told him fondly; "they say you are too old, and a fool, but I know that you are wise—" She bent over and kissed him. "I shall make you an enchilada—very hot with much chili—" She bustled away to the big brick range with its bright array of shining copper kettles.

CHAPTER VI
BILL BRANT'S GRANDSON

Sam Hally had faithfully kept Paula's secret. Not even Seth McGee and the Cotas knew the full story, although they were aware of the romance that had severed the friendship of Bill Brant and Ed Benson and why the former had ridden from the Valley of the Kings, never to return.

Shirley's mother could not forgive herself for the trick she had played the day she was forced to choose between Bill Brant and the man she loved, nor could she quite forgive Ed Benson for insisting upon so harsh a wager. Ed Benson had won the girl—and the full ownership of the ranch—but Paula had cheated in order that he could not fail to win. Which was why she had urged Sam Hally to become the custodian of the paper she found in her husband's desk and made him promise that when the right time came Sam would see justice done to Bill Brant's son's son.

There were times when Sam was tempted to break his promise to Paula and quietly put the deed on record and so secure her daughter's future undisturbed inheritance. He knew that Bill Brant had prospered on the Cimarron, that his grandson's huge holdings made him one of the wealthiest cattlemen in the Oklahoma Panhandle. Clay would have scorned to profit personally from the situation.

The time came when Sam was thankful he had kept his secret. Few remembered that Ed Benson once had a partner; he was regarded as the sole owner of the Box B ranch. In theory he was; in fact he was not, there being no documentary evidence of public record to show that Bill Brant had deeded to him his half interest. It was in this fact that Sam saw a weapon with which to break Sandell's stranglehold on Shirley Benson's inheritance. The various mortgages Ed Benson had placed on the ranch lacked the signature of the man who was still legally his partner. Sam knew that if he destroyed the deed signed by Bill Brant, the latter's grandson would be co-heir with Shirley to the vast acres of the Box B ranch. The appearance of such an heir would be a blow to Sandell's cunning schemes.

Maria Cota had promised Sam to keep him informed of events vitally concerning the ranch; it was from her that word reached him in the Spanish Sinks of sinister doings, the mysterious cattle raids, the murder of Ed Benson and his foreman at the hands of the rustlers.

It was then, and for reasons that would have astonished Shirley's mother, that Sam decided that the time had come to make use of the secret she had entrusted with him. Not for the sake of Bill Brant—but for the sake of Ed Benson's daughter.

Unfortunately for Morton Sandell he was no stranger to the Spanish Sinks cowmen. Sam and Seth knew him of old as a crooked gambler in San Antonio, despite Shirley's assertion that he was a New Yorker. The HM men had grave suspicions regarding the self-styled banker's activities in San Luis; suspicions further aggravated by a certain message from their old friend Pop Daly, pioneer hotel man in the town.

The affair at Poison Springs was warning that Sandell was aware of their interest in his schemes, that his spies had warned him of Sam's message to Clay Brant arranging the rendezvous at Indian Head.

Sam did not believe Sandell knew Clay was the lawful owner of an undivided half interest in the ranch, or that lacking the signature of the Brant heirs, the mortgages given him by Ed Benson were worthless pieces of paper.

Sandell's alarm would spring from an entirely different source, the HM men grimly realized. Clay had a reputation up in the Cimarron country. It was Clay who organized his fellow-cattlemen against the rustlers and drove them in terror from the Panhandle. It would be in the banker's mind that they had sent for Clay to investigate the many mysterious raids that had depleted the Box B herds and brought ruin to other cow outfits of the San Luis range. Unwilling to allow so formidable an enemy of the rustler clan in his domain, Sandell had sent his hired gunman, the luckless Whitey Joe, to lie in wait for the young Cimarron cattleman. Chico's attempt to impersonate his employer had made the attempt abortive and probably saved Clay's life.

By the time Clay and the two Spanish Sinks cowmen were within a mile of the Box B ranchhouse, Bill Brant's grandson was in possession of the facts.

"I've told you all I know," finished Sam.

"And that's a-plenty," Seth added grimly.

"You're sure this Sandell is the same man you ran across in San Antonio?" queried Clay.

"He's bleached his hair some," Sam answered, "barrin' the color of his hair he's the same feller—"

"I reckon his dang heart ain't bleached none," opined Seth. "I figger that hombre's heart is as black as it ever was."

"Does he know you two old longhorns?"

"He wouldn't remember us from them San Antone days," Sam was sure. "He knows us plenty, though, as old-time friends of the Bensons. His sending Whitey Joe to ambush you sure proves he's had his spies watchin' things in the Sinks for weeks." He chuckled. "We know that much—got one of 'em locked up out at the ranch now—a feller named Tulsa Jones. Hasn't talked

71

none yet but I figger he will when the boys git through with him."

"Any notion about some of these other spies— the ones you think are on the Box B payroll?" Clay wanted to know.

"That's what I aim to find out right soon," growled the big HM man. "I figger there's snakes sleepin' nights in the Box B bunkhouse."

"Traitors?"

There was a steely look in Clay's eyes.

"I got plenty good medicine for snakes—them kind o' snakes," purred Seth McGee.

"Sam," said Clay; he reined his horse; "I'm glad you sent for me. Between the three of us, we'll do some snake killing; but first of all we've got to lay some plans."

"The gal has promised she won't sign no papers for Sandell till we see her ag'in," Sam informed him. He shook his grizzled head. "Don't see how she can keep the old ranch on its feet even if she don't sign that quit-claim paper," he added dubiously. "Juan Cota was telling me them rustlers sure cleaned up on that last raid."

"Let's get down and talk it over," Clay suggested. "I've got some ideas."

They found seats on a boulder in the shade of a big oak tree and rolled cigarettes. In the distance they could see the clustering roofs of the ranch buildings. Smoke lifted lazily from the kitchen chimney, melted into the blue sky. A small herd of bawling cattle streamed slowly from the mouth of a distant canyon, urged on toward the corrals by the shrill yips of some half dozen riders.

"All that's left of the Box B," muttered Sam. "Juan told me he was aimin' to comb the west fork of the San Jacinto for strays. Reckon that's them."

"Sam, have you the paper my grandfather signed, deeding his half to Ed Benson?"

"Sure have, Clay"—Sam fumbled in a pocket—"fetched it along a-purpose for you."

Clay glanced at the paper briefly. There was no mistaking his grandfather's familiar handwriting. He folded the paper and returned it to Sam.

"Some day, Sam," he said, "we'll put this deed on record—after we've fixed Sandell's clock for him. In the meantime you keep the thing."

The two cowmen looked at each other, nodded approvingly.

"We figgered you'd look at it that way, son!" There was pride in old Sam's voice. "Figgered you'd not go back on Bill Brant's signed name."

"I've got plenty; and if I hadn't we'd let that deal stand, no matter what trick was played on my grandfather. He made the bet." Clay grinned at them. "The way it's turned out it's lucky for the Benson girl that it happened. Sandell is due for the surprise of his life when he learns those mortgages are worthless, which he will when he starts foreclosure suit—"

"Providin' the gal don't sign that dang quit-claim paper afore we kin head her off," worried Seth.

"Even if she does give him a quit-claim deed it won't be worth the paper it's written on," Clay argued. "You see, she can't sign away my rights in the old ranch, not so long as nobody knows about this—" He nodded at the paper in Sam's fingers. "The moment Sandell starts foreclosure proceedings, or if he wangles a quit-claim from the girl, he'll get a hefty piece of dynamite from my lawyer." Clay nodded thoughtfully. "We'll get off a note to Cimarron tonight—ask Kincaid to be all set for a war."

"Sandell's got the law eatin' out of his hand down in this county," gruffed Sam. "He'd have you licked, son, if you take him into court."

"He can't lick the Supreme Court of the United States," protested Clay. He stared thoughtfully at the broad reach of meadow lying between the low foothills undulating the length of the valley.

"Plenty of good grass." He nodded vigorously, as though he had arrived at a definite decision. "We'll start a trail herd down this way from the Cimarron, Sam. The Circle Dot can easily spare a couple of thousand cows—"

"Meaning you're going to show your hand to the gal?" asked Sam. "Meaning you're going to lay the cards on the table—tell her you're claiming your half interest in the ranch?"

"No"—Clay shook his head—"don't want her to *sabe* who I am, yet," he decided. "I want to keep under cover as much as possible, Sam. Right now, my notion is to hire on as a Box B hand, if you can manage it. There's a chance I can find out a few things, mixing with the outfit; maybe get a line on the men you suspect are in Sandell's pay."

"A right smart idea," admired Sam.

"And all I craves is the names of said skunks, when you gets wise to 'em," added Seth thinly.

Respect, affection, was in the look Clay gave the little HM man.

"You haven't changed, Seth," he said softly. "You're still the same two-gun fighting man my grandfather used to tell me about. Saved his life three times in one night, he said."

"The time Santana's gang jumped us just out of Tascosa," recalled Sam.

Seth grinned. " 'Twas fifty fifty, Clay. Bill Brant did the same for me, that night—reckon he never told you *that* part of the story, huh?"

Clay's gaze was following the pitiful remnants of the Box B's once great herds, slowly moving toward the corrals. He looked at his companions.

"We've got to make the Benson girl believe these Circle Dot cows are some stuff you two have picked up cheap for feeders, understand. The idea is she'll pasture them on shares. We'll have 'em road-branded by the time we get 'em here," he added.

The two HM men nodded approval. Clay continued:

"What about this man you say Miss Benson has put in as foreman. Is he one of us? Can we trust him?"

"Folks say lots of hard things about Juan Cota," Sam answered cautiously. "There's talk that he's a bandit chief, when he's south of the border, mebbe one of them revolutionary hombres; but I'm telling you, Clay, you can bet your last *peso* on Juan when he's on the old ranch. He'd give every drop of his blood for Shirley Benson—and the Box B *rancho*."

Seth nodded vigorous agreement.

"Juan sure'd never go back on the *rancho*," he declared. "Juan was born on the *rancho*; he'd die with his guns a-smokin'—for the old Box B."

Clay was satisfied to accept their guarantee of Juan's integrity. He knew the stern code by which these two grizzled old men lived.

"How about the others in the outfit," he asked.

"Maria Cota, and old Miguel can be trusted to the limit. They kind of figger Shirley's their own gal," Sam assured him. "Maria brought her up— same as she raised her mother"—Sam nodded— "you can trust them two. Old Maria's the queen bee on that ranch and all the other Mexicans do what she tells 'em. She and Juan'd have their scalps if they didn't play straight."

"Ain't a Mex on the place that don't kiss the ground the Benson gal walks on," averred Seth. "It's the bunkhouse fellers we got to watch out for," he grumbled.

"Meaning any one of 'em in particular?" questioned Clay.

"Referrin' special to a snake wearing the name o' Wes Droon," answered the little cowman grimly. "If poor Ed Benson had knowed about Wes Droon he wouldn't have hired him."

"This here Wes Droon hombre used to work for the Cross Knife outfit in the Spanish Sinks," explained Sam. "That was a couple of years back, when the Tandy gang was rustlin' the Sinks to the bone"—Sam chuckled grimly—"that is they *was* until we set a few of 'em to dancin' on air, including Tandy himself. Well, Don Mike Callahan of the old Cross Knife found out that Wes was one of the wild bunch, planted with the outfit a-purpose to git inside information for the gang. Wes made his getaway and 'twas only recent that we knowed he's with the Box B. We figger he's up to his old tricks—which mebbe explains a thing or two about the rustlin' going on in these parts."

"There's two other fellers I ain't trusting none," added Seth, "meanin' Pecos and his pardner, Red Hansen. I'd say they was hand in glove with Wes."

"Any others?" Clay wanted to know.

Sam considered thoughtfully. "There's a feller by the name of Vin Sarge," he went on; "Seth and me figger he's the big wind, next to Sandell. This Sarge hombre is foreman of the Bar 7 outfit, a ranch that Sandell's fake bank got away from old Pat Flynn. The Bar 7 was a good ranch, once, till the rustlers cleaned her out. Flynn was all mortgaged to the eyes and couldn't pay up 'cause his cows were stole. Sandell put Sarge in charge. Haven't got proof," added the old man, "but I'm plumb suspicious of Vin Sarge. He's a rustler—and in cahoots with Sandell."

Clay stared musingly at the bawling cattle slowly nearing the corrals.

"Does this Wes Droon know you two?"

The HM men nodded.

"If he sees you at the ranch he'll be suspicious."

Seth bristled.

"I'm cravin' to meet up with the snake," he announced.

The young cattleman shook his head.

"You no *sabe*, Seth," he smiled. "We want to make use of Wes Droon—right where he is, on the ranch—unless we think up something better. For the present we must not let him know that we suspect him."

"I git you," approved Sam. "He ain't to know there's anything doing. If he's secretly working with the gang he can tell us a lot of things when we're ready to make him talk—"

"Why not make him talk up fast," argued Seth. "No time to lose, way I figger the thing."

"We want to git the rest of the gang," explained his partner patiently. "We must give Droon rope to hang himself and—the hull passel of 'em. There's a heap we want to know," he added, "and one of 'em is the name of the man that shot poor Ed Benson and Clem Collins." Sam looked at Clay. "Clem was Ed's foreman."

Clay nodded, smiled at the sulking Seth.

"Sam's right, old timer. No use fooling with the hired henchmen. We want our ropes round the necks of the big chiefs—" Clay paused, an intent look in his eyes. "I've another idea coming up. We'll talk it over later. Leave it to me, Seth, and we'll work it out to smash this gang for good."

"I'm a dang fool," muttered the HM man. He gave Clay a sheepish grin. "Which same you ain't, young feller. Reckon the play is to keep Wes Droon for bait—like you say."

They rode on toward the ranch-house, circling to the left to keep the clustering trees between them and the corrals. It was home ground for Sam and Seth; and presently they drew rein at a small gate opening into a vegetable garden, where an elderly peon was irrigating a patch of young beans.

He straightened up at their approach and eyed

them wonderingly. It was not customary for horsemen to enter by way of the vegetable garden.

"*Buenas dias*," Sam greeted, "don't you remember me, Felipe?"

Recognition dawned in the Mexican's eyes. He nodded vigorously, a smile wrinkling his dark face.

"*Si, Senor . . . yo sabe usted*!"

"Sure, you know me," chuckled the old man. "Droon round the place?" he asked.

Felipe shook his head, replied that the *vaquero* Droon was over in the West Fork with Pecos and Red Hansen, repairing a drift fence. He added the information that Juan Cota would be at the corrals.

Sam looked at his companions.

"Seth and me'll leave our broncs here and walk through to the kitchen," he decided. "Don't want anybody to spot our HM iron—might be spies and tell Droon." He considered a moment. "Clay, you can ride round by the main gate. Juan'll know who you are, but to the rest of 'em you're just a cowpoke lookin' for a job, *sabe*."

Clay jerked a nod at them and rode away at a jog trot toward the corrals. The two HM men swung from their saddles and after a brief talk with Felipe led their horses into the vegetable garden, where the *mozo* found a snug hiding place for the animals under a shed used for storing his garden produce.

80

Sam removed the roan's bridle and loosened saddle cinch. Seth performed the same office for his bay horse.

"Give 'em some water when they've cooled off," Sam instructed Felipe. "You can give 'em some of them ears of corn, too," he added as he hurried away with his companion.

The path led them through the garden to a seldom-used side door opening into the kitchen. Sam rapped softly; they heard the familiar flop flop of old Maria Cota's soft shoes—the door opened an inch, revealing a peering dark eye.

"*Madre de Dios*!" they heard the old woman exclaim in a low, jubilant voice. "Miguel—they have come—they have come!"

In a moment the two cowmen were inside the great kitchen, the door closing behind them.

Maria stared, her eyes bright with tears, a shining copper pan in one hand.

"I was making an enchilada for Miguel," she told them in Spanish. "Now I shall make enchiladas for you, too!"

CHAPTER VII
SAM HALLY SINGS AN OLD SONG

Shirley was more perturbed than she cared to admit. She had a vast respect for Maria Cota's intelligence. The relationship between them was that of grandmother and granddaughter, rather than housekeeper and mistress. The untimely death of Shirley's young mother had left her baby girl to the tender care of Maria, her close friend and foster-mother. The devotion and love Maria gave to little Paula Wynne she had continued to give to Paula's infant daughter. It was to the good Maria that little Shirley had always taken her childish problems, and with the years the bond of affection between them had taken deep root in their hearts.

Shirley knew that the kindly, unselfish Mexican woman was her dearest friend; she would not have warned her so earnestly against Morton Sandell unless for some good reason.

Breakfast was impossible, the girl decided. She would take a shower, change into something cool.

The shower revived her spirits. Slipping into a white linen skirt and blouse she went out to the garden to cope with the problem of Morton Sandell and the quit-claim deed he was bringing her to sign that morning. He was to call at noon with the papers.

Shirley loved the big ranch garden—the old trees. A small park, really, with a tiny brook and pond, fed by the waters of San Jacinto creek. Maria Cota had told her that her father had planted the trees and dug the ditch that the years had transformed into a grassy-banked little stream with a waterfall emptying into the pool. The trees were huge, now; towering eucalyptus, giant oaks, sycamores and willows, with here and there the spreading branches of a hoary cotton-wood.

She stood for a time, watching the waterfall with unseeing eyes, her mind on the problem of the quit-claim deed. Morton Sandell would soon be arriving . . . she had promised Sam Hally and Seth McGee not to sign the papers—any papers . . . she must devise some excuse for putting Sandell off—some plausible reason. Writer's cramp . . . smallpox in the house . . .

The girl's lips curved in a sudden smile. They were a pair of old sillies . . . dear old sillies! But they had been so tremendously in earnest, those two old ex-Box B men! They did not want her to sign that quit-claim paper under any circumstances—not until after she had seen them again. She recalled Sam's mastiff growl at the mention of Sandell's name, the chill look in Seth's hard black eyes.

Shirley was suddenly conscious of a feeling of fear; perhaps, after all, she had been deceived in Morton Sandell!

Her thoughts went to old Maria, her insistence that Sandell was not to be trusted.

Perhaps Maria was right; perhaps she was the victim of a wicked conspiracy that was spreading sinister tentacles even before the murder of her father.

She crossed the little rustic bridge, wandered down the path—came to the rose garden, they had always called it.

She leaned on the gate, her gaze fixed on two slender white stone columns. A climbing rose entwined one of the marble shafts—her mother's. The rose clinging to the base of the other one was not yet in bloom. It had been planted only a few months—in memory of the slain Ed Benson.

There were other, smaller headstones in the little rose garden; two for the children of Miguel and Maria; and one for the slain sweetheart of their daughter, Carmel, the brave Clem Collins, late foreman of the ranch, who had died with a gun in his hand, fighting by the side of her father.

Shirley drew a quick breath. Died fighting—fighting for what? For the old ranch—*for the old Box B!* That was what her father—and Clem Collins had died for!

The thought thrilled her, stiffened her courage.

What was it old Sam Hally had told her only that

84

same morning—out in the rimrock overlooking the desert? He had said, "You couldn't be nothin' else but brave; to be brave is your inheritance—the brave ain't never been licked—"

Sam was right; courage was the heritage of Clem Collins, the heritage of her father—her mother. Courage was her heritage!

She pushed open the gate in the white picket fence and knelt between the two headstones, one hand touching a red rose that smiled from the slender column on the right, her other hand reaching to the cold marble on the left, where roses had not yet bloomed.

Presently she stood up. The weariness, the indecision, had left her. She knew now what she would tell Morton Sandell.

A thought came to her—the memory of a book she had once read—a book called *The Red Badge of Courage*. Shirley suddenly smiled, impulsively plucked the red rose her hand had caressed and pinned it to her blouse.

She saw it was nearly noon—time for Sandell's arrival. She closed the gate and hastened toward the house, pausing quickly as the winding path brought her in view of the little rustic bridge spanning the brook. Two men were waiting there.

One of them she recognized as Juan Cota, the ranch foreman; the other, a tall, younger man, was a stranger.

Juan greeted her with his customary bow and

brandishing of huge silver-braided sombrero. There was good Spanish blood in the Cota family, Shirley had always thought.

The cattle boss was a burly man of early middle age, a first-rate cowman. He had been away from the ranch for several years, supposedly serving as an officer with some revolutionary army across the border. Rumor whispered that actually those absent years had seen him in the role of bandit leader in Sonora until the *Rurales* made it too hot for him. Shirley was inclined to believe the rumor true. One sensed something of the savage in Juan Cota—the wild freebooter. A scar across one cheek heightened the harshness of his swarthy face when in repose. When he smiled he showed flashing white teeth under a short bristling mustache. He was attractive enough at such moments, his eyes warm and friendly. Shirley liked him and knew he could be trusted when it came to the honor of the ranch—the home of his parents—and his birthplace.

A glance told the girl that Juan's companion was obviously a cowboy, and unusually good-looking. In spite of his youthfulness there was a certain seasoned maturity in his bearing that was reassuring. She liked the steady gray eyes regarding her so calmly, the keen, sun-tanned face; and noticed with approval that his garb was simple, a faded dark blue shirt, dark pants, pulled over plain soft-leather boots and turned up at the bottoms. Scarred, much worn leather chaps indicated he had worked in the brush country. He wore a battered wide-brimmed hat, under which she glimpsed straight darkly-red, almost black, hair. Even the two guns, slung low in tied-down holsters, were plain serviceable weapons. Nothing of the dandy about this capable-looking young cowboy, Shirley reflected.

Juan was speaking in his voluble Spanish, from which she gathered he desired to hire the stranger.

"I don't know, Juan," she demurred. "The way things are I don't see how we can use another man. I think you must be crazy," she added.

The cattle boss was strangely insistent, it seemed to Shirley. He would discharge Pecos—and Red Hansen, he explained, both of them lazy good-for-nothings. The Americano would be worth a dozen such loafers.

Shirley hesitated, glanced down at the red rose flaming against the snowy whiteness of her blouse. She had made a resolution a few minutes ago, a resolution that meant a fight, she would need good men—men she could trust. And this young, steady-eyed cowboy seemed exactly that sort of man. She studied him thoughtfully, appraisingly.

"I'll be fair," she said to him finally, "there may be a lot of trouble on this ranch. We've been up against a gang of rustlers and what not. I'm planning to do something about it—just what I don't know—except that I'm going to get some cows on this ranch again if such a thing is humanly possible." Shirley's words came tumbling from her lips as she noticed that Juan was staring at her with mixed amazement and delight. "So it will mean a fight to keep those cows when we do get them," she finished a bit weakly.

The cowboy shrugged his shoulders, smiled gravely. "I don't hunt trouble, ma'am," he answered quietly, "but if trouble hunts me I don't run away from it."

Shirley smiled at him; she was feeling the least bit foolish—she had talked a little too confidently of the big things she would do.

"You don't look as if you would scare easily"—she hesitated—"Juan hasn't told me your name—"

"Clay, ma'am," he informed her, "Bill Clay—"

"I'm Shirley Benson," she smiled; "but of course Juan has told you." She gave him a sharp glance. "How did you happen to hit the Box B for a job? Did somebody send you—Mr. Sandell send you?"

"Always heard the Box B was a good outfit to work for," he explained. "No, ma'am, I've never met the man you speak of—this Mr. Sandell. I've heard of him," he added.

"Well," the girl's voice was rueful, "the Box B *was* a good ranch to work for—once." She shrugged her shoulders, looked at her foreman. "What do you think, Juan? Is he as good as he looks—and sounds?" She spoke in Spanish.

"*Si, Senorita! muy bueno!*"

The burly cattle boss grinned amusedly.

"He speaks as good Spanish as ourselves," he added. "I should have told you, Senorita."

Shirley colored, smiled apologetically at the tall cowboy.

"That is—is fortunate," she said, attempting to cover her momentary confusion. "It makes things so much easier for Juan if our men understand his own language."

"You mean I'm hired, ma'am?"

"I think so, Clay—that is if forty a month—"

Clay was looking at her rather than listening to her words, and thinking he had never seen so delightful a picture—this young girl with the gleaming pale gold hair, so slim and straight in her simple white dress, the red rose nestled above her heart, her direct, fearless eyes.

Shirley was nettled by his apparent hesitation.

"I'm afraid we can't pay more," she began coldly; he interrupted quickly:

"It's plenty, ma'am," he assured her, reddening under her cool stare.

Shirley nodded, looked again at her foreman.

"All right, Juan. I'll leave it to you—"

With a little nod at them she passed across the rustic bridge and continued toward the house.

Doubts assailed her. She wondered if she had gone quite crazy—putting a new man on the payroll when she honestly did not know how much longer she would continue to own the ranch. She had talked so big in front of Juan and Bill Clay . . . telling them she would re-stock the ranch. Where in the world could she raise money to buy cows. Sandell would be fairly entitled to any money she could manage to find. And what was she going to tell Mort Sandell? She had thought her mind was made up—that she would refuse to sign his wretched quit-claim papers. The little flare of courage had evaporated and left her in a panic.

Questions flung at her like wolves with bared fangs, tearing to shreds her bold resolve to fight for the life of the old ranch. By the time she reached the house she was in a state of near-hysteria—certainly in no mental condition for the encounter with Morton Sandell.

Maria Cota met her in the patio. There was a curious look of alarm in the old housekeeper's eyes.

"The Senor Sandell has come again. He waits in the living room," she told the girl with a toss of her head.

Shirley sank into a garden seat placed against the ancient adobe wall, festooned with gay scarlet bouganvilleas. She stared up at the older woman, fear, rebellion in her eyes.

"I—I can't see him, Maria. Tell him—tell him I've the smallpox—writer's cramp—" she laughed hysterically.

Maria gave her a frightened look. "Poor child! You—you are ill, my darling—"

Shirley pulled herself together with an effort. "No, I'm not, silly! I was just remembering something—something ridiculous. But I don't want to see Mr. Sandell—if you can get rid of him."

"I'll get rid of him," promised the old lady in a determined voice. Her white head bent low to the girl's ear: "You saw Juan, Senorita? He was looking for you." There was an odd excitement in Maria's voice.

"Yes, I met him down by the brook. Why, Maria?" Shirley eyed the woman curiously. "You seem so—so excited," she added wonderingly.

Maria denied this. "It is that Sandell hombre that upsets me. When he is here it is like having a snake in the house. I would trust a rattlesnake more than him." She shrugged her plump shoulders. "And you hired the young *vaquero Americano*, Senorita? Juan said he would be a good man to have on the *rancho*."

Shirley studied her shrewdly. Maria's voice was *too* casual. There was some mystery behind the interest in the new cowboy.

"I believe you put Juan up to it!" she charged. "What is all this excitement about the man?"

"He is so nice," confided the housekeeper, "so young—such a boy"—Maria lifted an expressive shoulder—"Carmel will be so pleased if you have hired him. She saw him when he rode into the yard on his beautiful black horse—such a handsome *caballero!*"

Shirley thought she saw the light.

"Maria Cota!" she exclaimed, "you dear old plotter! You are scheming to find Carmel a new sweetheart—a husband!" She jumped up and gave the old housekeeper a hug. "Yes—it's all right; I told Juan to put your handsome Americano on the payroll. Now go and get rid of Mr. Sandell."

The beaming Maria hastened away, soft shoes padding on the worn bricks of the long gallery. Shirley relaxed on the seat, vaguely conscious of a disturbing dismay.

So the mystery was explained. She understood now the eagerness of Juan and his mother to have the good-looking young cowboy on the ranch. Carmel was the answer. Carmel had seen him—taken a fancy to him!

A suave, mellow voice broke into her meditations. Shirley turned a startled face.

"Why, Mr. Sandell!"

The San Luis banker smiled down at her, mopped his face with a large silk handkerchief.

"Happened to see you pass the window," he explained. "I thought I'd join you out here. A charming little retreat, Miss Shirley; a little bit of Paradise cloistered inside these old gray walls. I remember your father telling me that he planted that huge old pepper tree with his own hands nearly forty years ago."

Mr. Sandell's approving gaze traveled around the patio, came back to the girl leaning against the ancient wall. Admiration crept into his eyes as he looked at her.

"And may I say that you make an exquisite picture in that white frock—against the background of those beautiful red bougainvillea—"

She frowned, struggled back to some semblance of poise.

"You startled me," she confessed. "Won't you sit down, Mr. Sandell?" She made room for him on the bench.

The banker said he would be delighted and beamingly seated himself.

"Yes, indeed," he continued smoothly, "this pleasant little retreat is a bit of old Mexico. Ah, my dear young lady, *there* is a picturesque land for you—such color, charm, romance with a capital R. No doubt your father gained his inspiration for this delightful little garden from some old Mexican hacienda."

Shirley answered that she had no idea. She felt like telling the verbose Mr. Sandell that he was rather rubbing it in, raving over the charms of the home he was planning to take from her.

For the first time she was suddenly aware of an intense dislike for Mr. Sandell. He was too smooth and oily, under the circumstances. She knew that Maria distrusted him, and that Sam and his partner had expressed bluntly unfavorable opinions, but now she was herself certain that Mr. Sandell was not the friend he had pretended to be. She gave him a sideways glance from under lowered dark lashes and wondered how it was possible for her ever to have liked the man. His piggish, close-set pale eyes, his beefy, perspiring face and wispy hair parted down the middle. Shirley found herself contrasting him with a certain tall, good-looking young cowboy named Bill Clay and was suddenly cross with herself. She would leave it to Carmel Cota to let her thoughts stray in *that* direction.

Mr. Sandell leaned comfortably against the gray wall, pudgy hands folded over pudgy stomach, short plump legs stretched out. His immaculate pongee suit was beautifully tailored, his tan shoes beautifully polished. He wore a large diamond ring; a big diamond pin winked and blazed in a white cravat. Mr. Sandell had prospered since his arrival in San Luis some five years earlier. He had many irons in many fires, and kept all of them hot. His suave voice brought Shirley back to her unpleasant dilemma.

"It is all arranged," he was saying blandly, "the trustees were delighted when I suggested they offer you the school—Ed Benson's daughter, you know. They agreed you would make an ideal teacher."

"You are most kind," Shirley heard herself answer.

"Not at all, my dear young lady," protested the banker. He was fumbling in his coat pocket. "Regarding the matter of the quit-claim deed—I have the papers with me. Perhaps you will care to glance over them before I have Mr. Cone in. He's the notary. I suggested that he wait in the buckboard until we had finished our little talk—"

The papers made a sinister rustling noise as he spread them open. Shirley suddenly felt cold. She wanted to leap to her feet, scream for him to take himself and his papers out of her garden. Her feet, her tongue, seemed paralyzed. At that moment she could neither move nor speak. She could only listen in a sort of trance.

From the long gallery sounded the soft pad of Maria Cota's slippered feet. The old housekeeper hurried into the patio, came to an abrupt standstill as she saw the banker seated by the girl's side. She stared for a moment, a picture of consternation, then turned quickly away, the soft pad of her feet on the bricks quickening to a rapid beat as she sped down the gallery to her kitchen.

Her brief glimpse of Maria Cota, the distress

in the latter's eyes, her hasty flight, served to increase Shirley's misery, her indecision and helplessness. What had become of her will-power, she wondered numbly; her brave resolutions to defy Morton Sandell? In a daze she heard his oily voice explaining some of the clauses in the several mortgages her father had given years ago.

"You will understand how distasteful all this is to me," he finished; "but I'm not alone in the matter—the bank must be considered."

Mr. Sandell shook his head sadly. "Business is a hard master, Miss Shirley!" He sighed. "Now if you'll glance over the papers, we'll have Mr. Cone in to witness your signature. Mr. Cone is our new justice of the peace, you know."

Shirley took the stiff, crackly paper into her hands, stared at it with unseeing eyes.

Was she going to sign the thing after all, she wondered frantically? Was she? . . . *was she?*

She felt Sandell's piggish little eyes watching her closely, saw that he was holding out a fountain pen. She looked at it dumbly.

"If you're satisfied it's all in order I'll call Mr. Cone," he said with sudden bruskness.

Shirley did not hear him; she was listening to a voice lifted in song—hauntingly familiar words; a deep hearty voice she knew well—Sam Hally's voice; and the song was one he used to sing to her when she was a child, a song of the brave

96

days when sturdy pioneers fought Westward Ho across a savage wilderness.

Like one in a dream she listened.

"Oh, Susanna, oh don't you cry for me,
I'm off to Californy wid a banjo on my knee—"

Sam! Sam Hally had come! He was there in the kitchen, waiting to see her! She had promised not to sign any papers until he had seen her again. The old song was his message to her, a reminder of her promise!

Shirley's paralysis fell from her. She felt new strength pouring into her; she felt suddenly cool, contemptuous of Morton Sandell. She heard his odious voice as from a far distance.

"I'll have Judge Cone in," he was repeating in an annoyed voice.

Shirley rose quickly, thrust the papers and pen into his hands.

"No," she told him composedly, "don't trouble about Mr. Cone. I've quite changed my mind about the matter; in fact I don't care to sign the papers, Mr. Sandell." She gave him a cool smile. "I think you can find your own way out to the buckboard—"

Ignoring his furious splutterings the girl sped lightly down the long gallery, heels clicking merrily—like castanets on the worn old red bricks.

Breathless, Shirley paused in the doorway. It seemed dark in the vast old kitchen, after the bright sunlight of the patio; for a moment she could see nothing. A low, familiar chuckle reassured her; she saw the big cowman smiling at her from the dim corner near Miguel's chair. She closed the door, ran to him and seized his reaching hands.

"Oh, Sam!" Her voice was self-reproachful. "One moment more and I'd have signed that quit-claim paper! I almost forgot my promise not to sign anything until I'd heard from you—but"— she shivered—"he seemed to hypnotize me—I felt so helpless—alone—"

"I figgered mebbe you was forgettin', when Maria run in and told us Sandell was out there with you"—Sam chuckled—"sort of figgered you'd *sabe*—"

"I was in a trance," she confided, "it was hearing you sing that old song you used to sing to me years ago when I was little, that brought me to my senses. Thank you, Sam."

Shirley laughed softly, patted his hands.

"You should have seen Mr. Sandell's face when I told him I wouldn't sign his old papers," she went on; "oh, Sam—he looked like a fiend." She shivered and clung to Sam's big hands. "I'm frightened when I think of that look. He's a—a devil—"

"Don't you fret about him," comforted the old

cowman. His glance went to the door. "Here comes Juan. Reckon we can have a sort of council fire right here in the kitchen and figger out the best thing to do."

"*Si!*" old Miguel said, from the depths of his big chair, "the time has come for us to talk—and *do!*"

There was a fierce exultation in the aged ex-vaquero's sonorous voice, a curiously expectant light in his sunken eyes.

CHAPTER VIII
COUNCIL FIRES

Shirley was frankly surprised when Sam Hally suggested that the new cowboy be invited in for the council of war to be held in Maria's kitchen.

"We really know nothing about the man," she demurred. "He seems all right," she shook her head, "and yet—he may be just—another spy—"

"No, Senorita!" Juan spoke earnestly. "He is a good man, this Clay hombre! You can trust him as you trust me. He has had much experience with rustlers up in the Cimarron. He is young—but wise. The Senor Hally's idea is good."

"Sure," rasped Seth McGee, "let's have the feller in. Sam and me 'll look him over. If we don't like his style we'll talk out loud." Seth grinned at his partner.

Still Shirley held back from the idea, her glance going from one to the other of them—the wrinkled mahogany face of old Miguel, huddled in his huge chair, watching her with sunken inscrutable eyes; the anxious Maria, sitting very straight on a small bench near the great kitchen range with its shining array of copper pots and pans; the burly Juan, pacing like a lithe jungle cat up and down the worn red bricks of the floor; the

100

two veteran cowmen, dusty hats on their knees, lined weathered faces impassive. They all of them were her devoted friends, she well knew, and wiser than she, especially Sam Hally and his taciturn fierce little partner. They would never purposely advise her wrongly.

"We can use a good man, Miss Shirley," Sam said in his deep voice. He smiled at her. "Reckon it's a right good idea to have him in so Seth and me can look him over."

She nodded assent; Juan grinned, hastened from the room and Shirley caught an exchange of looks between Maria and Miguel—read ill-concealed elation in their eyes. For some reason she was resentful. Could it be possible their interest in the good-looking Bill Clay was not entirely unselfish; that it was because of the pretty Carmel, rather than for her own interests the Cota family were so eager to include Clay in what was practically a family council of war? Was it a deliberate attempt to make him important in Carmel's eyes?

Shirley inwardly fumed for a moment, then thrust the thought aside as ungenerous. That aspect of the matter was of no consequence to herself, she reflected scornfully. She was not in the least interested in the good-looking Bill Clay, save his ability and his worthiness to work for the ranch. And that was something she could blindly trust old Sam and Seth to decide for her. Just the same she rather wished Carmel Cota could be in the kitchen when Clay came. She would have liked to see their reaction. Perhaps they had met during Carmel's recent visit to Dallas; which might explain why Clay had turned up at the ranch asking for a job.

As if in answer to Shirley's wish, the pretty, dark-eyed Carmel suddenly entered from the patio. She paused at the sight of the silent, sober-faced group, smiled apologetically and turned away. Shirley spoke quickly:

"Come in, Carmel. No reason why you shouldn't. We're talking about the ranch—sort of a council fire. You have as much right here as any of us."

The young woman obeyed, took a seat near her father.

Carmel was several years older than Shirley and decidedly attractive with her shining black hair and demure madonna face. Ed Benson had been generous with Maria's youngest child and allowed her the same gentle rearing and education given his own daughter. Carmel had come to fill the place of a devoted elder sister in Shirley's life.

There was nothing in her languidly appraising dark eyes to indicate that she and Clay were old friends, or even acquaintances, Shirley decided, when the tall cowboy followed Juan Cota into the room. Nor did he give Carmel more than a brief glance. Rather his eyes were all for herself, Shirley realized with a curious little start of surprise.

He came forward, smiling, self-possessed.

"Juan says you have something to tell me—"

"Yes, Clay," Shirley gestured toward the solemn-faced HM men; "I want you to meet two old friends of mine—and of the ranch. Sam and Seth were with my father when he brought the first herd of longhorns into the Valley of the Kings." She smiled faintly. "That was many years ago, before I was born, so you can imagine how long they've been friends."

Not a quiver of an eyelash betrayed the three men as they gravely acknowledged the introduction.

"Yes, young feller, Seth and me has knowed the old Box B ever since she was a cow outfit," confirmed Sam, offering a huge hard hand. "We used to work for Miss Shirley's pa till five or six years back when we started our own outfit over in the Spanish Sinks. Our HM ain't so big, but she's good for a few hundred prime steers come fall round-up."

"Seems to me I've heard of you two old timers before," Clay responded solemnly. "Glad to meet you both." He turned quickly to the girl as Seth's left eyelid showed signs of dropping a sly wink.

"I think you have met Maria Cota, and her daughter, Carmel," Shirley continued; "and this is Maria's husband, Miguel"—she threw the aged Mexican a fond look, wondered a bit vaguely at the unusual fire in the old man's eyes—"they have both been with the ranch ever since it's been a ranch, as Sam says, and they are trusted friends, too."

Clay admitted he had met them for a few moments while waiting to see herself.

"And of course, Juan, you already know," Shirley resumed her seat and gazed rather helplessly at Sam. The latter spoke deliberately.

"Miss Shirley says as how she's put you on the payroll, Clay. Seth and me bein' old friends like she tells you we kind of wanted to look you over. Down from the Cimarron country ain't you?"

"Was born up there," admitted Clay briefly.

"You use pretty good lingo for a cowpoke," put in Seth with a malicious grin. His left eyelid quivered perceptibly.

"Used to work for a man who'd been to college," Clay explained solemnly; "taught me how to spell and write some if you must know, mister."

"Well," drawled Sam, giving his grinning partner a hard look, "a mite of l'arnin' don't hurt nobody. Reckon you'll do, young feller. Juan says you've got a fancy saddle on your bronc that you won ropin' and ridin'. We got no call to doubt your ability." Sam's voice was suddenly grave. "Only thing we wanted to know was if you was a man Miss Shirley can trust." He glared again at his partner. "What you chokin' for, mister? Swallered your chewin' terbaccy, or something?"

In spite of the fact that it was all a play staged for the girl's benefit, Clay was suddenly uncomfortably aware of an appealing wistfulness in the look she gave him. He felt that she was pleading with him to be all that Sam had said—a man in whom she could place her full trust—pleading that he would not betray her trust; that she was in trouble and surrounded by traitors. He began to regret the decision to keep his identity concealed from her. The safety of his plans demanded secrecy. The Cotas, excepting Carmel, knew that he was Clay Brant, and so did the HM partners. The secret was safe with them. Shirley was different, a young girl, and young girls were apt to be impulsive. The less she knew of his real purpose the better for his plans. For the present his role must be that of an honest cowboy . . . soon the role would be more difficult— more dangerous—and one that was going to hurt her.

"It's a poor man who'd double-cross his outfit," he said, looking at the girl. "Juan told me he planned to have me do some secret work—track down some rustlers."

"It's worse than rustlers," answered Shirley; "we have traitors and murderers on this ranch,

I'm afraid. I hope you can track them down, and oh, Clay, we do so need men we can trust . . . and something tells me that we *can* trust you."

Clay flushed. It was worse than he expected, this desperate appeal to his loyalty. He looked quickly at Sam and Seth; they were staring guiltily down at their boots.

Juan Cota broke the momentary silence.

"It is settled, then," he said quickly in Spanish. "Clay's work will be to track down these rustlers—learn the name of their leaders."

"Reckon we can make a pretty good guess," Seth put in dryly.

"What we aim to get is proof—and find out where them Box B cows is hid." Sam looked at Shirley. "Talkin' of cows, Seth and me has a chance to pick up a couple a thousand two-year-olds cheap if we'd a place to graze 'em. We figgered mebbe we could fix it with you to trail 'em up here to your range. A fifty-fifty deal," he added.

Shirley's eyes questioned her cattle boss. Juan nodded vigorously.

"*Si, Senorita*! It is a good plan. We have the good grass going to waste. *Si*, it is a good plan the Senor Hally suggests!"

"Sounds like a fairy tale! Oh, Sam, you take my breath!" Shirley gave the old cowman a starry look. "I've been nearly crazy—trying to work out some way of re-stocking the ranch."

Sam's glance flickered at Clay, caught the latter's slight nod.

"We'll start a trail herd moving this way right soon," he promised.

"What—what if they are stolen—like the others?" queried the girl, suddenly dubious.

"Not this herd," purred Juan softly, his gaze on the other men.

Sam chuckled, looked at Clay. "Reckon the man we're gettin' them cows from'll send two or three good fightin' cowpokes along, wouldn't you think, young feller?"

"I'd say he'd do that to oblige you, if he's a good cowman," Clay agreed.

Sam rose and moved toward the side door. "Well, folks, Seth and me has some business to 'tend to—"

"Why, Sam! you're not going so soon?" Shirley's voice was disappointed.

"Sure do hate to ride off so quick," he assured her. "Seth and me has got a date in town, huh, Seth?" Sam chuckled, sent Juan and Clay a significant look from his keen old eyes. "Mebbe Juan'll explain . . . and mebbe he won't. You just leave things to us, Miss Shirley." He tramped out, followed by his partner.

Shirley looked at the cattle boss questioningly. "What did he mean, Juan?"

"We have a little plan"—he hesitated, threw a worried glance at Clay—"but it is hard to explain, only that it will be wise for Clay to meet some of the hombres whom we suspect—"

"Oh!" The girl's voice was dubious, "I suppose you know what you want best"—she suddenly smiled mischievously—"if you see Nora Daly while you're in town please give her my love, Juan."

"It is possible we shall eat at the Daly House," admitted the cattle boss with great dignity. He hastened out by way of the side door, and Clay, with a brief parting smile, followed at his spurred heels.

Shirley looked thoughtfully at Maria Cota. "I've a queer sort of feeling," she confessed, "the strangest notion that I've seen him in this old kitchen a long time ago; that he went out through that same door into the vegetable garden and that he smiled at me over his shoulder the way he did just now, without a word—not even an *adios*."

They stared at her in silence, Carmel's dark eyes wondering, the two old people curiously unamazed.

"Didn't you feel something queer about him—about Clay?" persisted the girl; "you, Maria, and you, Miguel—you never took your eyes off him! I couldn't help but notice how you two watched him . . . and you seemed—well—excited."

Carmel spoke quietly. "He is a good-looking young man, this Clay," she shook her sleek dark head, "but no, I have no such strange feeling that

I have seen him before, as you say, Shirley."

"Why don't *you* answer me, Maria, and *you, Miguel?*" demanded the girl. She stared at them with mounting wonder. "Answer me—did you feel the way I did—that he'd been in this kitchen—a long time ago?" Shirley's voice had a bewildered note. "I had the queerest sensation that there was a ghost in the room."

"*Quien sabe?*" muttered old Miguel in his sonorous voice. "Who knows, my Senorita? Stranger things have happened."

"*Si!*" echoed Maria in an awed tone; "who knows?" Her large dark eyes filled with tears and suddenly her arms went round the girl. "Yes, my Paula's child, the same thought did come to us, to Miguel and me," she went on in her soft mother-tongue; "we seemed to see again that same tall, splendid young man—here in this room—"

"It's the strangest thing," marveled the girl. "It's—it's uncanny!" she declared.

"We must not seek the answer, yet," old Maria told her in a hushed voice. "We must believe that the good God has heard our prayers; that he has sent us a flaming sword to deliver us all—the *rancho*—from the hands of evil men—"

"The thought of any help at all—the coming of dear old Sam and Seth, has been too much for us," decided Shirley, striving for the practical. She gave the old housekeeper a hug. "We mustn't let our nerves play tricks; although," she candidly confided, "I will admit that I have hopes this Bill Clay man proves all he seems. What do you think of him, Carmel?"

Miss Cota shrugged her attractive shoulders. "If looks count for anything I think he is much of a man," she murmured.

Shirley eyed her thoughtfully, wondering if the girl's apparent indifference was a pretense. Maria had hinted vaguely of a possible romance. She wondered if Carmel's lack of enthusiasm was merely a clever pose. Shirley was suddenly annoyed at herself for her wild conjectures. It was of no importance what Carmel thought of Bill Clay, or what he thought of Carmel.

"I'm going to the pool for a swim," she announced abruptly. She smiled at her foster-sister. "Are you coming, Carmel?"

Carmel declared the idea was already in her own mind.

"It is good to forget our troubles," she said wisely. "A swim will cheer us up."

As the patio door swung behind the two girls, Maria Cota looked at her husband.

"It is a miracle," she said softly. "He is our Bill Brant in the flesh, this young grandson! I could have sworn that he is the same brave Bill Brant whom we served so many long years ago, whom we last saw in this kitchen when he said *adios* and rode away—never to return. Is it not a Blessed Miracle, Miguel?"

The aged Mexican nodded solemnly.

"In this young man the soul of our own Bill Brant truly lives again," he pronounced in his surprising voice. He wagged his head sagely. "He will do much, this young Clay Brant. It is indeed a miracle, Maria mia."

"They have plans we do not know," mused the old woman. "Or is it that you know this plan Juan just now spoke of?" She eyed her husband shrewdly.

There was a curious gleam in Miguel's sunken black eyes and for a moment a smile wrinkled his leathery mahogany face.

"Do not worry," he reproved gently; "what is in the young Senor Clay's mind to do will be good. He will be guided by the wisdom that is in him and that comes from the man who was his grandfather, the Bill Brant who first rode into the Valley of the Kings."

Bill Brant's grandson was at that moment in the old bean shed, listening with stern face to Sam Hally's rumbling tones.

"Mebbe you're right, son," grumbled the old cowman, "but the gal's going to feel awful bad. Sure will be a shock to her when she learns you're a rustler and that we been mistook in you."

"She sure will make it plenty tough for Sam and me," mourned Seth. "Won't take *our* word for nothin' no more, Shirley won't. Here we go and tell her that we size you up for a good hombre she can trust to the last bullet and you go and turn rustler on her." Seth shook his head dolefully. "Mebbe it's a right smart play, feller, but it's awful tough on us—and the gal."

"It's for her own good, the good of the ranch," reminded Clay curtly. "The only way for me to uncover the trail of these thieves and killers is to gain the confidence of the gang."

"We ain't disputing you there," interrupted Sam. "It's the idea of keeping Shirley in the dark. Seems kind of cruel—havin' her fret and mebbe git sick 'cause she don't understand. She's going to feel awful bad when she learns you're one of them murderin' bunch of rustlers." He shook his head sadly. "Shirley won't trust nobody!"

"Dang it!" groaned his partner, "she won't even trust me and you, Sam!"

"I'm here to clean up this gang of killers," argued the young man. "I know what I'm about. I've got to make Sandell believe I'm the sort of rascal he can use. If he and Vin Sarge think I'm one of the old Gillis gang I can get a job with the Bar 7."

The two cowmen nodded grimly.

"You've done a lot of talking about this Bar 7 outfit," continued Clay, "and you, too, Juan"—he looked at the Box B foreman—"and if what you say is true the place is Sandell's recruiting station for all the border scum that rides this way, and Vin Sarge is his right bower."

Again they nodded glum agreement, and Clay said:

"It's tough on the girl, I'll admit, but it's for her own good, and remember she is only a girl—a young girl and we don't know what she might say or do, unthinkingly"—his voice hardened—"don't forget that my life will be at stake. We don't want too many people wise to our plans."

He smiled grimly.

"She'll get over it, when she knows the truth—when we've got these rustlers on the run."

Sam surrendered.

"Reckon what you say makes good sense, son," he said reluctantly. "We'll not give your play away to her; nor nobody, till you say so." He swung up to his saddle. "Seth and me 'll be there at the Red Front," he promised.

"Don't let Sandell know you're in town," reminded the young cattleman.

"We'll lay out there in them tule flats back of the Daly House," Sam told him. Now that the matter was settled he was his genial calm self again. "Climb your saddle, you old smoke-eater," he chuckled to his partner; "shouldn't be s'prised none if them six-guns of yours see plenty action tonight."

"Suits me," grunted the veteran ex-gunman.

He grinned hopefully and spurred after his tall companion.

Juan Cota said softly to Clay, in Spanish: "I do not know how good he is now, but in the old days on the Box B, no man was as fast with a gun as that little Senor McGee." Respect and admiration was in the burly Mexican's voice. "The wisdom of a serpent, the cunning of a fox, the courage of a lion—it is theirs, Senor Brant," he added. "It is good they are on our side, our friends, those two old men."

They stood watching from the ancient garden gate until roan horse and bay vanished with their riders into the depths of a coulée. Clay glanced at the westering sun.

"Time we're on our way, Juan." For all his cheerful smile, there was a steely glint in his gray eyes. "I've an idea we'll have some excitement when we meet our friends in town tonight."

"*Si!*" Juan Cota's teeth gleamed. "*Si* . . . one beeg time, Senor!"

They hurried toward the corrals, avoiding the rambling old house, where they would have seen Carmel and Shirley emerging from the patio on their way to the swimming pool. The girls, though, saw them riding swiftly away.

"It is Juan—and the new *vaquero*!" exclaimed Carmel. "They ride to San Luis, as Juan said."

Shirley halted, gaze following the disappearing horsemen. A troubled look darkened her eyes.

She wished Juan had not been so secretive—had explained the purpose of this mysterious and hurried trip to San Luis. Morton Sandell was all-powerful in San Luis.

She shivered, was vaguely aware of a frightening presentiment of threatening evil.

"I'm not going to the pool," she suddenly told the other girl.

Carmel's eyes widened.

"I'm going to town," Shirley announced. "I simply must know what they are up to. I'm sure to find Juan at the Daly House."

"I'll go with you," Carmel said quietly. "It will mean staying the night, there, and you can't stay alone—in that dreadful place."

They hastened back toward the house.

CHAPTER IX
POP DALY WANTS TO KNOW

The Daly House was a sizeable two-story frame building with an upper balcony fronting the dusty main street. A fresh coat of whitewash made a brave attempt to conceal a certain decrepitude brought on by the ravaging years. Despite warped boards and sagging windows one sensed that here was a smiling, hospitable old lady, gallantly bedecked with her best false curls and finery to greet the transient guest.

It was Pop Daly's custom of an evening to sit on his hotel porch, ancient armchair tilted back against the wall. Pop was the sole and proud owner of the Daly House, and the undisputed father of the little border town of San Luis. Like the once straight and strong pine timbers of his hotel his own former tough and wiry frame had become somewhat shrunken and warped, and a pronounced stiffness in his joints obliged him to use a stout cane of polished manzanita wood.

In his lusty youth he had been fur trader, buffalo hunter, wolfer, and finally freighter, which latter calling had led up to the historic event he delighted to relate to any newcomer who chanced to occupy an adjacent porch chair.

It was when he was freighting supplies across the desert to the new mining camp of Oro Grande that he was jumped by a small war-party of Apaches. Pop put up so desperate a defense from the barricade of his ponderous Conestoga wagons that the marauders were content to stampede the livestock and call it a day. A hollow victory for the pugnacious little Irishman, despite the three painted warriors left on the field of battle, mute evidence of his deadly marksmanship. The loss of his mules seemed nothing less than a major disaster. There were tons of freight in the two huge wagons—Pop's hard-won savings.

What to do was a problem that made him scratch his red head all that long sleepless night.

With the coming of the dawn he buried his slain and scalped Mexican swamper and grudgingly performed the same office for the three red men. He had no liking for the company of the dead while standing guard over his precious freight.

The evening of the same day found a small wagon-train making camp on the bank of the creek—gold seekers bound for the new bonanza at Oro Grande. They were in need of various and sundry supplies which Pop Daly sold them at bonanza prices. The following day brought others traveling the same rainbow trail, ready cash customers for the stores of general merchandise stowed away in the great Conestoga wagons. Pop was prospering in spite of hell and high water. He went into conference with himself.

One of the wagons held a consignment of Sibley tents. He dug them out and before the sun set that day Daly's Camp had sprung into existence.

The largest tent bore a sign, DALY'S GENERAL STORE. A placard above another tent advertised DALY'S SALOON. Two barrels of whisky unloaded from his wagons backed the enticement. A group of four tents were set aside for the accommodation of any weary transient desiring a brief rest before braving the perils of the desert. Willow and alder trees supplied poles and rails for DALY'S FEED CORRALS. Another, and the biggest sign of them all, erected some hundred yards up the new road being beaten into the earth by the increasing horde of gold-seekers, told incoming Argonauts that they were approaching DALY'S CAMP.

In this manner Pop Daly became the father of the little town that in later years was to be known as San Luis. A humble beginning—rising from the ashes of a stunning defeat—for most men, but not for the indomitable little Irish freighter. Pop was not the one to accept defeat. He literally hung his dusty old hat on a willow tree, spat on his hands and proceeded to build a town.

The past decade had seen a steady dwindling of Pop's power and prestige. Where once his word had been law, he was now held in good-natured contempt by the newer element, of which Morton Sandell was the accepted leader. The little cow town on the banks of the peaceful San Luis Creek had undergone a sinister change since the arrival of Mort Sandell. The steady influx of undesirables considerably perturbed old Pop Daly. San Luis was fast becoming a rendezvous for the lawless. While it was true the town was conveniently close to the border for those seeking to avoid the long arm of justice, Pop was not satisfied this quite explained the increasing numbers of hard-faced men who made Frenchy Larue's Red Front saloon their headquarters. Frenchy Larue was another recent addition to the population, a beady-eyed French-Canadian, whose breezy geniality wise old Pop Daly shrewdly suspected cloaked a heart darkly spotted with avarice and treachery.

The growing lawlessness weighed heavily on the old Irishman's heart. He had been dethroned and it was in his mind to track the unknown usurper to his lair. Pop seemed helpless enough, sitting there in his ancient porch chair, lean terrier jaws leisurely working on his cud of plug tobacco—just another old man peacefully dozing. Which was far from the truth. Nothing escaped those keen blue eyes, nor was that astute smooth-working brain of his idling the hours away.

It was like a baffling picture puzzle. Slowly, patiently, Pop was assembling the scrambled pieces; gradually the picture grew—vaguely revealing a certain sinister likeness to Morton Sandell. It was then that a message traveled into the west, across the San Dimas mountains, into the great basin of the Spanish Sinks to the HM ranch—to Pop Daly's old friends, Sam Hally and Seth McGee.

No answer had come from that message, but Pop was not alarmed. He knew Sam Hally did things in his own way. He was content to sit in his porch chair, content to watch—and wait. None suspected the fierce determination animating that shrunken old frame, the keen probing brain behind those mild blue eyes. A harmless old dodderer who lived in a dim, long-gone past, they said. The thought afforded Pop grim amusement. Some day, soon, when it was too late, they would learn that Pop Daly's fighting days were not done. He chuckled, stared with sudden interest at the two horsemen riding up the street. The burly, swarthy man he knew was the Box B's foreman; the tall young rider was a stranger—or was he a stranger?

Pop sat up, peered intently at the approaching horsemen, a puzzled light in his eyes.

Juan Cota espied him, drew rein with a cheery salute.

"*Buenas dias*, Senor Daly," he greeted, "*como esta usted*?"

Pop assured him that he was feeling first rate.

There was a curiously excited look in his eyes as he continued to stare at Juan's companion.

"We plan to sleep under your roof, tonight," the cattle boss informed him. "You have a bed, eh, Senor, for Bill Clay and me?"

"Shure and if the house is full there's always the hay," chuckled the old man. "Maggie'll be knowin' more than mesilf." He pounded the floor with his manzanita stick. "Maggie!" he called in a shrill voice, "is it full up ye be this evenin', Maggie?"

His daughter, a middle-aged buxom woman with a pleasant smiling face, came to the door. Juan greeted her with his elaborate flourish of sombrero—a flash of white teeth.

"The Senora is looking *muy buena, esta dia*," he complimented.

"You and yer blarney," smiled Pop's daughter, "and shure we always have a room for our friends, Juan Cota." Mrs. O'Grady's smiling gaze went approvingly to the good-looking young cowboy. "And who is yer friend, Juan?"

The Box B foreman introduced his companion. Clay removed his Stetson, politely expressed his pleasure.

"Ah!" Juan told him in Spanish, "wait until you meet the young Senorita Nora, my friend!" He rolled his eyes romantically, "such loveliness—"

"Go on with yer nonsense," laughed Nora's

pleased mother, "I *sabe* yer lingo, Juan Cota! My Nora will pull yer hair for ye!"

They continued on their way to Daly's Feed Stables, where they turned their horses over to Jake Weems, an elderly, silent, saturnine individual. Pop Daly was still in his chair when they returned to the Daly House and made for the dining room. The old man was apparently dozing, but as the two men jingled past him his eyes opened in a sharp look at the disappearing straight back of Juan's companion.

" 'Tis him," he muttered, " 'tis the lad himsilf. Sam got me message . . . and now, Mister Sandell—ye'll be payin' the piper right soon, I'm thinkin'." Pop Daly smiled contentedly, fumbled in a pocket for his tobacco.

The Daly House dining room was rapidly filling. Mrs. O'Grady was famed for her excellent meals and most of the unattached males in San Luis swore by her cooking. Also the dark-haired, blue-eyed Nora was not hard to look at, which was one more good reason explaining the popularity of the Daly House cuisine. It was Nora who found a table for the Box B men. There was no mistaking her interest in the glamorous Juan Cota.

Morton Sandell and his friend, Judge Cone, took a nearby table. Two other men presently joined them. One of the newcomers wore a town marshal's star pinned to black vest. His companion, tall, heavy-shouldered and middle-aged, wore the garb of a cowman.

There was an ugly gleam in the banker's eyes as he stared at Juan Cota whom he recognized with a curt nod. Shirley Benson's unaccountable defiance had left him in a vicious mood. Her refusal to sign the quit-claim deed worried him. He scowled.

"Who's the stranger?" he asked the man with the star.

"Never seed the jasper before," the town marshal answered, after a brief scrutiny. "What about him, Mort?" The marshal grinned. He was an undersized, skinny man with thin sneering lips and short flat nose and pale unwinking eyes.

"It's your business to know who he is," complained Sandell. "What did I make you town marshal for, you fool? Didn't I tell you to watch out for strangers?"

The marshal gave him a sulky look. "How do I know who the hombre is when I never laid eyes on him till now," he protested with an oath. He turned his scowling death's head face for another scrutiny of Juan's companion. "Wears two guns," he muttered. The marshal's eyes suddenly glittered triumphantly; he looked at Sandell. "Say, Mort, if you ain't likin' the feller's looks I can throw him in the lockup for totin' guns in a public eatin' place without a permit from me." Town Marshal Bat Brimms grinned at Justice of the Peace Cone. "Ain't we got a new law that says it's a crime to tote guns in this town without a permit?"

Judge Cone voiced the opinion that in view of the times such a statute would be of benefit to the town of San Luis.

"All right!" Sandell's smile returned. "Write it in the book tomorrow. In the meantime it's the law." He gave his hireling marshal a significant look. "It's up to you, Bat, to see that strangers don't break the laws of this town."

The gunman smiled grimly, pushed back his chair and got to his feet. There was a sudden hush in the long dining room, and Juan Cota, sensing the man's intention, darted Clay a warning look.

"Already they are worried about you—those men," he said in Spanish. "Be on your guard! This man who comes is dangerous—a snake that strikes without a warning." Juan's voice was suddenly loudly genial.

"Ah!" he exclaimed, "the Senor Breems of the law! *Buenos dias*, Senor!"

The town marshal nodded curtly, fastened a cold hostile gaze on Clay.

"Stranger here, ain't you, mister?" he wanted to know.

"You might call me that," Clay admitted mildly.

Brimms nodded grimly.

"Mebbe that explains why you wouldn't know it's ag'in the law to wear your guns in this town without you got a permit from the town marshal." His voice grew menacing. "Ain't rememberin' giving you a permit to tote guns, mister," he added.

"Ha! I 'ave not know thees law," broke in Juan Cota. His smile was frankly skeptical. "I always carry the gun when I come to thees town."

"You mind your own business!" Brimms gave the Box B foreman an angry glare. "This here new law is for strangers and as an officer I'm dooty bound to arrest any stranger as wears his shootin' irons in defiance of same."

Clay interrupted him. "I'm willing to take out a permit," he drawled good-naturedly. "What's the tax, marshal?" He reached in his pocket.

"Five dollars," Brimms told him. He grinned. "Keep your money in your pocket, mister. We don't hand out no permits after six o'clock, so I'm taking your guns now. You can call for 'em at my office in the morning."

"I'd feel awful lonesome without my guns, marshal," argued Clay. "Juan Cota can vouch for me. I'm workin' for the Box B, he'll tell you."

"He speak the truth," the Box B foreman assured Brimms, nodding vigorously, "thees hombre—he weeth the *rancho*."

"Since when?" Brimms sneered. "You're under arrest," he told the young man. "Reach for the roof, mister . . . you, too, Cota!" The marshal's curved fingers hooked over gun butt—death peered from slitted eyes.

The Box B men reluctantly lifted their hands, for reasons that did them honor. A shooting affray in that crowded dining room was unthinkable. Unnoticed by the tense, breathless spectators, Mrs. O'Grady appeared from the kitchen, stood watching the scene with growing indignation.

"Turn round!" rasped the town marshal, "and keep them hands elevated."

He moved closer, reached for Juan Cota's gun, his own weapon threatening them. There was a rustle of crisp starched skirts—a girl's indignant voice.

"Bat Brimms! You leave Juan Cota alone! How dare you take his gun?"

Nora O'Grady was suddenly between the marshal and his victim, blue eyes sparkling wrathfully, her face flushed with anger.

"How dare you make a disturbance in our dining room—scaring folks to death."

He gave her a deadly look.

"Back up there, gal! Don't you interfere with the law!"

"You little runt!" stormed the girl; she lowered her voice, "don't you and Clay make a move, Juan! He's just wild for an excuse to pull the trigger—the coward!" Nora's voice rose to a shrill scream. "Mother!"

Mrs. O'Grady was already hastening across the

room, very pink of face and drying her hands on her kitchen apron. Brimms threw her an uneasy glance.

"Stand back there!" he warned with an ugly scowl. "I'm only doing my duty!"

Mrs. O'Grady eyed him angrily, hands on her ample hips.

"An' when did I ever take orders from scum like you?" she wanted to know.

A second gun suddenly appeared in the marshal's hand.

"You're under arrest, Mrs. O'Grady," he blustered, "the gal goes to jail with you for interferin'—"

There was a scraping of chairs as men came to their feet.

"Don't you go too far, Brimms!" growled a voice. "Mrs. O'Grady and her gal has plenty of friends in this town—"

"I'm needin' no help to teach the little man his manners," shrilled the enraged Mrs. O'Grady. Her hand fastened on a large water jug. "Start a row in me own dinin' room, will yer?" she cried and flung the contents of the jug in the marshal's face. A second swing crashed the jug against his head. Brimms staggered, gasping and spluttering.

"Grab the spalpeen, Nora!" shouted the militant Mrs. O'Grady, "into the street with him!"

The two women were on the town marshal like a pair of clawing she-panthers. "Arrest us, will yer?" panted Mrs. O'Grady as she gained a strangle hold round the luckless man's neck.

Helpless in their hands the marshal was hurried across the room to the accompaniment of loud cheers from the delighted audience. The screen door banged and the rapid beat of booted feet on the board walk told all that the town marshal of San Luis was in full and ignominious flight.

The two Box B men resumed their seats. It was in Clay's mind that the attempt to disarm him betrayed the fine Italian hand of Mort Sandell. He was already under suspicion, not because Sandell knew that he was Clay Brant, but because he feared that any stranger in the town *might* be Clay Brant. The fact that no word had come from the assassin sent to ambush the Cimarron man would worry Sandell. He would be on the alert for any stranger in town.

Clay smiled at Nora who had joined them at the table for a cup of coffee to "quiet her nerves," she naively explained.

"Plucky thing you did, Miss O'Grady," he thanked her.

Nora tossed her dark head.

"That rat!" Her voice was scornful. "I wouldn't be surprised if we had a new town marshal by tomorrow morning!" She stared across the way at Mort Sandell.

Somewhat to Clay's surprise the banker turned a blandly smiling face. "Nor I, Miss Nora," he agreed, "the man's conduct was outrageous, a blot upon our fair community. I believe that Brimms was—was drunk." Mr. Sandell's shocked gaze went to the Box B foreman who was smiling contemptuously. "Juan," he went on pompously, "I trust you'll not take this unfortunate incident too seriously. Brimms should have been more discreet."

The Mexican shrugged his broad shoulders. "*Si*, Senor. We *sabe!*"

Mr. Sandell missed the sarcasm. "Brimms took the matter too seriously . . . this new gun law, you know"—he frowned—"mustn't blame Brimms . . . he was only doing his duty. These killings and cattle raids have made us jumpy."

The Box B foreman interrupted him with a gesture. "*Si*, Senor. We *sabe*. You no need have scare from thees hombre. He knew vaquero. I know heem—the *muy bueno*—good hombre."

"Fine, Juan!" congratulated the banker. "Miss Benson needs good men on the ranch these dangerous days." He pushed his chair back and got to his feet. "Well, *adios*. My compliments to Miss Benson, Juan."

Followed by his two companions the banker strutted from the room. Clay's glance was on the tall, heavy-shouldered cowman. Juan read the question in his eyes.

"Vin Sarge," he muttered, "the Bar 7 man. A dangerous hombre, that one."

Clay nodded and with a parting smile for the dimpling Nora went out to the porch. Old Pop Daly was still in his chair, lean terrier jaws meditatively working on his navy plug. Clay felt, rather than saw the old man's quick glance.

"You set a good table, Mr. Daly," he complimented.

"Maggie knows her business," chuckled the hotel man. "Sit ye down and chat whilst ye're waitin' for Juan Cota." He gave Clay a knowing smile. "Shure now, and the way Juan Cota takes his time with his supper. Wouldn't be s'prised at all if Nora's give him a second helpin' of her pie." Pop laughed quietly, darted a sharp look at his attentive listener. "And what did ye say was yer name, me lad?"

"I didn't say," Clay smiled at him.

"Shure now," cackled the old man, "I remember that Juan said yer name was Bill Clay." He stared with ill-concealed interest at the younger man. "There's a look about ye that calls me back to an old friend of better days, me lad. Ye might be his brother, or son—or grandson."

"We'll hope he was a *good* friend," commented Clay.

"The best in the world," declared Pop, suddenly vehement. He sat up and gave the cowboy a probing look. "Ye're the image of him, lad—the image of Bill Brant!" Pop leaned forward, his voice a hoarse whisper. "I'm wagerin' ye knowed him, lad!"

"Bill Brant was well known where I'm from," admitted Clay cautiously.

Pop winked slyly. "The same wager goes that ye know an old longhorn they call Sam Hally," he ventured.

"Most of us have heard of Sam Hally—and his partner, Seth McGee," Clay again admitted. "Those two old timers have trailed too many longhorns out of Texas not to be known—at least by name."

"I'd swear ye was Bill Brant himself by the careful way ye answer a question," chuckled the old hotel man. "Bill never was one to speak too freely. And so ye're with the Box B outfit, Juan Cota tells me. A good outfit," he went on, not waiting for a reply, "a fine ranch it was in the old days"—Pop wagged his head—"and shure 'tis hard times with the Box B—now that Ed Benson is lyin' in his grave." He gave Clay one of his sharp looks. "There's wicked scoundrels—wolves— snarlin' at Miss Shirley's heels—poor lass."

Juan Cota came jingling out to the porch and looking very pleased with himself.

"It is time we attend to our business," he said in Spanish to Clay. "On with the drama, eh, my friend?"

Curiosity brimmed in Pop's eyes; he stared shrewdly at the Mexican.

"What divilment is the pair of ye up to?" he wanted to know. "Ye forgit I talk yer lingo, Juan Cota."

"Juan means we're going to try our luck at the Red Front," interposed Clay hurriedly.

"*Si.*" The Box B foreman laughed softly. "We feel lucky, tonight, Senor Daly."

"Ye're a pair of fools, the two of ye," grumbled the old man. "Frenchy Larue's a crook. There's no luck for ye when he's around."

Juan smiled, patted his holstered .45 significantly. "We carry strong medicine for crooks," he assured the proprietor of the Daly House in his own Spanish.

They strode across the street, toward the big swinging kerosene lamp that lighted Frenchy Larue's Red Front saloon. Pop Daly's gaze followed them thoughtfully.

"Now what in the mischief is the pair of 'em up to?" he muttered. "I'm thinkin' it's no game of poker takin' thim two over to the Red Front this night." Pop reached for his manzanita stick. "Shure do wish old Sam would come!"

With a worried shake of his head the hotel man rose stiffly from his chair and was about to hobble into the lobby when the smothered thud of horses' hoofs made him look over his shoulder. The riders were two girls and they were drawing rein in front of the hotel. Pop Daly's eyes brightened with delighted recognition.

"Shure and it's yersilf, Shirley lass!" he cackled heartily, "and Carmel Cota!" He lifted his voice. "Maggie! 'tis visitors from the old ranch we've got this night . . . *Maggie!*"

The girls slid from their saddles and hastened up the steps to the porch.

"Pop!"

Shirley's voice was brittle, quite unlike the soft low tone familiar to the old hotel man's ears.

"Has Juan been here?"

Her breath was coming unnaturally fast, Pop observed, a sign of fear—terror. The symptoms were an old story to him. He had seen animals gripped with the same elemental emotion . . . a rabbit suddenly menaced by the crushing jaws of a hound, a trapped buffalo wolf, a mountain lion brought to bay. No matter the degree of their courage, the defiance of death in their eyes, there was always that same quick labored breath. He answered her cautiously.

"Shure, lass. Juan's been here to supper—him and his frind. I'll call Maggie," he added. "Maggie and Nora 'll be glad to see the pair of ye they will."

"Where—where are they, now?"

Pop shook his head. "Ye'll not be seein' thim this night, I'm thinkin', lass. 'Tis not five minutes since they wint over to the Red Front for a bit of an evenin' with the cards, they said."

"Oh!" The girl's face fell and she looked at

her companion. "What *shall* we do, Carmel?"

"What else can ye do but stay the night now that ye've come," declared the voice of Mrs. O'Grady, suddenly making an appearance. "Bless yer hearts, colleens! 'tis good fer sore eyes to see ye both!" The motherly Mrs. O'Grady beamed. "Come right in. I've a nice big room for ye, with two beds, the best in the house, and by the time ye've washed up there'll be a hot supper ready for yer."

She bustled them into the lobby.

"Oliver Scott's in the dining room," she archly informed Carmel Cota, "him and old Dr. Kirk."

"I'm not in the least interested in the whereabouts of Mr. Scott," Carmel told her coldly.

"He's such a nice young man," protested Mrs. O'Grady, "he's always askin' if I've seen ye— bless me—here he comes now, and the doctor, too!"

The two men emerging from the dining room halted as they saw the girls following Mrs. O'Grady to the stairs. The younger man's eyes lighted.

"Carmel!" he exclaimed.

She ignored him, went on up the stairs. The young man's face was suddenly pale.

"I'd say that was rather a snub, Oliver," chuckled his companion. "What's wrong between you and the little Cota girl? You used to be good friends."

"Perhaps *you* can tell me, doctor." The young man's tone was despondent.

Dr. Kirk, a genial, ruddy-faced elderly little man, gave him a shrewd glance. "I think, Oliver," he said sorrowfully, "that you are not being honest with yourself, if you pretend you don't know why Carmel Cota does not care for your friendship these days."

Oliver Scott nodded gloomily.

"She doesn't like my association with Morton Sandell."

"You can't blame the girl for not wanting the friendship of Morton Sandell's lawyer," commented the doctor dryly.

Upstairs in their room Shirley was questioning her foster-sister.

"I thought you liked Oliver Scott," she wondered.

"I do like him, a lot"—Carmel colored—"but he's Mr. Sandell's lawyer—and—you can understand—friends of your enemies can't be my friends."

Downstairs old Pop Daly was slowly limping into the lobby. There was a troubled look in his eyes.

"There's bad business brewin'," he muttered, "the lass was all stirred up, she was . . . and so eager to see Juan Cota. Shure would like to know

135

where Sam Hally is this night—him and his fire-eatin' partner."

Shaking his head worriedly, Pop limped slowly toward the dining room.

CHAPTER X
SANDELL SMELLS DANGER

Sam Hally looked at a fat silver watch, holding it cupped in his hand under a soft vagrant moonbeam that stole for a minute from behind the cloud drift.

"Most nine," he muttered. "Soon be time for us to start our play."

"That clock of yours!" jeered his partner. He glanced at his own old-fashioned timepiece. "Won't be nine for a good half hour."

Sam shrugged his massive shoulders, thrust his watch away. "You're too doggone lit'ral, Seth. Wasn't claiming it's nine o'clock. Was only trying to git it into your thick head that it's time for us to be on our way. We're due at the Red Front afore Clay and Juan gits there." He rose gingerly. "Ain't so spry as I was forty years back, Seth," he grumbled. "Seems like I heerd a crik in the j'ints—or mebbe 'twas your own old bones crackin'," he added with a chuckle.

"You're plumb out of your head," retorted Seth indignantly. "No bones creakin' yet, old timer. What you heard was your brains rattling."

With muttered good-natured gibes, the two veteran HM cowmen left their tethered horses and climbed up the steep, boulder-strewn slope.

Lights twinkled from the rear windows of the Daly House separated from them by the river flat, a stretch of sandy wasteland dotted with clawing cactus and clumps of willows.

Cautiously they continued across the sandy strip, drifted from bush to bush with the silent stealth of stalking Indians. Not a pebble rattled under their bootheels from which had been removed big-rowelled spurs, not a twig of dry shrub crackled; they might have been shifting shadows that came and went under the fitful light of the cloud-draped moon.

There was good reason for their caution. They were aware of the risk in venturing into Sandell's stronghold—were too wise and experienced to underestimate a foe. A certain Tulsa Jones, now a prisoner on the HM ranch had sullenly admitted that Sandell had marked them for death. Which piece of news in no way daunted Shirley's two faithful old friends. Their presence in San Luis was necessary—they had made a promise . . .

Unaware of the nearness of the two men he had come to dread Morton Sandell glowered at the papers littering his desk.

Disquieting premonitions disturbed him. Like a wary old wolf he smelled danger in Shirley Benson's startling refusal to sign the quit-claim papers. He had not expected such a show of courage from the girl.

He swore softly.

Sam Hally and Seth McGee! There was the answer explaining her sudden defiance! She never would have dared to thwart him unless sure of the support of the two Spanish Sinks cowmen. They were old friends of the Box B ranch. Hard customers, those two old longhorns.

Sandell chewed viciously on his cigar.

They would pay dearly for their interference if he could ever locate them. It was a mystery where they were hiding out. He had instructed Bat Brimms to be on the watch for them if they showed themselves in town, and Wes Droon had similar orders to let him know if they visited the Box B. The fact that no word had come from Tulsa Jones would indicate that the HM men had not left their Spanish Sinks ranch. He was beginning to worry about Tulsa Jones—his long silence. It was possible, more than possible that Tulsa was in trouble; that old Sam Hally and his partner had been too clever for him.

Sandell would have been even more worried had he known that his vague suspicions were correct—that Tulsa Jones was at that moment in the custody of two hard-eyed HM cowboys and therefore quite incapable of supplying further information regarding the movements of Sam Hally and Seth McGee.

There was another matter causing Sandell no small concern—the prolonged absence of Whitey

Joe. The weasel-eyed little killer had never failed him before. His non-return from the desert was perturbing.

"Should have sent Bat Brimms with him and made sure of the job," the banker mused worriedly. "If this Cimarron man is all they say he may have been too smart for Whitey Joe. No telling what will happen if Clay Brant connects with Sam Hally."

Sandell's florid face was suddenly a pasty gray; he hurled his maltreated cigar aside and wiped his moist brow with a large silk handkerchief. Whitey Joe's failure to report was ominous, a matter to be looked into without delay. From all reports this Brant was formidable. He wished he knew more about the man, what he looked like—if he were young or old. His information had been annoyingly meager. Practically all he knew was that Brant had organized his fellow-cattlemen against the Gillis gang of rustlers and exterminated them. Sandell surmised from this that the Cimarron man was no callow youngster, or a veteran like Sam Hally would not have sent for him.

His seething mind went back to the scene in Mrs. O'Grady's dining room. Was it possible the stranger with Juan Cota could be the mysterious Brant? He shrugged the thought aside. The fellow was scarcely more than a youth—nothing formidable about *him.* Just the same he must find out about the fellow, how long he'd been with the Box B outfit. Not long, or he'd have heard from Droon.

Sandell bit savagely into a fresh cigar. One more incident to stir up disquieting premonitions. Bat Brimms had made a hash of things and a fool of himself. He shouldn't have tried to force the issue against the opposition of the O'Grady women—should have waited for a more opportune time to throw the young stranger into jail. They had worked the trick more than once when wishing to force some unknown to disclose his identity.

Sandell stared morosely at the papers on his desk. The Benson girl's refusal to sign the quit-claim deed was a stunning blow to his immediate plans, but not a fatal one. There was nothing she could do to prevent him from taking full possession of the ranch eventually. She was a fool to fight him; she could not stave off foreclosure proceedings.

He ground savagely on his cigar.

His plans would not allow the long-drawn out process of foreclosure, the maddening delay of a year. Immediate possession of the fertile Valley of the Kings—the water-rights—was necessary for the fulfilment of his ambitions.

"I should have offered her a fat bonus," he reflected sourly. "Worth a couple of thousand— worth ten thousand to have her clear out."

He mulled the idea over in his mind, nodded thoughtfully.

"I'll do it," he decided, "I'll go out to the ranch in the morning and shake a few thousand under the brat's nose."

He slumped loosely in his chair, cigar cocked from moist thick lips, a curiously vacant stare in his pale eyes. Already he could visualize the shining steel rails of the new railroad thrusting down through the long valley. Where cattle had roamed for so many years would be hundreds of neatly-tilled, prosperous farms. Not only the Valley of the Kings, but the rich mesas of the San Jacinto, controlled by the Bar 7, once the domain of spendthrift O'Flynn, and a dozen other big ranches that had fallen or would soon fall into the clutches of the San Luis Stockman's Bank. All paying rich tribute to the Stockman's Bank— to Morton Sandell, supreme lord of the town of San Luis! In the picture he saw the dusty sordid little border cow town magically expanded into a thriving city on the banks of the Rio San Luis— paved streets, tall business blocks, parks. A city of countless thousands, all paying golden tribute to Morton Sandell—Man of Destiny—Lord of the Western Border country.

The smirk of triumph was suddenly a twisted snarl of fury. A dream, phantasy, unless he gained possession of the Valley of the Kings!

Again the banker dabbed a moist brow with

his silk handkerchief. There was a chance in a thousand—but a chance—that Shirley Benson's stubborn defiance might prove the rock upon which his ship of dreams would crash to destruction. News of the railroad's as yet vague plans might leak out, reach the ears of Shirley Benson—her friends! Or this mysterious Brant of Cimarron—this nemesis of rustlers—might prove a relentless hound clinging to a blood-stained trail that would lead to the killer of Ed Benson, lead to the plunderers of the Box B ranch.

Sandell stared at the cigar between his fingers. His hand was trembling. Muttering an oath he hurled the cigar to the floor.

"I'm a fool!" he told himself savagely. "No sense letting my nerves play tricks. What can a brat of a girl or a pair of senile old mossy horn cowpokes do to stop me now? As for this Brant of Cimarron! I've handled 'em tough before and I can do it again."

A malignant grin spread a mask of ferocity over his habitually bland face, revealing for a moment the stark wickedness of the man.

He glanced at his watch, hurriedly thrust the litter of papers into a drawer and crossed the room to a large Navajo blanket draped on the wall. It was one of several gay Indian blankets and rugs adorning his rather luxurious private quarters in the rear of the bank building's second floor.

So far as was known, Sandell was a bachelor. Few save his intimates knew of the secret concealed by the folds of the Navajo rug.

He passed through, pulled the door shut and felt his way cautiously down a dark flight of steps built in between the side walls of the bank building and the Red Front saloon. He moved slowly, a monstrous bloated spider, creeping furtively through the blackness.

He came to the last step and continued along the cramped passage until his fumbling hand touched the cold iron of a door fastening. In a moment the bolt was drawn, the door opening to his gentle pull. It was a thing of battened boards, really a section of the wall cut out and swung on hinges, and so low that he was forced to stoop and literally crawl through on all fours.

Puffing slightly, Sandell got to his feet and struck a match; in another moment the dim light of a kerosene lamp revealed that he was in a small meagerly-furnished office.

He went to the door opening on the rear alley and satisfied himself that the bolt was in place and also examined the lock on the curtain-draped window, then he rolled the desk in front of the secret opening in the wall.

Few people knew of the dingy little room in the rear of the saloon. It was here that Sandell preferred to confer with his various lieutenants. He was seldom seen in the saloon and never publicly betrayed more than casual acquaintance with the members of his lawless gang.

Again Sandell glanced at his watch, then crossed the room to a framed picture of a buffalo head. He pushed it to one side, uncovering a peep hole in the wall. Satisfied by his brief inspection of the barroom he unlocked the door. The shifting of the two ponderous bolts would operate a signal familiar to the ears of Frenchy Larue, or his bartenders. None could enter the secret conference room in the rear of the saloon until Sandell had first thrown the two bolts on the heavy intervening door.

Again he watched through the peep hole, saw one of the bartenders whisper to the saloon man. The latter nodded briefly, casually upended an empty liquor glass on the bar. Sandell turned back to the desk. He knew that his signal had been heard—and answered.

He unlocked a drawer and took out a small derringer. Sandell had an aversion for firearms. He preferred to hire his shooting done for him—when possible. His newly-aroused apprehensions urged him to take added precautions. It was not always feasible to keep a paid gunman at his elbow. It was best to be prepared.

He examined the stubby little weapon carefully, thrust it with an ugly grimace inside an inner pocket. A low satirical laugh jerked his head round. A man was standing inside the doorway, watching him with mirthful eyes. Sandell's face reddened.

"Makes me think of one of those wolverines of your own north country the way you creep up on a man with the ugly snarl of a grin on your face," he said sourly.

Frenchy Larue shrugged a contemptuous shoulder. He was a broad-backed, compactly-built man. He had sleek black hair and when he smiled, which was often, he showed glistening white teeth under a bristling short-cropped mustache. Despite his smiling geniality there was cunning and greed in his intelligent, watchful beady eyes; a cat-like stealth in his every movement. He wore a black silk shirt, open at the throat, and a loosely-knotted red silken scarf. His tight black trousers were tucked into half-boots of shiny black leather and a wide belt of black leather, fastened with a broad silver buckle, clasped his lean waist.

"You look disturb, my frien'," he greeted ironically. "You 'ave ze beeg scare, eh?" He sank into a chair, leaned forward and tapped the pocketed derringer. "A toy," he added contemptuously, "a play-t'ing for a boy."

Sandell drew the weapon from his pocket and eyed it reflectively. "It's killed a man," he said softly.

Frenchy looked skeptical. "Ah, I 'ave not theenk you 'ave ze courage, my frien'," he murmured. His teeth gleamed in a sneer.

"I tell you this little gun has killed a man! I should know—" Sandell broke off, gave the smiling saloon man an angry, uneasy look and returned the derringer to his pocket.

Frenchy laughed noiselessly, suddenly whipped a long-bladed knife into view. "For me—I lak ze knife," he told the other man, "no noise—always ze point in ze 'eart—ze t'roat—before ze gun in ze 'and. Queek—like zat—" The blade flashed from slim brown hand, was suddenly quivering in the opposite wall. The saloon man laughed again. "More better zan leetle gun, eh, my frien'?"

"For you, maybe," admitted the banker. "The trouble, Frenchy, is that most of us can't throw a knife the way you can."

Sandell's glance went to the alley door. "Sounds like Brimms—and Vin Sarge. Let 'em in, Frenchy."

The town marshal swaggered into the room, followed by the big Bar 7 foreman. Sandell eyed them with a frown of annoyance.

"Where's Droon?" he asked the foreman.

"Wes figgered he needed a drink," Sarge answered. "Says he'll be in later."

Sandell snorted peevishly. "Who does Droon think he is?" He looked at Frenchy Larue. "Go get him in," he told the saloon man. "He ain't drinking till he's talked with me; and you can tell him I said so."

Frenchy nodded, made his noiseless exit into

the barroom. Sandell's attention went to the town marshal. "You made a fool of yourself in the dining room, Bat," he grumbled. "You'll never hear the last of it, letting those women chase you into the street."

The marshal scowled. Sandell regarded him thoughtfully.

"Might as well turn in that star, Bat. Can't have folks laughing at the town marshal."

Brimms sprang from his chair.

"Ain't carin' none for the way you talk, Mort Sandell," he said angrily. "If it hadn't been for them fool wimmen I'd have slammed both them hombres in the calaboose! Couldn't pull my guns on them fee-males, could I?"

"You could have pulled some plain horse sense and used it," sneered his chief. "There are times for gunplay and times for using good horse sense."

The town marshal glowered at him.

"Horse sense!" he snorted, looked at the Bar 7 foreman. "You were thar, Vin," he appealed, "you saw the play them wimmen pulled on me. Wasn't nothin' I could do but sort of retire. Wimmen don't take no stock in horse sense no how."

The big-shouldered Sarge considered for a moment. "The way it looked to me, Bat, I figger you was plumb out-played," he decided judicially. He spoke in a deep rumbling voice. "I'd say there weren't nothin' you could do but sort of draw in your horns."

Brimms gave Sandell a triumphant look. "You heerd him, Mort! You heerd Vin back me up, didn't you?"

Sandell seemed to have a high regard for the Bar 7 man's opinion. He nodded reluctantly.

"Wasn't much you could do with those O'Grady women clawing you," he acknowledged. "Just the same, Bat, this town won't soon forget the picture of our town marshal being chased down the street like a yellow pup with a can tied to him."

Vin Sarge's long mustaches twitched in a faint smile.

"Reckon not, Mort," he agreed.

Brimms glared at them, his face scarlet. Muttering an oath he tore the star from his vest and flung it on the desk.

"I'm resignin'," he announced indignantly.

"The only thing you can do, feller," approved Vin Sarge.

The little gunman resumed his chair and began making a cigarette. Sandell watched him for a moment.

"It won't mean you're through, here," he soothed. "You'll have a chance to get even with Juan Cota—and that young feller he's riding herd with. They're your meat, Bat."

Brimms nodded, an ugly gleam in his eyes.

"I git you, Mort."

His smile was wicked.

A sudden wave of sound beat at their ears—men's voices, the stamp and shuffle of booted feet, the clink of glass and bottle, a girl's shrill laugh mingling with the dissonant clamor of a tinny piano—a cacophony that came and went as Frenchy Larue opened and closed the barroom door. A heavy-set, sandy-haired man followed him into the office, a whisky bottle clutched in one big freckled hand. Sandell sprang to his feet.

"What's the idea, Droon? I told you to lay off the drinks!"

The sandy-haired man shrugged dusty shoulders.

"Ain't takin' more'n a swaller, Mort," he said sullenly. "Sure et plenty dust ridin' in from the Box B. Ain't nothin' cuts dust as good as whisky."

There was a look in the cowboy's hard eyes that warned Sandell not to press the issue.

"What's the news?" he wanted to know. "Had any word from Tulsa Jones? And who's this young puncher Juan Cota's put on the Box B payroll? Why haven't you sent in word about him? That's what you're out there for."

"You're sure askin' a mouthful of questions," growled Droon, "an' the same answer covers the hull lot of 'em."

"Meaning just what?" demanded Sandell impatiently.

"Meanin' I ain't heerd no word from Tulsa and

150

don't know nothin' about the new puncher 'cept his name is Bill Clay. Was over to the West Fork when he was hired and I ain't laid eyes on him."

"He's in town now," Sandell informed the sandy-haired cowboy.

Droon nodded.

"That's why I come on the jump. Sure aim to learn a thing or two about that Bill Clay hombre—and why Juan went and fired Pecos and Red—"

The other men exchanged startled looks. Sandell was suddenly pale.

"Any notion why Juan fired them?" he asked in a troubled voice. "Would you say that Juan was wise to Pecos and Red?"

Droon shook his head.

"No *sabe* a-tall," he declared. "Juan just told 'em they was fired. Didn't give no reason, 'cept that he was cuttin' the payroll."

"Which same explanation don't tally with Juan puttin' this Bill Clay feller on the payroll," voiced the Bar 7 foreman.

"Sure don't," concurred Brimms.

They exchanged uneasy looks. Sandell spoke thoughtfully:

"Whitey Joe hasn't got back from that little trip into the desert," he told Wes Droon. "I—I'm wondering what's happened to him—if he ran into that Clay Brant's lead—"

The sandy-haired cowboy swore softly.

"That makes two of 'em missin'," he muttered. "Tulsa Jones—and now Whitey Joe. Don't look so good, boss!"

"And now the Benson gal gives Pecos an' Red their time," added Brimms significantly.

"Looks like she smells a rat," surmised the taciturn Vin Sarge in his deliberate voice.

"That's not all you know"—Sandell clenched his fist—"the Benson girl says she won't sign the quit-claim deed—"

They stared at him, and the big Bar 7 foreman said slowly, judicially, like one carefully weighing evidence:

"Too many queer things happenin' at the same time, Mort, to figger up natcheral." He held out a big hand and counted on his fingers: "Fust off, say, there's the Benson gal gettin' high and mighty with you—tells you to go to hell, huh?"

"You can call it that," grunted Sandell in a surly tone. He bit savagely into his cigar.

Vin Sarge went on deliberately: "Then there's Wes Droon tells us he ain't had no word from Tulsa Jones like was arranged when you sent Tulsa over to the Spanish Sinks to keep a eye on them old longhorns at the HM ranch. You figgered 'em in 'cause they was friends of Ed Benson an' used to work for the Box B outfit."

Again Sandell nodded.

"We got you checked, Vin," he grunted.

"Thirdly," continued his foreman, warming up

to his work and obviously enjoying his summary of the situation, "thar's your own statement submitted and sworn to, which said statement made of your own free will and without prej'dice, is on record that Whitey Joe ain't been seen nor spoke to, nor heerd from since his dee-parture for Poison Springs—"

"Say, feller, where d'you think you are?" peevishly interrupted Bat Brimms, vaguely aware of a certain would-be legal phraseology. "This ain't no court room, nor more'n you is a lawyer." He snorted. "Cut out your oratin' and git down to facts."

The big Bar 7 man's cold slate-gray eyes fastened reprovingly on the fretful little gunman.

"Mebbe this ain't no court o' law, mister, but I'm warnin' you here and now to shut your big mouth onless you aim to have same filled with plenty hot lead. And speakin' of court rooms," he added severely, "I'm tellin' you that my dad was a justice of the peace down on the Pecos and I was eddicated for a lawyer till I was most fifteen. It comes plumb natcheral for me to use lawyer lingo."

Brimms subsided. While he knew nothing of Vin Sarge's legal ancestry he was completely aware of his readiness to meet any challenge. He satisfied himself with a sneering, "All right, Mister Lawyer, and what comes after the ree-corded statement likewise presented and filed in this dang court—"

Sandell flung him an angry glance. "Don't mind him," he told Vin Sarge, "seems like Bat gets nervous when there's talk of the law."

"No call for him to get thataways," growled the Bar 7 man. "Bat won't never face no jury."

"Meanin'—" Brimms glowered at him.

"Meanin' you won't live that long," chuckled Sarge. "Plenty hot lead waitin' for you, feller." He frowned. "If you've done shootin' off your mouth I'll finish what I aimed to tell yuh—" Sarge gave the former town marshal a hard look. "We got three points made and established in this here mysterious case," he continued solemnly, "the Benson gal, Tulsa Jones and Whitey Joe, which draws us down to Pecos and Red Hansen. The Benson gal has give 'em their time—fired 'em—"

"Ah, ze leetle Shirley—she smart!" Frenchy Larue rolled his expressive eyes, laughed softly. "Me—I would 'ang thees Pecos and Red Hansen on a beeg tree ver' queek—"

"—she give 'em their time," rumbled the Bar 7 foreman, wisely ignoring the gibe. He was aware of the French-Canadian's dexterity with a knife; "and then she goes and puts this Bill Clay hombre on the payroll, which don't make no clean tally of this here round-up of facts and figgers."

154

"Any idea where Pecos and Red are by now?" Sandell asked Droon.

"Said they was headin' for town soon as they got their pay." Droon laughed. "You know them two; like as not they're back in the bar right now. They sure like their likker, those hombres."

"I want to send Red and Bat out to Poison Springs and see what's happened to Whitey Joe. Thought I'd give Pecos the town marshal job." Sandell grinned at Brimms. The latter gave him an ugly look.

"Pecos is right fast with his guns," Vin Sarge declared, "most as fast as Bat." He shook his head dubiously. "Trouble with him, he likes his likker, as Wes jest said." Sarge paused and slapped his thigh a resounding whack, "Say! I clean forgot! Took on a new hand today—fellow that calls hisself Chico Lopez. Says he's from the Cimarron country—"

"What's that?" Sandell pricked up his ears. "From the Cimarron, you say, Vin? What sort of looking man is he?"

"I'd say he was Mex and Injun," Sarge told him. "What I'm gittin' at, Mort, is that he's the man for your town marshal job. I had him show me what he can do with a six-gun afore I hired him and he's sure fast—got Bat Brimms faded when it comes to a quick draw—"

"Fellers has made talk like that," sneered the gunman. "Me—I ain't met up with any of 'em."

155

"Like I says this Chico has Brimms faded," went on the big cowman unperturbed by the interruption, "he's your man, Mort. Him bein' a stranger is all to the good. We can spread it round that he's a killer and plumb bad medicine."

"Any chance he's this Brant we've been hearing about?" worried Sandell.

"Not a chance," Sarge was positive. "Chico's a half-breed."

"All right, Vin. Send him in. I'll look him over." Sandell lighted a fresh cigar. "This Brant man has me worried," he confided. "No telling what might happen with Brant nosing round." The banker stared hard at Wes Droon. "Sam Hally and Seth McGee were old friends of Ed Benson. They'll never quit the trail of the man that killed him. That's why they sent for Brant."

The sandy-haired cowboy grinned contemptuously. "You're not scarin' me none, mister," he retorted.

"We know from Tulsa Jones that Sam Hally sent for Brant to come down here. We know that Brant is head of the Cimarron Vigilantes that strung up Sig Gillis and a dozen others for rustling." Sandell's voice was grim. "We've got to do something about this Brant—or we'll get the same medicine they gave Gillis."

There were grim nods from his attentive henchmen, and Vin Sarge said with finality, "Mort's right as rain, fellers. We got to git

Brant—or he'll git us. Not only that—we don't want him nosin' round after them Box B steers."

"No chance," scoffed Wes Droon. "Only one way into the Painted Valley. Brant wouldn't find the Bottle Neck in a hundred years."

"Who've you got posted on lookout at the Bottle Neck?" Sandell asked the Bar 7 foreman.

"Shorty Riggs and Tom Painter."

"Better double the guard there," Sandell decided. "Can't take any chances while Brant's running round loose." He thought for a moment. "I'll send Pecos and Red out to you soon as they get back from Poison Springs."

"A right good idee"—Sarge nodded approval— "Pecos won't git no likker out there—'cept what we send to the Painted Valley—" The foreman's gaunt frame suddenly tensed. "Guns a-smokin'!" he said softly. "Frenchy—sounds like trouble back thar in your place—"

The saloon man was on his feet and moving swiftly toward the barroom door. Brimms and Droon started to follow him. Sandell waved them back with a low curse, gestured toward the rear door opening on the alley. Vin Sarge was already throwing the bolt; he vanished into the outside darkness, Brimms and Droon at his heels.

Sandell stood listening, head cocked toward the barroom. All seemed quiet again. The sound of roaring six-guns in the Red Front was nothing to arouse alarm—ordinarily. He knew the shooting perhaps signified nothing more serious than a common dance-hall brawl, but the past hours had left Sandell's nerves jumpy.

He went swiftly to the rear alley door and locked it, and threw the big bolts of the barroom door, then cautiously slid the buffalo head picture from the secret observation hole in the wall and peered into the long dance-hall.

What he saw brought a gasp to his throat.

There was something strangely familiar about those two old grim-faced men backed with drawn guns against the barroom wall. He had seen them before, Sandell unhappily recalled. He had reason to remember them—the same pair who had put the fear of death into him one night in San Antonio—the same cowmen whose cold nerve and ready guns had exposed his crooked card game and sent him in terror-stricken flight across the border.

Sandell's blood turned to ice as shocking realization came to him.

He had never learned the identity of the men who had driven him from San Antonio, but now he knew them at last for Sam Hally and Seth McGee of the Spanish Sinks—the two men who, next to the unknown Brant of Cimarron he had come to fear as the greatest menace to his schemes.

His fascinated eyes began to absorb further details. Pecos and Red Hansen seemed to be sitting in curiously frozen attitudes at a table near the Spanish Sinks men. He could see other groups clustered back from the zone of gunfire— the white tense faces of frightened dance-hall girls—the two barmen and Frenchy Larue; and, backed against the long bar, the tall cowboy, Bill Clay, a gun in either hand, his watchful gaze on Sam Hally and his partner. Sandell saw now that the burly Mexican standing close to the HM men was Juan Cota.

The latter was speaking in low fierce tones, addressing his remarks in Spanish to the cowboy. Sandell did not understand Spanish. He could only surmise that Juan was attempting to force his new rider to relinquish what might prove a fatal quarrel with the aged Spanish Sinks cattlemen. There was a deadly threat in the way the cold-eyed young cowboy held his two guns—a threat that promised quick death to Sam Hally and Seth McGee.

Sandell silently cursed Juan Cota for his interference.

The scene perplexed him. What could be the young stranger's quarrel with the Spanish Sinks men? They were old-time allies of the Box B and Shirley's loyal supporters.

One tremendous fact stood out against all his doubts and fears. No matter what Bill Clay did, Sam and Seth were cornered in the Red Front— doomed to die before the blazing guns of the men who had just left him. In a few moments Vin Sarge, Wes Droon—Bat Brimms, would be surging through the swing doors from the street.

Sandell had no wish to see the murder. He hurried back to the desk and snuffed out the lamp.

In a few moments he reached his apartment by way of the secret stairs. His watch told him it was nine o'clock. He smiled. Judge Cone and Dr. Kirk were due for their nightly game of poker.

Smiling complacently Sandell went to the door in answer to Judge Cone's familiar knock. The little poker party was opportune, an unshakable alibi that he was enjoying a game of cards with friends in his own rooms at the time two aged cattlemen from the Spanish Sinks were slain in the barroom of the Red Front saloon.

Sandell always liked a good alibi.

CHAPTER XI
GUNSMOKE

Seth McGee's chunky frame squirmed restlessly on the hard seat.

"Ain't so much, this Red Front dump," he sneered, scorn was in his roving black eyes. "Too dang peaceable," he complained bitterly; "things ain't like they used to be when we was young fellers." Seth wagged his head dolefully. "Tascosa, Abilene—Dodge," he chanted the names softly, "them was the roarin' days, huh, Sam?"

His big partner shifted long legs to a more comfortable position under the small table.

"Wasn't no frost in our hair in them days, nuther," he reminded with a tolerant smile.

"What you mean? Your talk o' frost in our hair?" Seth bristled like a terrier. "We ain't senile yet!" He glared indignantly. "No moss growin' on *our* horns, mister!"

"There you go ag'in," remonstrated Sam. "Growing old don't mean we're growing plumb useless, you old galoot. Mebbe we change some and git wise about things as make life worthwhile." The big cowman's gaze traveled distastefully up and down the long noisy barroom. "We come here to keep a promise," he went on, "else you and me would be back at the HM—boots off and feet restin' up on a chair"— Sam chuckled—"and you across the table, your ugly moon face all scowlin' 'cause you never could play a smart game o' cribbage like me."

"You're a dang liar!" fumed his incensed partner, "can wallop you at cribbage blindfolded any time you say!" He returned to his first grievance. "Sure am weary sittin' here—pretendin' to lap up this bilge they sells for whisky. Wish the fireworks 'd start. I crave action . . . plenty action!"

"Mebbe you'll git your wish pronto," Sam said softly. "Reckon we done seed that hombre some place, ain't we?" He jerked his chin at a heavy-set, sandy-haired cowboy expostulating with a sleek, swarthy man who had suddenly appeared from a door at the far end of the long bar.

"Wes Droon!" muttered Seth. "Sure we done seed the coyote afore! He's the hombre used to work for the Cross Knife outfit till Callahan found out he was helping Tandy's Bear Creek gang rustle Cross Knife cows." Seth's eyes glittered. "He hightailed it from the Sinks the time we put them rustlers out of business and stretched Tandy's neck for him."

"He's got him a job with the Box B," Sam reminded grimly. "He's one of them bunkhouse snakes—pullin' off the same play he done at the Cross Knife—like Juan suspects."

"Who's the jasper he's talkin' to?" Seth wondered.

"Fust time I ever seed him but I'm bettin' a new hat he's Frenchy Larue," was Sam's belief.

"Looks like a hard hombre," appraised Seth.

"Sure hope Wes Droon don't see us settin' here," worried his partner. "Droon's the only feller here as would know us. Ain't wanting Sandell to know we're in town—not yet. Would spoil our play."

"Frenchy's taking him into the back room," reassured Seth. "Reckon he didn't spot us settin' way over here in the corner. Kind of dark over here."

"Lucky for us he didn't," muttered Sam. He drew grizzled brows in a grim frown. "I'm bettin' another hat that Sandell's back in that there room, which sure proves that Wes Droon is one of the gang. The sneakin' spy!"

The big cowman suddenly refilled his glass from the bottle at his elbow and leered drunkenly at a scantily-clad girl who came drifting up to their table.

"No, sister, we ain't dancin' none till we done likkered plenty," he hiccoughed.

Painted lips parted in a mechanical smile and the dance-hall siren turned away with a scornful lift of gleaming bare shoulder.

Sam grinned at his companion, slyly emptied his glass into the big spittoon between their chairs. Seth chuckled, carelessly brushed his sleeve against his own glass, spilling its contents over the table. To all appearances they were a pair of mildly inebriated old cowmen out for an evening's relaxation.

"Wish Clay and Juan'd git here," fretted Seth. "Wonder what's keepin' 'em?"

"Should be here mos' any minute," observed the more patient Sam Hally. "You allus was one to start a sweat when you had to wait," he chided.

For a few moments the two old men watched the milling crowd—miners from the Oro Grande district; cowboys, sheepherders, desert prospectors; border ruffians, sombreroed Mexicans—the butterfly flutter of gaily-clad dance-hall girls whirling in the arms of male companions to the music of fiddle and guitar. Things were humming in the Red Front, despite the early hour.

Sam peeped surreptitiously at his fat silver watch, glanced hopefully at the swing doors. The newcomers were two cowboys, dust-covered and stiff-legged, obviously just off their horses.

Exchanging curt nods with several of the hard-faced fraternity lounging near the bar the pair made for a table near the one occupied by the HM partners.

They were an unprepossessing couple, with the hard vicious faces typical of their breed. Alkali dust lay thickly on battered wide-brimmed hats and sweat-stained flannel shirts—lined the creases of their brush-scarred leather chaps and boots. It was plain to Sam and Seth's experienced eyes that the pair had ridden far and fast.

For a minute or two they sat in sullen silence, fingers busy with cigarette papers, gaze fastened on the bar. A barman came over with bottle and glasses.

"Purty good at mind readin', ain't you, Fat?" grinned the smaller one of the cowboys. He was a bow-legged man with a thin dark face. Cunning and cruelty looked from his narrow-slitted eyes and his grin exposed protruding upper teeth that gave a sinister sneer to thin lips.

"Saw you come in, Pecos," laughed the bartender. "Figgered your throat was plumb arid. Looks like you an' Red have been churning plenty dust, huh?"

The cowboy cursed and drained his glass, sighed and wiped wet lips with the back of a dust-grimed hand.

"Wes Droon been in?" he asked.

The barman's gaze rested suspiciously for a moment on the two old men at the next table. The pair were arguing drunkenly. He lowered his voice. "He's in the back room," he told Pecos, "he just went in with Frenchy. Sarge and Brimms is back there, too. Reckon there's somethin' up, huh?"

Pecos drained a second glass, scowled at his quarreling neighbors.

"Sure have taken on a load, them two old mavericks," he commented sourly. "Fust thing we know they'll be goin' for each other with their guns." He looked at the bartender. "Did Wes tell you me and Red has been fired from the Box B?"

The man shook his head.

"Red and me figger there's somethin' back of us gittin' fired," Pecos continued. "Seems queer Wes Droon wasn't fired, too."

"Sure does," agreed the barman. He frowned. "Mebbe that new man Wes says Juan Cota's hired is back of this funny business."

The cowboy's protruding teeth showed in a wolfish snarl.

"Next time I meet up with that Mexican there's plenty lead flyin'." He patted the heavy gun clamped against his thigh and grinned at his companion.

Red Hansen, heavy of face and dull-eyed, shrugged burly shoulders.

"He's my meat," he grunted, "and I won't use no gun on the greaser." He flexed a powerful arm significantly.

The bartender's gaze flashed to the swing doors, rested for a moment on the two men entering from the street. Alarm was suddenly in his protuberant eyes.

"Don't you fellers start any trouble," he warned in an agitated voice. "Too many customers in the place for gunplay!"

He sidled hastily from the scene. Pecos and Red looked round at the cause of his startled retreat. The thin-faced cowboy muttered an exultant oath.

"Juan Cota!" Murderous hate peered from his narrowed eyes. "I'm bettin' the feller with him is that Bill Clay jasper—"

Fingers curled round whisky glasses the two punchers gloatingly watched the Box B foreman and his companion push their way to the crowded bar. A low voice spoke to them softly:

"Keep your hands on the table—if you aim to keep on livin' a while longer—"

Pecos and Red were too experienced not to know when Death whispered in their ears.

Careful to keep their hands in plain view they slowly turned incredulous startled faces, stared with venomous eyes at the two old men seated at the table behind them. For all Sam Hally's gentle smile, the cold light in his eyes quite backed up the threat of the huge six-shooter in his steady hand.

"Git their guns, Seth," he said in the same quiet tone.

The bleak-faced little man reached over and deftly emptied the low-slung holsters.

"Now you two hombres set there and behave," admonished Sam. "Seth is sure cravin' to do some snake-killin', and that's what he'll do if you make a move." He chuckled grimly. "Mebbe you've heard of Seth McGee, huh?"

The desperadoes exchanged dismayed looks. Seth McGee! and Sam Hally! The two men they had been instructed to kill on sight!

"We'll set," mumbled Pecos, all bravado gone. His big companion nodded dully, fascinated gaze on the gun in Seth McGee's hand.

"Mind you do," rasped the latter, "killin' fellers like your kind ain't no worse than killin' pizen rattlers. All right, Sam," he added in an undertone, "you start the play like we planned. I'll keep these babies quiet—"

"I've an idea," grunted his partner. He addressed Pecos and Red: "Shove your hands behind you—one hand each side of the center bar—"

They obeyed sullenly. Seth's smile was beatific.

"A right smart idea at that," he admired. His big .45 menaced the prisoners from the side of the table. "Fust one of you that squawks gits a hunk of hot lead in his gizzard," he warned in a chill voice.

The unhappy Pecos and his companion froze in their seats, hands tightly clasped around the rungs of the chair-backs. Sam produced a couple of the short rawhide tie ropes often carried by cowmen and deftly bound the extended wrists, making it impossible for Pecos and Red to move without carrying the chairs on their backs. Fortunately for Sam's idea the two tables were in a darkened angle of the wall nearest the street door—the full width of the room between them and the bar. Only close scrutiny would have given rise to suspicion that all was not well with Pecos and Red Hansen. Casual glances in their direction only saw two rather weary-looking cowboys leaning back in their chairs, apparently vastly interested in the low-voiced comments from the stocky little cowman seated at the adjoining table.

A girl swinging past in the arms of a burly Oro Grande miner threw a smile at the strangely subdued pair in the shadowy corner. She was the same blonde who had spoken to Sam a few minutes earlier.

"Pecos looks awful quiet," the girl commented to her heavy-footed partner. She sent a frowning glance over her bare shoulder. "I'll bet him and that pig-faced Red Hansen is plannin' to get them old geezers' bankroll away from 'em—and that old fellow so nice—makes me think of my grandpop—" She whirled on down the long room.

"All right, feller, start your play," whispered Seth. "I'll watch things back here."

Sam nodded dubiously and there was a curiously sober look in his eyes as he slowly pushed his way through the crowd toward the bar. Juan Cota espied him; delight spread over his dark face and hastily putting his glass down he grasped the old cowman's hand.

169

"Ha!" he exclaimed, "eet ees my frien' Sam Hally from the Spanish Sinks! *Buenas dias, Senor! como esta usted*?"

An ominous hush followed the Mexican's exuberant greeting; hard-faced men exchanged significant looks, men to whom the name of Sam Hally was anathema; a barman glanced nervously toward the inner room door.

Sam was eyeing Juan's tall companion intently. It was plain to the tense bystanders that the cowboy was restive under the old cowman's scrutiny. The latter spoke softly:

"Seems to me I've seed you afore some place, young feller."

"Reckon not, mister?"

"I sure have," insisted Sam, his voice suddenly hard. "I remember you now and it was down in Sonora I seed you." He turned on the rather bewildered cattle boss. "Juan, how come you know this hombre?"

"He weeth the *rancho*," stammered the Mexican, "thees hombre ees Bill Clay—he work for the Box B—"

"You don't tell me!"—Sam's tone was withering—"I'm warnin' you, Juan, you'll be shy plenty cows if he works for the Box B long enough."

Juan flung a startled glance at Clay, saw the young man look nervously toward the street door, as though premeditating a hasty exit.

"What—what ees thees talk, Senor?" he asked worriedly, "what ees thees theeng you say about Bill?"

"I mean he's a onery rustler—a killin' coyote," declared the old man loudly. He pointed an accusing finger at Clay, whose hands were stealthily lowering to holstered guns. "This feller was one of the Gillis gang as the Cimarron Vigilantes run out of the country and his name ain't Bill Clay by a dang sight. Last time I seed him he was wearin' the name of Texas Jack and I reckon you've heard of *that* killin' cow thief!" Snorting wrathfully Sam turned back to his table.

Rage convulsed the Mexican foreman's swarthy face; he swung furiously on the accused man.

"You treek me!" he shouted, "*Dios*—you are fired *pronto, sabe usted*!" The indignant cattle boss hastened after Sam.

There was a sudden stir, a rush for cover as two men standing at the upper end of the bar jerked guns from holsters. A girl screamed; Clay whirled, guns leaping into his hands and belching flame and smoke. As his .45s roared the two men dropped their weapons, stared stupidly at bullet-shattered hands. One of them began to curse.

"You fool!" he shouted, "we wasn't drawin' on you—it was the big feller—"

"How did I know?" retorted Clay. His gaze

swept the crowd menacingly. "Ain't taking chances," he warned grimly.

They eyed him fearfully. There were honest, courageous men in those huddled groups, but for the moment none cared to risk sudden death from those smoking guns in the hands of the cold-eyed youth whom Sam Hally had exposed as Texas Jack, notorious desperado—Texas Jack, ruthless killer.

Frenchy Larue came in hurriedly from the rear room.

"W'at ees ze trouble?" he demanded angrily and staring incredulously at the two wounded men. He knew their reputation for fast shooting.

"We was tryin' to help that feller an' he started smokin' his guns at us," muttered one of the men in a disgusted voice.

The saloon man gave Clay a wicked look.

"Who are you?" he wanted to know in a cold voice.

"None of your business, mister," retorted the young man.

A bartender whispered in Frenchy's ear. The latter muttered an exclamation, flung Clay a startled glance, then stared at the two old HM cowmen standing at bay with Juan Cota across the room. His black eyes glittered. Sam Hally's voice boomed at them.

"Lucky for Seth and me you mistook their intentions, Texas. Them varmints was all set to fill us with lead. Ain't that true, you coyotes?"

They glowered at him and Clay said regretfully:

"If I'd known it was you they were gunnin' for I'm sure sorry I spoiled their play." His face darkened. "I'm advisin' you two old meddlers to clear out of this town before I get real peevish and finish what they set out to do."

"You low crawlin' snake!" rasped Seth; he fell into a crouch by Sam's side, "we leave when we git ready to leave," he screeched.

Only a keen observer would have observed that Seth's watchful eyes were on certain lowering faces rather than upon the man he was defying. Standing near the HM men was Juan Cota, keeping an alert eye on Pecos and Red bound to their chairs; a needless precaution. Pecos and Red were content to remain silent for the time rather than have their ridiculous plight exposed to jeering spectators.

"I'm advisin' you to clear out," repeated the pseudo Texas Jack, "you, too, Cota—"

"Come on, fellers," muttered Sam, "no sense us foolin' round here—"

He started toward the door, halted abruptly, genuine dismay on his face as the board walk resounded to the clatter of men's booted feet; the swing doors flew violently open and Bat Brimms rushed into the barroom. Crowding at his heels were Vin Sarge and Wes Droon.

Glimpsing the young cowboy he had unsuccessfully attempted to arrest earlier in the evening, the deposed town marshal's gun roared—a split second too late. Clay's .45 was already belching leaden death. With a muttered curse Brimms staggered, fell sideways against Vin Sarge as the latter charged in; in turn the big Bar 7 foreman lurched against Wes Droon and both men went sprawling over the cursing little gunman.

Again there was a frightened scream—from the blonde girl, the same whose sympathies had been aroused by old Sam Hally because he reminded her of her grandfather. Clay spun on his heel, saw Frenchy Larue balancing his deadly knife, baleful gaze on Sam plainly indicating his murderous purpose.

"Drop that, mister!"

Clay's smoking guns menaced the saloon man; and Frenchy, with a vicious look in his beady eyes, sullenly obeyed.

The fallen men were struggling to their feet; other men furtively edged near the two HM partners, their courage somewhat restored by the presence of Frenchy and Vin Sarge. Things began to look perilous for Sam and Seth—the Box B foreman. Tight lines appeared around Clay's mouth as he realized that their carefully-planned little drama was likely to result fatally for the Box B *rancho*'s staunch friends. His guns went up, roared—one of the big hanging kerosene lamps collapsed into fragments; Seth's ancient six-gun crashed—the second lamp spurted splintered glass . . . darkness . . . the startled shrieks of frightened girls . . . the heavy breathing of tense, listening men.

CHAPTER XII
DARK HOURS

Shirley and Carmel were in their rooms overlooking the river flats when they faintly heard the double report of Clay's guns. They were busy freshening up before going down to the hot supper promised by Mrs. O'Grady. Shirley turned a startled wet face from the wash basin.

"Carmel! did you hear?" Her voice was apprehensive, her eyes wide with fear.

The other girl pulled a comb through her thick shining black hair.

"Only some wild cowboy shooting off his guns to let the town know he's arrived," she reassured with a shrug of her shoulders.

"I can't help feeling worried," confided Shirley. "It seems so—unwise for Juan to come to this town when he knows how things are. If Mr. Sandell is as bad as Sam suspects there is real danger here. I don't like it, Carmel!"

"Juan always could take care of himself," smiled her foster-sister. "Don't you worry about him, or about that young Bill Clay. He seemed quite a capable sort if you ask me."

"They are up to something mysterious," complained Shirley. "I think I have a right to know what is going on. I don't like mysteries."

176

She finished her toilet in silence and sat on the edge of her bed waiting for the more deliberate Carmel.

Again the roar of six-guns came to their ears—a woman's frightened scream.

Shirley sprang to her feet.

Silence followed the burst of gunfire; they could hear the frogs down in the river flats, then suddenly the uproar of men's excited voices, the heavy clatter of running feet on the board sidewalks.

Shirley ran to the open window and leaned out; Carmel joined her.

"We can't see the street from this back window," Shirley said impatiently. She drew back. Carmel cautioned her with a look.

"S-sh!" she whispered, "somebody is coming this way, I think—"

The sound was nearer—stealthy footsteps, and two vague shapes materialized from around the corner—took form in the tricky vagrant moonlight—became men.

One of them was tall, his companion, short and stocky. Shirley held her breath. Sam Hally—and Seth McGee!

Shirley fought a mad impulse to call down to them. Their caution told her that great danger threatened the two old men, warned her not to do anything to draw the attention of their pursuers. She pressed close to Carmel.

To the astonishment of the girls Sam and his partner came on swift, noiseless feet to a small door almost directly under their window. Indians could not have made a more silent approach. Shouts and cries floated from the street; they could hear the heavy pounding of feet as men scattered in search of the quarry; horses' hoofs went hammering into the distance.

The watching girls clung to each other, frantic with apprehension as Sam and Seth paused under the window. Almost instantly, to their surprise and vast relief, the door opened and for a moment they glimpsed the white head of old Pop Daly. The HM men vanished inside.

Scarcely had the door closed behind them when two men came running around the corner of the building. The girls drew back.

The searchers halted, stared across the river flats.

"Couldn't have come this way," declared one of the men. "No time for 'em to reach the willows yonder."

His companion growled an oath.

"Sure funny where them hombres got to so quick," he grumbled. "Like you says they ain't had time to git into the willows, which means they're still in town somewheres."

They hurried on, circling the rear of the hotel.

Shirley turned quickly from the window. Her face was pale.

"Did you hear what those men said?" She rushed on, not waiting for an answer. "It means the hotel will be searched! Oh, Carmel! we've got to do something!"

"They wouldn't dare search *our* room," Carmel began.

"That is exactly what *I* am thinking!" Shirley broke off, ran into the hall; she knew the little door below was the entrance to a flight of stairs leading up to the rear hall adjacent to their bedroom.

Carmel overtook her, grasped her arm.

"Shirley! what are you trying to do?"

"S-sh! they're coming—"

They peered down the dark stairway, saw Pop Daly cautiously mounting the steps, cane in one hand, a ponderous six-shooter in the other. Close in the hotel man's wake were Sam and Seth. The three men halted abruptly, startled faces upturned to the girls dimly visible above them.

Shirley beckoned reassuringly.

"Hurry!" she urged in a whisper, "I think they are going to search the hotel! We heard some men talking—"

"It's the lassie," they heard Pop mutter to his friends; "bedad, give me a start, she did."

He came limping up to the landing, the HM men at his heels.

Men's loud voices reached them from the street—from the lobby. They could hear Mrs.

O'Grady indignantly denying any knowledge of the fugitives.

"Quick!" implored Shirley; she fled back to the bedroom, gestured from the doorway. "In here—*please! They daren't look for you in our room!"

Pop Daly nodded approval.

"A good head she's got on her pretty shoulders," he applauded.

He motioned for them to hurry.

"I'll let ye know when the coast is clear," he promised as the two old cowmen somewhat reluctantly tiptoed into the room. With a relieved grin Pop limped down the hall to the front stairs. Maggie was having a time of it down in the lobby. He could hear her shrill protests—Nora's indignant voice.

Shirley turned the lock, stood with her back pressed against the door.

"Sam," she faltered, "what does it all mean? This shooting—these men—hunting for you and Seth?"

The veteran cowmen exchanged embarrassed grins. They were not accustomed to find themselves in a bedroom with two young women.

"Now don't you get all fussed"—Sam cleared his throat, glared at his sheepish partner—"you do some talkin', mister! What you standin' there so dumb for?"

Seth returned his glare with compound interest.

180

"She spoke *your* name, the same bein' *Sam,*" he reminded peevishly. "I'm leavin' the oratin' to your own self."

"I don't care which of you does the talking!" Shirley flared. "All I want is the truth." She looked at Sam Hally. "*Please* tell me what has happened—what all that shooting means, and why these men are hunting you down! Is—is it Sandell?"

"Seems like Sandell don't much care for Seth an' me being in San Luis," admitted Sam cautiously.

"Were Juan—and Clay, mixed up in the trouble?" she wanted to know. "Please tell us, Sam," she added unhappily. "Have—have they been hurt?"

"Juan an' the young feller come in while we was there," Sam again admitted, reluctantly. "No—they didn't catch no bullets," he added quickly as he saw the alarm in the girls' eyes. He hesitated, glanced at his cold-eyed partner.

"Juan—he had his bronc handy . . . reckon he's headed for the ranch by now—"

"I don't understand," interrupted Carmel in a troubled voice; "my brother is not the man to desert his friends—"

"He didn't!" explained Seth McGee. "Juan played his hand like was planned. Nothin' else for him to do but high tail it outer town." He grinned. "Sam and me would have been givin' him our dust if we could have got to our own broncs down in the river bed."

"Oh," murmured Carmel, puzzled, but relieved. "I just knew Juan wouldn't run away. I do think, though, you should tell us how the trouble started. What do you mean by saying that Juan 'played his hand like was planned'?"

The HM partners exchanged perturbed looks. Shirley's heart was suddenly curiously heavy.

"You're keeping something from us," she accused. "Why don't you tell us what happened to Bill Clay?"

"Young Clay?" Sam seemed strangely hesitant, "you mean that there new rider?"

"You know well enough whom I mean, Sam Hally!" Shirley eyed her old friends perplexedly. It was not like Sam to resort to subterfuge with her. He seemed oddly ill-at-ease; and Seth, too, was strangely fidgety. Sickening premonitions overwhelmed her. "Please, Sam," she begged unsteadily, "please tell me what has happened . . . I—I'd rather know—"

"Well"—Sam took a deep breath—"sort of hate to tell you 'bout him, Miss Shirley—" He broke off, looked quickly at the door. "Looks like maybe you'll have visitors," he added.

Footsteps resounded in the hall, the heavy tread of booted feet. Doors opened and slammed. They could hear Mrs. O'Grady's indignant protestation—men's curt, gruff voices. Sam and

Seth exchanged looks, went swiftly to the open window. There was no balcony, but by standing on the window ledge it was possible to grasp the cornice of the flat roof above. Sam swung up with surprising agility and reached a hand down to the shorter Seth; for a moment the little man's feet dangled precariously, then vanished as he pulled himself up to the roof. Shirley flew to the window, noiselessly closed it.

The searchers were at the door. There was a loud knock, and more indignant protestations from Mrs. O'Grady. Carmel went to the door.

"Who is it?" she called softly.

"Open up—we're taking a look in your room," answered a gruff voice.

"Don't you mind the man, colleens," shrilled the voice of Mrs. O'Grady. "Get on away from this door!" she stormed at the intruders; "ye'll not be disturbin' and insultin' the young girls! Black shame on the pack of ye!"

Shirley came close to Carmel's side. "What's the trouble, Mrs. O'Grady?" she called. "We're undressing—we can't open the door—"

"Shure, I don't be knowin' what it's all about," wailed Mrs. O'Grady.

A snarly voice interrupted her. "Git a move on and open the door or we'll bust her wide," it threatened.

The girls exchanged astonished looks.

"Pecos!" gasped Shirley, "it's Pecos—out there!"

"Makes matters worse," Carmel whispered. "He knows Sam and Seth are our friends—"

Shirley lifted an indignant voice. "How dare you threaten me, Pecos! You get away from that door! You know well enough who I am!"

"Sure, I know who you are," answered the voice of Pecos; "that's why I aim to take a peek in your room. If them two old side-winders is any place in this hotel it's in your room. Me and Red sure aims to take 'em apart for what they done to us. Ain't taking your orders no more, since that greaser foreman fired us from your outfit," he added sneeringly.

"What did they do to you, Pecos?" questioned Shirley from her side of the door, desperately striving for time.

"None of your business!" The maddened cowboy beat savagely on the door with the barrel of his gun. "Open up pronto—"

Hurried steps approached down the hall. "Get away from that door, you coyotes! What's the idea—disturbing these ladies?"

Shirley's heart thrilled as she recognized the curt, incisive tones of Bill Clay. In a moment she had turned the lock, pulled the door open. A gun in each hand, Clay was confronting the two former Box B riders. Other men were hastening up to the scene, Oliver Scott, Morton Sandell and a big man the girl vaguely recognized as Vin Sarge who she knew was foreman of the Bar 7 ranch. Bringing up the rear was Pop Daly, leaning heavily on his cane as he limped along. The old hotel man was frothing with rage.

"Ya yellar-livered spalpeens!" he shrilled, "I've a mind to fill yer with hot lead—" His big old-fashioned .44 menaced the two cowboys.

Pecos looked at Vin Sarge. "Was only wanting to take a peek into the room," he grumbled. "Red and me figger them two old Spanish Sinks buzzards is holed up in there—"

"Get out of here, you two," interrupted Sandell curtly. "I'll attend to this matter."

Pecos flung a malignant glance at the girl framed in the doorway and slunk away, the ponderous Red Hansen lumbering at his heels.

The banker smiled urbanely at the two young women peering nervously from the bedroom door. Sandell was again the smooth-tongued financier, the polished, suave New Yorker. "A most deplorable incident," he regretted, "although perhaps somewhat pardonable, considering the circumstances."

The girls looked at him wonderingly. It was hard to picture this bland rotund, genial-faced person as the ruthless chief of lawless men. Sandell continued:

"It seems this man, Hally and his partner, created a disturbance in the Red Front with the result that several men have been shot—one of them, our town marshal Brimms, perhaps fatally."

Shirley looked quickly at Clay, could read nothing in his grimly-set face, his averted eyes.

"Mr. Sandell is telling you the truth, ma'am," confirmed Vin Sarge in his heavy tones; "this Sam Hally hombre and his pardner sure went hog-wild and we aim to land 'em in the calaboose if we can get our hands on 'em."

"They're not hiding in our room, I tell you," Shirley persisted. Clay's strange lack of support secretly perturbed her. Again she sought his eyes; again he avoided her look.

"As a plain matter of duty—of justice," purred Sandell, "perhaps it is best that you permit us to assure ourselves. We realize," he added with a smile, "that Hally and McGee are old friends of yours and might have imposed upon your friendship under false pretenses—"

"Oh, look if you must—" Shirley drew aside with an offended shrug of slim shoulders.

Carmel stood her ground, refusing to budge, and said loftily: "I think you are all very rude, doubting our word." Her dark eyes swept them a scornful look, rested for a moment on the fair-haired Oliver Scott.

He flushed, took a quick step toward her.

"Please—you must not think that I—that I—" He stammered, gave Carmel a woeful look. "I merely chanced to learn you were being annoyed by those men and came to—offer you my help— if necessary."

Carmel eyed him more kindly. *"Gracias,"* she murmured.

To their surprise it was Clay who stepped quickly into the room. "Not here," he curtly informed the others. "Reckon those two old scoundrels got away from us after all."

His very apparent regret, his strange words, sent a chill through Shirley; she stared at him, aghast, scarcely believing her senses. Sandell saw her perturbation, smiled somewhat wolfishly.

"Come on, feller," growled Vin Sarge angrily, "we've gotta git them hombres if they're still in this cow town." He hurried away, spurs rasping on the floor.

Clay and Sandell exchanged glances, and the latter said, "Come on over to my office—I want to talk to you."

They hurried down the hall.

Oliver Scott lingered, ignoring the impatient glances from Pop Daly and Mrs. O'Grady. "I trust," he said earnestly, "I sincerely trust that you will pardon my apparent rudeness—this intrusion. As I explained I was really alarmed for you when I heard you were being annoyed by those half-drunken cowboys." He looked almost imploringly at the dark-eyed Carmel.

"I'm sure we have no reason to doubt you, Mr. Scott," demurely smiled the girl; she began to close the door.

The young lawyer turned away reluctantly but was halted by Shirley's voice.

"Perhaps you can tell us just what did happen in the Red Front," she begged.

Oliver frowned. "I'm not quite sure myself," he confessed. "It seems those two old men, Hally and McGee, accused one of your cowboys of being one of a gang of cattle thieves recently driven from the Cimarron country." The lawyer shrugged his tweed-clad shoulders. "It was the man just now in your room, I believe."

"Bill Clay!" Shirley gave him a shocked look. "It—it can't be true—"

"I—I'm rather afraid that it *is*—true," worried the young lawyer. His tone was sympathetic. "I gather you have regarded the man as highly trustworthy, Miss Benson—"

The girl nodded unhappily, looked at Carmel. "Juan's say-so," she confided; "Sam—and Seth, both backed Juan's say-so, didn't they, Carmel?"

"They did," conceded her foster-sister with a puzzled frown, and staring a bit coldly at the lawyer; "what you have told us about Bill Clay seems unbelievable, Mr. Scott."

"Nevertheless," maintained Oliver a bit stiffly; "the story is going the rounds, and"—he glanced at the old hotel man—"and Mr. Daly will confirm what I have told you—and so will Mrs. O'Grady," he appealed.

Pop scowled. "Shure I'm not denying there's

talk like ye say buzzin' 'round," he admitted gloomily; "but let me put a word in yer ear, Mr. Scott; 'tis wisdom to remimber there's two sides to anny sthory, me young bucko." The veteran ex-bull whacker and founder of the town of San Luis looked at his plump daughter. "Ain't it true, Maggie?"

"All I've got to say is I wouldn't believe the worrd of anny man in this town," declared Mrs. O'Grady, "excusing yerself, Mr. Scott, and referring more 'specially to that tricky Mort Sandell and the pack that runs to his beck and call."

The young lawyer gave Mrs. O'Grady a disturbed look, bowed and strode away.

Mrs. O'Grady shook her head pityingly. "A nice young man he is, I'm thinking," she confided to the others. " 'Tis a shame he's so friendly with that Sandell." The good woman gave the two girls a shrewd look. "Mighty queer—all this frantic business about old Sam Hally and Seth McGee! Sandell and his hired men can't make me believe those two old timers did a thing but what they was forced to do in self-protection." She smiled knowingly. " 'Tis lucky they weren't hiding in your room, colleens, or is it the truth that you pulled the wool over the eyes of thim rascals?"

"Ye should be down at the desk, Maggie," her father somewhat peevishly reminded.

"Ye don't need to tell me when I'm not wanted," retorted Mrs. O'Grady complacently; "just the same," she added with another shrewd smile at the girls, "I do be thinking the pair of ye is too upset to come down for the nice hot supper I'd fixed for yer—" She nodded her head. "I'll send it right up to yer," she announced mysteriously. "I'll tell Nora ye've worked up appetites for at least twice the two of ye." Mrs. O'Grady bustled away.

Pop Daly hesitated, saw Shirley's urgently beckoning hand. In a moment he was across the threshold and the door closed.

"Phwat become of thim?" he wanted to know; "shure, and me heart was in me mouth whin thot young rascal searched yer room, bad luck to him!"

"Pop!" Shirley slumped down on the edge of one of the beds. "Pop—they went up on the roof—"

The old man chuckled. "Trust Sam for thinking quick," he admired. His glance went to the closed window. "Ye heard Maggie, didn't yer. She's sending up hot supper for more'n you and Carmel." Pop laughed noiselessly. "Tell thim two old longhorns to come down from thot roof, lass. They'll be needing a bit to eat for the ride back to the Box B."

Shirley obediently went to the window, quietly pushed it open; and in response to her cautious signal, a pair of booted legs lowered to the window ledge. Shirley and Carmel reached out steadying hands and in another moment Seth McGee was scrambling through the window. In turn he helped his partner down the perilous descent. The big HM cowman gave them a weary smile.

"Ain't so spry as I was," he said ruefully; "this monkey business don't come so easy no more, huh, Seth?"

"Don't trouble me a-tall," denied the little man crossly. "Me—I can outfight, outclimb or out-do anything any o' these young fellers can do."

"Out-do anything but out-run 'em, eh, Seth?" chuckled Pop Daly. "Ye never was one to run, old timer."

Shirley was holding Sam's hands in a tight clasp. "Sam," she begged, "Sam—tell me it is not true—what they say about Bill Clay—"

The old cattleman's face was suddenly pale. "I—I reckon it's best we don't talk about him, honey," he evaded; "mebbe there's things we don't quite *sabe*—yet—"

Shirley stared at him for a moment, read the misery in his eyes. "So, it *is* true—" She turned away and threw herself face down on the bed.

CHAPTER XIII
THE PAINTED VALLEY

Clay reined in the buckskin, eyes swiftly appraising the possibilities of the little gully. A perfect hiding place for the buckskin; sheer, heavily-brushed cliffs on three sides and only the fifteen foot bottle neck to barricade. By stringing his rawhide riata across the bottle neck and piling armfuls of the prickly dry brush against its length he would have a tiny enclosure, well grassed and with a spring of running water. He could leave the buckskin snugly hidden for days and without the worry of food and drink.

Clay worked at furious speed. He was anxious to make the ascent of the Porcupine before sunrise. Preliminary explorations had sharply etched the topography on his mind; there were certain stretches, barren of brush or timber, that would be dangerous to negotiate in the bright light of day. The elusive shadows of early dawn were necessary for the success of his plans. Vin Sarge's reluctance to trust him had dangerously delayed matters. Clay wondered uneasily if he had done something to arouse the big Bar 7 foreman's suspicions—if the latter doubted his story of the Circle Dot trail herd. He could recall no false move he had made since that night in the

Red Front when his carefully-staged drama had convinced Mort Sandell and the latter's friends that he was a rustler and a former member of the notorious Gillis gang. The affair had been a risky bit of play-acting, not alone for himself, but for Sam and Seth, and Juan Cota. A narrow squeak for all of them, but so far the plan had worked smoothly.

Clay grinned as he stripped off saddle and bridle from the buckskin and carried the gear to a little brush-concealed cave under the beetling brows of the cliff that formed the blind wall of the gully. He had had a time of it, convincing Bat Brimms and those two others who had tried to gun Sam and Seth that he thought it was himself they were trying to shoot. His deadly marksmanship had favorably impressed Sandell and Vin Sarge, however; they had quickly quietened the resentful victims of Clay's not unnatural error. Vin Sarge had taken him aside, suggested that Clay might find a connection with the Bar 7 more than highly profitable. "Can use smart fellers like your sort in my outfit," the stoop-shouldered Bar 7 foreman had told him with a sly smile. Such a connection being the goal he had in mind, Clay's assent was fairly prompt, after a proper amount of the cautious inquiries to be expected from a hunted and notorious outlaw. Vin Sarge had only grinned at his questions. "No call for you to worry none," he had assured Clay. "We don't hold it 'g'inst a hombre if he's on the dodge from the law. We got other fellers in the outfit in your own fix and they make right smart riders for us. All we ask is they ride on the up and up for the outfit they draws their pay from, *sabe*?"

To Clay's casual question if Mort Sandell had instigated the offer of a job with the Bar 7, Vin Sarge had snorted indignantly. "Mort Sandell is boss of the bank that owns the Bar 7," he informed his new hand. "I do all the hirin' and the firin' that's done, mister."

The next day had found Clay out at the Bar 7, a fully accepted member of the outfit. That Vin Sarge himself sponsored the new man was assurance enough for the other riders. That Bat Brimms, perhaps, would have made matters unpleasant. The gunman's quarrel with Clay was now a personal affair. For the time being, the surly little ex-town-marshal was still in town, under the care of Dr. Kirk, as were the other two victims of Clay's fast guns. Clay would not have been so content with the outcome of the Red Front fracas had he known that Chico Lopez, the one man who would recognize him, was a recent Bar 7 recruit. Clay would have been more than worried had he known that Chico Lopez was still in the neighborhood, would have deeply regretted he had not followed Seth McGee's grim advice a few mornings earlier in the shadows of Indian Head.

With a last satisfied glance at the snug hideout for the buckskin, Clay left the place and began worming his way over the smooth round boulders of a dry arroyo. He carried a rifle, supplementing two .45's in his holsters; also a small knapsack containing a pair of powerful binoculars and a supply of beef sandwiches. The water canteen he left behind with his saddle gear; he was bearing weight enough, and he knew water was still plentiful in the springs.

Presently he left the arroyo and began a direct ascent of the rugged slope, climbing laboriously until he came to a nearly obliterated narrow trail winding round the breast of the giant ridge. It was precarious footing, at times no footing at all; and then he was forced to literally crawl, cling to tough brush roots and jutting cropping of granite. He knew from the signs that it was an old wild game trail originally, later used by the Indians and finally abandoned with the coming of the white man. There were many such trails, some that the white man had found safe shortcuts through a seemingly trackless wilderness and adopted for their own. It made easier travel than forcing his way through the hostile brush—the dense growths of cherry-limbed manzanita.

The sun had tipped the hills at his back by the time he had gained the summit—and the concealment of the giant spruce trees. The old trail became impossible to follow, littered with leaves and rotting remains of timber. Clay was not disturbed; he had an idea of his general direction. After a few minutes' rest he went swiftly forward, growing alertness in his roving gaze. He suspected that somewhere beyond this top of the world he would find the answer to a mystery.

An antlered buck broke from a thicket, went crashing back into the thick undergrowth at sight of him. Clay came to a standstill. Noise was something he did not like. Sound traveled and might convey a warning to keen ears. He moved on, more cautious, and with increasing watchfulness. A bear suddenly materialized from behind a great rotting tree trunk where it had been nosing for grubs. Clay halted again, eyed the huge animal prayerfully. He was stalking creatures more dangerous than any four-footed quarry; he was reluctant to use his rifle upon a mere bear. One shot from his weapon could not fail to reach the keen ears of those against whom he was pitting his own skilled woodmanship.

As if suddenly deciding there was no harm in the two-legged intruder the big bear lumbered away, not hurriedly, but with the bored indifference of one who had something more interesting on his mind than a lot of grubs to worry about. Clay moved on; and soon had worked his way through the thick growth of timber. Again he started a slow ascent, up the steep barren sides of the peak that had been his goal from the moment of leaving his concealed horse.

He began to regret his canteen of water. The sun was scorching his back; his breath came in labored gulps, and after the first hundred yards he unbuckled the heavy cartridge-laden holsters and six-shooters and left them under a boulder, together with the knapsack, retaining only rifle and binoculars.

Another thirty minutes brought him to the great cleft in the pinnacle. Breathless and sweating, Clay sank down in the gloom of the chasm. It was cool, here, with the draft of air drawing between the split shaft of the peak.

Presently he proceeded deeper into the cleft. He had to climb and scramble over great jagged boulders and at times squeeze between crevices scarcely large enough to admit his shoulders. He began to wonder if the fearsome passage had an ending—if perhaps it wound back on itself. Of one fact he was sure—no man's feet had in his lifetime ever traversed this boulder-strewn chasm piercing the lofty summit of the peak.

He went doggedly on, rounded a sharp turn, was suddenly rewarded by a faint penciling of light that lay like a delicate blue vein against the face of the crowding darkness—the blue of the morning sky.

Clay climbed over the boulders to the crevice-like opening. The crack, or cleft, ran up at an angle from the floor of the passage; he could see nothing as yet save the ribbon of blue sky. He drew himself up to the ledge and crawled through the crevice to the outer edge. Although not unprepared for something of the sort, the panorama that burst into view held him spellbound.

The floor of the valley lay nearly five hundred feet below his lofty perch, a phantasy of color, lush green in the lower meadows where a creek wove a pattern in silver thread to a lake that lay like a mirror framed by the deeper green of marsh-land. On the upper reaches the grass was yellowing, broken by darker splashes that were clumps of live-oaks; and, rimming the grasslands, again the deeper tones of low brush-clad hills. Surrounding valley and foothills rose sheer cliffs, their barren steeps splashes of color—reds and greens and shades of yellow—the chalk-white of limestone.

For long minutes Clay crouched motionless in his eagle's aerie, rapt gaze on the scene stretched below him. He knew he had found the answer to the riddle he had set himself to solve.

He had not been many days at the Bar 7 ranch before suspecting the existence of a mysterious hiding place for stolen cattle. Bits of overheard gossip between members of the outfit, sly allusions to the Bottle Neck. Curly Smith's unguarded answer to Clay's carefully casual question regarding Vin Sarge's two days' absence from the ranch . . . "Vin—he's got business over to Painted Valley." Curly had suddenly thrown him a sullen, suspicious look and clumsily turned the conversation. The name had stuck in Clay's mind.

Painted Valley! Apparently nobody had ever heard of the place. He had put the question to Juan Cota and the HM partners when he met them at a secret rendezvous. Juan had declared that not in his lifetime had he ever heard of such a place. Sam and Seth corroborated him. It was apparent that the secret of Painted Valley was known only to members of the rustler gang. It also grew on Clay that the Bottle Neck had some connection with the mysterious hidden valley, was no doubt the gateway into the rustlers' stronghold.

Curly Smith, some days later, had given Clay his first opportunity. The cowboy's hasty departure, after a lengthy secret conference with Vin Sarge, had struck Clay as significant. Curly and a companion had ridden away after night-fall, taking with them three heavily loaded pack horses. Leaving a dummy, supposed to be himself soundly asleep in his bunk, Clay followed the trail, only to lose it in the rugged foothills of the Porcupine. Carefully marking the oddly-shaped peak with its split cone he managed to get back to his bunk before dawn discovered his absence to his fellow riders. He learned later that the peak was known as the Devil's Pitchfork.

Clay had soon realized that Vin Sarge was keeping him under close surveillance. To the outfit he was Texas Jack, notorious border desperado with a price upon his head; at the same time it was apparent that the big Bar 7 foreman desired further assurance that Texas Jack was yet to be trusted with certain secrets. He was, in Vin Sarge's eyes, a novitiate; until he had proved himself by some act in keeping with his character. Clay decided he must himself supply the further necessary proof that would convince the others of his lawlessness.

Clay chuckled as he recalled the new respect with which Vin Sarge had listened to his exaggerated account of the great trail herd on its way from the Cimarron to the Box B ranch. The big foreman had questioned him closely as to the source of his information. Clay's answer had been plausible enough.

"What do you reckon give me the notion to hire on with the Box B outfit for?" he retorted with a knowing grin; at which Sarge had nodded admiringly.

"*I sabe*, young feller," he chuckled. "You knew 'bout this here trail herd afore you headed for this part of the country your own self, huh?"

"Sure did, mister," drawled the pseudo Texas Jack, whose name Clay had felt entirely safe in using for his purposes. Texas Jack's sinful career had come to a violent end on the same night that the Cimarron vigilantes hung Sig Gillis to a convenient cottonwood tree. He gave the attentive Bar 7 man further interesting details.

"Was laying low down in Juarez when I met a hombre used to work for the Circle Dot outfit. Seems he'd been fired and was awful sore. 'Twas him told me 'bout the Circle Dot sending these cows down to the Box B—"

"Circle Dot, huh," muttered Sarge thoughtfully. "Reckon that's the outfit owned by that there Brant hombre, huh?"

Clay nodded. "Sure aim to get that feller some day," he promised darkly. "Brant's the hombre as organized them Cimarron vigilantes and run us out of the country—after makin' poor old Sig Gillis dance on air."

"You're plumb certain these cows is heading for the Box B?" Sarge had persisted. "Where from would the Benson gal be raising money for a big deal like you say?"

"Them old HM coyotes is mixed up in the deal, way I figger it," was Clay's ingenious fabrication; "this feller I was telling you 'bout that I met down in Juarez, says the big hombre, Sam Hally was up there at the Circle Dot. You and me knows plenty that Sam and that gun-slinging runt of a pardner of his are old friends to the Benson gal." Clay simulated a fierce scowl that would have done justice to the late unlamented Texas Jack himself.

"Reckon that's why the old wolf jumps me that night in the Red Front," he reminded; "looks like he suspicioned why I come down here and got me a job riding for the Box B."

Sarge's ready acceptance of Sam Hally's mythical visit to the Circle Dot afforded Clay a certain grim satisfaction.

He had more than one reason for wishing news of the impending cattle drive to reach the ears of Sandell. Coming from himself, it strengthened his pose as one of their own lawless breed—made good bait to lure Sandell and his lieutenants into a trap from which there would be no escape. The Bar 7 foreman's more friendly manner was proof that he no longer doubted Clay; even though he had not thawed out enough to become confidential.

"I've gotta run into town," he had finally mumbled; "want to ride in with me, young feller?"

Clay assuredly did not want to ride into San Luis. The foreman's absence would give him the opportunity he had been chafing for. Somewhere in the heart of the rugged Porcupine mountains was a mysterious hidden valley he yearned to find. He looked regretful.

"Sure would like to make a night of it," he mourned, "didn't have much chance to spread myself last time that I was at Frenchy's place."

"Fork your bronc an' ride with me," invited

Sarge genially. He hesitated, "Mebbe a man I knows in town 'll be a heap interested in your story of this Circle Dot trail herd."

For a moment Clay was tempted, then realized that even if the man proved to be Mort Sandell he would still lack the proof he needed. Most important at this time was some definite information regarding the secret of Painted Valley—the Bottle Neck. He shook his head.

"You're the boss of this outfit, Vin," he grumbled, "and you ain't doing right luring me to the gay lights when I should be down at the Perdido Canyon camp come nightfall. That trail herd'll come in by way o' Perdido Pass, sure as you're born—"

"Mebbe you're right, Tex," admitted the foreman after a moment's frowning concentration on the matter. He stared not unkindly at his new rider. "Meanin' you'd like to take on the job watching for their dust, huh?"

"Well, I tipped you off, didn't I?" drawled the young man. "I'd figger the job was mine, Vin, wouldn't you?"

"Sure should keep a lookout down at the Perdido," mused Sarge, "only trouble is, Tex, I sortta figger it's a job for a man I knows more than I knows you, *sabe*?"

"Kinda looks like you ain't trusting me much," Clay told him with another Texas Jack scowl. "If that's the way you feel 'bout me, Vin, reckon I might as well climb on my bronc and play a lone hand with that trail herd."

"No call to go on the prod," remonstrated the foreman. He shrugged his wide, stooped shoulders. "All right, feller," he agreed with some reluctance, "the job's yours. Git what supplies you need from the cook and hightail it for the Perdido pronto."

Which Clay had lost no time in doing. If he had known that Vin Sarge, always cautious, had left certain instructions with Wes Droon, now a member of the Bar 7 outfit, he would have been more wary. Not knowing it was the crafty foreman's inflexible rule never to trust an important mission to any single man of his outfit, Clay did not dream that Wes Droon, suspicions aroused, was stalking the trail to the Devil's Pitchfork.

CHAPTER XIV
THE DEVIL'S PITCHFORK

From somewhere far down the valley a meadow lark's triumphant alleluia to the morning sun floated up to Clay—a range bull sent out a thunderous challenge; thin blue smoke lifted lazily above the log house half hidden in the willows near the creek. Life was astir in Painted Valley.

Clay crawled cautiously from his precarious perch in the mouth of the crevice. The place was too conspicuous for safety, even though the most alert of sentries would hardly be watching for intruders by way of the Devil's Pitchfork. Even so, Clay knew that any movement on the bare face of the cliff might readily arouse curiosity and draw a high-powered rifle bullet in his direction. He inched himself along the narrow ledge, was suddenly motionless as another sound drifted up to his tensely-listening ears—the bang of a door. For a full minute he flattened against the ledge, as a lizard flattens when sensing danger. A man appeared, paused for a moment in the doorway, and then went leisurely toward the horse corral. Clay got to his feet and made a dash for the big clump of greasewood that had been his objective.

Three more men appeared from the basin and

went to the corral where the first to arrive was preparing to rope one of the milling horses. Clay could hear their voices plainly, but was unable to understand what was said. Presently two of them rode away, splashing across the creek where the willows quickly hid them from view. One of them Clay recognized as the man who had accompanied Curly Smith when the latter had made his hurried departure from the Bar 7. He shifted his glasses to the remaining pair now returning slowly to the cabin.

There was no mistaking the short squat Curly Smith. Clay smiled mirthlessly. The hard-faced Curly was Vin Sarge's top-hand rider and close friend; his presence in mysterious Painted Valley only confirmed Clay's belief that the Bar 7 foreman was the active leader of the rustler gang, of which Mort Sandell, according to old Sam Hally, was the brains. Clay was interested in Curly Smith and his fellow desperadoes only so far as they led to the undoing of the ringleaders— the men responsible for the murders of Ed Benson and Clem Collins. He had followed the trail to Painted Valley for more important reasons than such as Curly. It was in this secret stronghold that the rustlers probably were holding cattle stolen from the Box B and other ranches. So far all had been surmise. Clay wanted facts, wanted actual proof that the stolen cattle were in the valley, wanted to learn the secret of the mysterious

Bottle Neck. He suspected that the two men who had ridden across the creek were on their way to the Bottle Neck, to relieve the night shift.

Curly Smith suddenly reappeared from the cabin, followed this time by four companions. All of them hurried to the corral. Apparently the business of the day was about to begin. A sixth man, apron-clad, lounged negligently in the doorway and stood watching the others roping and saddling their horses. Clay surmised he was the outfit's cook. Eight men, he had counted, with at least two more on the night shift at the Bottle Neck, a total of ten. There might be others on lookout at different vantage points, Clay reflected; he thought not. The rustlers would feel reasonably safe from discovery as long as vigilant guard was kept at the Bottle Neck.

Curly and his companions rode away at a jog trot, spreading out in fan formation as they neared the low hills to the north. Their purpose was plain to Clay's experienced eyes. As the men on the left neared the northern rampart they would swing in and slowly force the gathered cattle toward the eastern wall, to a point almost directly under the Devil's Pitchfork. Here the herd would be held and brands worked over. He could see the very place the rustlers used for the purpose—a semicircle of low ridges that formed a series of small natural corrals; an ideal set-up for a limited crew. Clay trained his glasses on the spot and without much trouble was able to locate the ashes of the branding fires—even the irons—leaning against a boulder. He was in luck. He would have no difficulty reading the old brands before they were blotted out. He was confident that the cattle now slowly swelling into a herd would carry the mark of the Box B. What the new brand would be he had no idea; certainly not the Bar 7. It would be difficult to turn a Box B into a Bar 7—entail too much time and work. Whatever the rustler's mark was he would soon know.

Slowly the gathered herd, some two hundred in number, drew nearer, urged on by the shrill yips of the riders. One of the men now left his companions and came loping toward the point almost directly under Clay. He swung from his saddle—set to work building the fires. All would be in readiness by the time the small herd arrived. He had never seen the man before.

The bawling cattle were pushed into a run by the yelling riders. The haste struck Clay as significant, perhaps explained why Curly Smith had been rushed to the valley. The brand-blotting was to be speeded up, the stolen cattle removed to some distant range.

Painted Valley was only a temporary holding place until brands could be changed. There were at least five or six thousand head in the valley, he estimated, too many to be kept long without destroying the feed needed for the spoils of raids to come. He knew from Juan Cota's figures that Shirley's losses had been close to five thousand, which meant the greater part of the cattle now held in Painted Valley were Box B cows.

The pungent smell of wood smoke drifted up from the branding fires, the sharp impact of the cook's ax as the latter replenished his fuel box. Voices sounded from the willows and two riders emerged from the thicket, came splashing across the creek shallows. The relieved night men in from the Bottle Neck, Clay decided. He studied them through his glasses, was unable to recognize either as men he had met at the Bar 7. They swung from saddles, loudly demanding their breakfasts. The cook dropped his ax and hurried back to his kitchen, wiping hands on his apron.

Clay estimated at least an hour had elapsed since the day shift had left the camp to relieve the night guards. The Bottle Neck was evidently two or three miles down the valley. He was puzzled from his high vantage point, why he had not been able to spot the men, going or coming. He had a clear view over the tops of the creek willows; the men would have been in plain sight if they had ridden west from the stream. There was only one explanation, Clay decided. The route closely followed the winding course of the creek and traversed the opposite bank. He would be forced to penetrate further south for an unobstructed view down the west bank of the stream. He would make the attempt as soon as he had identified the brand carried by the approaching cattle. It was also important to learn the new brand that would replace the old; by this time most of the stolen Box B cows would have been re-marked; it was necessary to know the new brand for purposes of identification.

Crouched behind the greasewood Clay trained his glasses on the herd now within three hundred yards and approaching at a right angle. Almost instantly he picked up the mark on the left flank of a big steer. It was a Box B. He studied the sides of several other steers.

"Every one of 'em Box B," he exulted. "Mister Vin Sarge, I thought you were a rustler—and now I know it for sure." He lowered the glasses, waited for the brand-blotting to begin.

The rustlers worked quickly. Much practise had made them expert in the art of changing a brand. Clay soon had the information he wanted from the first indignant bawling victim. A circle inside the box made the old mark into a Box OB.

Satisfied he had nothing more to gain by remaining longer, Clay's mind took up the problem of the Bottle Neck.

It was soon apparent to him that he must abandon his first plan to penetrate south for a clear view down the west bank of the creek. The sides of the cliff were too sheer, the vegetation too sparse for concealment. His only alternative would be to return to his sequestered horse, circle the base of the Porcupine and approach the valley from the west slope. He had learned enough to know that the Bottle Neck was located somewhere on the west slope, probably near the place where the creek forsook the valley for its plunge down to the plains.

He studied the winding course of the creek through his glasses. Somewhere at the far end of the valley, at the point where the stream disappeared into the narrow gorge, lay the key to the hidden entrance. There was no other way for the men to have ridden unseen; he was convinced the trail to the Bottle Neck followed the creek for the entire distance, was quite concealed from view by the thickly growing willows.

He started carefully up the short steep ascent to the crevice. It was not possible for the men at the branding fires directly below to see him; the danger lay in a possible loosened falling stone attracting their attention, or a chance glance from alert eyes at the log house. Rifle held high to avoid knocking it against the stones, Clay crept toward the ledge that made a sort of platform in front of the crevice. He reached up, pushed the rifle, barrel foremost, toward the crevice, craning his head for a look back at the log house. The recently returned night men were still at breakfast, he saw with relief. He swung up to the ledge, stooped for his rifle . . . the gun had vanished.

For a moment Clay stared unbelievingly at the spot where he had placed the rifle. He knew it could not possibly have slipped from the ledge unnoticed. There was but one answer to the mystery. Slowly he lifted his gaze—stared coolly into the sneering, malignant eyes of Wes Droon crouched in the semi-gloom of the cavern. Clay's rifle lay at his feet, a gun was in his hand. Clay gave him a nonchalant grin, crawled through the narrow opening.

" 'Lo, Wes," he drawled, "how long you been here? Reckon you must have followed me from the Perdido, huh?" He reached down casually for the rifle. Droon put a big boot on it. "Leave it lay," he said harshly.

Clay pretended surprise.

"What's eatin' you, feller?" he wanted to know. "Peeved 'cause I wasn't at the camp when you got there?" He shrugged his shoulders. "Wasn't 'specting Vin to send you to keep me company at the Perdido or I'd have left a note telling where I'd gone."

Droon seemed unimpressed; if anything the menace in his unwinking stare was more pronounced.

Clay continued, fumbling in shirt pocket for cigarette papers and tobacco: "Figgered the Devil's Pitchfork might be a mighty good place for us to keep a lookout for them Circle Dot cows Vin maybe told you we was to watch for—"

A savage grin distorted the other man's face. "Sounds like them cows is purty close, feller." He jerked a thumb at the cliff. "Sure sounds like cows bawlin' down there—"

"Sure does," admitted Clay frankly; "only they isn't Circle Dot cows, Wes. Was going to ask you about that outfit down in the valley yonder. Didn't know there was a cow outfit back here in the Porcupine. Fact is, Wes," he confided, "I figger there's something underhand going on down there, from what I seed back on the hillside"—he winked knowingly—"something you and me should horn in on."

Droon's stare was stony, disbelieving.

"You know me, Wes," continued Clay a bit desperately, "you know well enough I was right-hand man to old Sig Gillis afore he got strung up by that Cimarron bunch. You know who I am and why Vin Sarge put me on the Bar 7 payroll. My idea is that one of us hightails it pronto for the Bar 7 and tell Vin what's going on in this valley. Vin—he won't be so awful pleased to know there's competition in this terr'tory."

"Meanin' just what?" asked Droon in a chill voice.

"Meanin' there's a bunch of rustled cows in this valley," Clay told him; "also meaning our own outfit can hop over here and horn in on their play—run those fellers outer the country and take the cows for our own selves." Clay gave the other man a knowing grin, bent casually down to the rifle. Again Droon's six-gun menaced him.

"Leave it lay," he rasped. He stared with cold, sneering eyes at the pseudo Texas Jack. "You can talk awful fast, mister, but what you say don't ring the bell with me," he said contemptuously.

"You ain't acting sensible, Wes," Clay remonstrated mildly. "If you don't believe me take a look your own self. Them fellers is changing brands right now"—he gestured through the crevice. "Take a look," he urged.

"Don't need to take a look," sneered Droon, "I know what's going on down there, and so do you, mister." His voice shook with passion. "You ain't fooled me none, feller! I got you figgered out; you come up here to spy on what's doin' here in Painted Valley—"

"That likker you mops up sure gives you funny notions," jeered Clay, again fumbling with tobacco sack. He shook the little bag impatiently. "Gets awful hard packed, this onery terbaccy," he grumbled. "Talk sense, Wes," he complained. "What you mean—I'm a spy? Ain't liking your talk much?"

"I've got you figgered," repeated the man, a murderous look in his eyes. "Your name ain't Texas Jack—"

"This terbaccy sure is a mess," muttered Clay,

seeming not to hear Droon's accusation. He gave the little sack another impatient knock, spilling out the powdery yellow contents into his palm.

"Listen, you!" growled Droon angrily, "Vin Sarge wasn't so sure 'bout you and your story, which is why he sent me down to the Perdido to keep an eye on you. I git to the Perdido and find you've sloped. . . . I'm some tracker—didn't take me long to pick up your trail!" Droon laughed mirthlessly. "Been watching you almost all the time you been here and while I was watching you I've been doing some figgerin' like I said." He paused, thrust his head forward, eyes glittering with triumph—"I know who you be; you're the feller the Big Boss told us to watch out for—your name's Clay Brant—" Droon's gun lifted.

Clay read the purpose in the man's deadly look; he knew that it was to be his life or Droon's— knew that the gloomy cavern must be the tomb for himself or the man confronting him with drawn gun. What a fool he was to have left his own six-guns down on the mountain side! He spoke quietly: "What you aim to do with me, Wes, s'posing I am Clay Brant?"

"I'm killin' you same as I'd kill any coyote!" snarled the man. He gestured with the gun. "Git a move on—you're crawlin' through that hole—"

It came to Clay that prompt compliance meant a minute longer to live—and many things can happen in less than a minute. Refusal to obey

215

Droon's curious command would only mean instant death. There was no mistaking his murderous intention. With a last regretful glance at the rifle clamped under Droon's big boot he turned his back and wriggled through the crevice.

"Stand there plumb on the aidge of the rock and keep your back to me," came the voice of his enemy. "I've got you covered," he warned.

Clay stood in silence, aware now of the doom planned for him, even before Droon spoke.

"I'm giving you your choice," the latter told him as he squirmed through the narrow passage, "you can jump off the cliff—or you can take a slug in your back"—his laugh was mirthless—"no difference to me whut you do . . . either way you take a five hundred foot drop." He laughed again with relish. "Some s'prise for Curly and the fellers down there. Sure will give 'em a laugh."

"This is cold-blooded murder, Droon," Clay said in a low voice. His gaze went to the distant mountains. They seemed very beautiful, at that moment; and the little valley in all its painted splendor seemed to draw in close to his eyes, as though bidding him take a last look at life. "Cold-blooded murder," he repeated in the same low, scarcely audible voice.

Droon laughed again, softly, maliciously. It was obvious that the cruelty in him revelled in the situation; that he desired to prolong the scene for the sheer pleasure it gave him.

"You won't be the first man I've killed," he boasted, "not by a damn sight, mister"—his sinister laugh came again—"don't mind telling you 'twas me that killed old Ed Benson the night of the raid." His voice hardened, was suddenly impatient. "Well—are you taking the long jump—or is it hot lead in your back?"

"Droon!" Clay spoke quickly; "there's five hundred dollars in bills, tucked away inside my shirt pocket. It's yours for a chance to smoke a last cigarette."

"Huh!" Surprise, cupidity, was in the man's voice. "Five hundred dollars—in your pocket—"

There was a brief pause, and then Droon said reflectively, "No sense sending five hundred dollars down there for Curly and the boys. All right, mister . . . turn round so I can watch while you get that money outer your pocket and if it's like you say, I'll give you time for your smoke."

Clay turned slowly, stood with his back to the precipice. One look at Droon's evil grin told him there would be no last cigarette once the man had the money.

"Hurry, you," grunted Droon, watching him sharply, gun ready for any desperate move on the part of his victim.

Clay fumbled in a shirt pocket, slowly drew out a roll of bills—he actually had the amount he said, carried for emergencies—and eyed the other man inquiringly. "Want me to count it, so you'll know there's five hundred dollars?" he asked.

"No!" grunted Droon impatiently; greedy fingers reached for the money, "give it to me—" He muttered an oath, instinctively shifted his gaze as the roll of bills apparently accidentally slipped from Clay's fingers and landed close to the edge of the cliff. For a fleeting moment greed triumphed over caution; and as Droon impulsively stooped to rescue the money, Clay opened his clenched palm, flung the handful of powdery cigarette tobacco full into the man's eyes. With the same lightning speed his other gripped Droon's wrist, forcing the gun down.

Cursing luridly, blinded and in agony for the moment, Droon fought to break Clay's hold; the gun dropped from his hand and the next instant the two men were locked in each other's arms.

They fought furiously, in silence, save for the sobbing gasps of their labored breathing.

The big sandy-haired rustler was quite as powerful as Clay, and considerably heavier; his long, mighty arms wrapped like steel cables around his opponent, tried to force him back to the crumbling edge of the precipice; Clay resisted the maneuver desperately, one foot slipping precariously for a moment. With a tremendous heave he swung Droon around and now the latter found himself battling for a foothold. From below came the bawls of the cattle, the hoarse cries and shouts of Curly's men at the branding fires. Clay's powerful arms tightened their hold, held the other man helpless on the brink. Droon's face was pasty-white under his sunburn, horror looked from his bloodshot eyes.

"I've got you, Droon!" Clay's voice was breathless. "So you killed Ed Benson, did you?"

"I—I was jokin'!" gasped the rustler.

"You lie! You killed Ed Benson," panted Clay. "You told me the truth when you boasted about it, Droon. I've a mind to send you over the side—"

"No! No!" pleaded the man huskily, "ain't wanting to die thataways—down thar on them rocks—all smashed and bloody—"

"It's too easy a death for your kind, Droon. You're going to hang, soon as I get you to the Box B ranch. There are men there who'll want to help pull on the rope."

"I can tell you things you want to know 'bout," gasped Droon, "let loose of me and I'll talk plenty—"

"I'm making no promises," Clay assured him grimly, "but it won't hurt you to talk all you've a mind to talk—about what you know." He darted a glance at the fallen six-gun, saw it was beyond his reach.

"Let loose of me," begged Droon, reading his mind, "I'm giving you my word I won't make a move; if you want to reach for the gun."

Clay considered the matter briefly. He was like a man who holds a bull by the tail, afraid to let go. His trust in Droon's word was one hundred per cent below par. He was in a quandary. Any second might disclose them to a chance look from the men at the log house. His one hope to gain possession of the gun lay in taking Droon by surprise, seizing the gun before Droon realized his intention. He saw the man's glance flicker downward, guessed his thought.

"Don't try it," he warned. "They couldn't hear you even if you yell your head off—with all those cows bawling. If you do try, you'll land down at their feet about as quick as your yell gets there."

Droon nodded, face ashen.

"I'm letting loose of you when I count ten, Droon," continued Clay; "or you can do the counting," he amended, hopefully believing the mental labor of counting might distract the man's attention. "When you reach ten, I'm turning you loose and both of us can go for that gun, *sabe*?"

Droon nodded, a sudden gleam in his eyes, a gleam that told the other how much mercy he could expect if the man got his hand on the weapon. Clay smiled grimly; he had no intention of waiting for the final count of ten before loosing his hold and make his lightning leap for the gun. "All right," he said, "start your count, Droon."

"One," began the man, "two—three—four—"

A low infuriated animal cry burst from his lips as Clay's powerful grip suddenly fell away and the latter whirled in a swoop for the weapon. A savage oath in his throat, the big rustler made a tiger-like bound toward the stooping body of his opponent. Clay saw his danger and flattened full length; taken by surprise the man tripped over him, plunged headlong against the face of the cliff. Dazed by the impact, half blinded by the blood streaming over his eyes from a gash in his forehead, Droon turned like a maddened bull, big hands reaching out for his enemy. Again Clay avoided his clutch by a quick sideways roll and carried along by the violence of his infuriated charge Droon went plunging over the precipice.

His face pale, shaken by the sudden and ghastly termination of the affair, Clay crouched there on his knees, grasping the gun. He had no need to look to be able to visualize that hideous descent to death on the rocks five hundred feet below. He knew by the sudden hush of men's voices that Curly Smith and his men were gazing with stupefied shocked eyes at something lying near the branding fires. He got to his feet, made haste to regain the concealing gloom of the cavern, somewhat surprised to find that his knees were strangely weak. A loud yell floated up to his ears. Crouched low against the opening he listened tensely. Curly Smith's voice, excited, bewildered.

"It's Wes Droon!"

Another stunned silence, broken only by the monotonous bawl of the milling herd. Men came running from the cabin, the two punchers—the camp cook, apron flapping about his legs.

"Sure is Wes Droon!" marveled another voice. "Wonder what he was doing up there, Curly?"

"Sure is queer—mighty queer," answered Curly's voice. "Mebbe we'd best take a look up there, fellers. You and Slinger stay with the cows. . . . Rest of you fork your broncs. Only way we can git up there is to ride round the Porcupine—"

In a few moments Clay saw four riders burst into view from under the cliff. He was not worried. He could reach his horse and be gone long before the rustlers would have time to reach the Bottle Neck—make the long ride around the mountain. He settled comfortably back against a boulder and fished out the depleted sack of tobacco. Enough for a smoke or two, he saw with relief.

He made a cigarette, lighted it, inhaled gratefully, his gaze on the roll of bills still lying where it had fallen close to the edge of the precipice. He smiled grimly. No need to leave it there for Curly Smith and his men to find. In a few minutes, when things had quieted down he would crawl once more through that narrow crevice. It was worth the trouble—for five hundred dollars—the five hundred dollars that had hurled Wes Droon into eternity.

CHAPTER XV
CHICO LOPEZ TALKS

Oliver Scott emerged from the narrow hall stairs leading to his office above Meeker's general merchandise store. After a moment's indecision he crossed the dusty street to the Daly House and mounted the warped sun-blistered steps to the porch. Pop Daly was dozing in his big chair, at least the young lawyer thought he was dozing. Oliver hesitated, turned to enter the lobby. Pop's voice swung him around.

"Ye was wantin' ter speak ter me, lad?"

"I thought you were sound asleep, Pop." Oliver took an adjoining chair and looked at the old man with worried eyes. There was a drawn expression about his mouth, Pop noticed. It was obvious that some knotty problem was disturbing him.

"I sleep with one eye open, these times," the veteran ex-bullwhacker said a bit grimly. "There's little that goes on in this town that I don't know about. Phwat's on yer mind, Mr. Scott?"

"Mr. Daly"—the young lawyer's voice was troubled—"what is your opinion of Morton Sandell?"

"I thought 'twas him on yer mind," muttered

Pop, gaze idling across the street to a swarthy-faced man lounging in the doorway of the town marshal's office.

"What do you think of him?" persisted Oliver.

"The words I'd use wouldn't be decent for yer ears," Pop told him; "an' don't act too serious, lad . . . thot new town marshal, Chico Lopez, has got thim snaky eyes of his fixed on us." Pop snorted wrathfully. "The rascal is nothin' more nor less than Mort Sandell's private bodyguard—his hired killer, Mr. Scott."

"I've had a shock," confided Oliver in a low voice; "in fact, Mr. Daly, I've made up my mind to leave this town—as soon as I have attended to a certain matter—"

Pop nodded, gave the lawyer a shrewd glance. "I knowed ye was too decent to do Mort Sandell's dirty work for him." His gaze again sought the new marshal's indolent figure across the street. "I take it thot ye've had words with Sandell, the way his gunman watches ye."

"Pop!" burst out the young man, "Sandell is a crook—and I told him so!"

"He's wuss than thot, I'm thinkin'," muttered the hotel man.

"He's plotting to get possession of the Box B ranch," Oliver went on, lowering his voice, "and it seems he's struck a snag in the fact that Miss Benson is not the sole owner. He's starting foreclosure suit against her and now learns that Ed Benson had a partner years ago. The claimant is this Brant's grandson, Clay Brant, and his attorney asserts the several mortgages are worthless because they were not signed either by old Brant or his heirs."

Pop's eyes gleamed. "An' phwat does Sandell think he's goin' ter do about it?" he wanted to know with a pleased chuckle.

"Possession of the Box B ranch is necessary to Sandell's schemes," explained the lawyer; "the railroad is planning to come this way; he needs the water rights controlled by the Benson holdings in the Valley of the Kings—"

"Ye don't say!" gasped the old hotel man, "the railroad—buildin' into San Luis!"

"Sandell plans to colonize the Valley of the Kings—and other ranch outfits he has foreclosed," Oliver told him; "he must own the Box B or his scheme is wrecked. Clay Brant's refusal to acknowledge his mortgage rights has him about crazy."

"An' phwat does Sandell think he can do about it?" Pop seemed hugely pleased.

Oliver glanced across the street at the town marshal leaning against his office door. "Listen, Pop"—he leaned closer to the old man—"Sandell says he has an old deed, supposedly signed by Clay Brant's grandfather years ago—claims he has two witnesses who are ready to swear they were present when Benson and Brant made the deal and saw Benson pay Brant in cash for his half interest in the ranch—"

"'Tis possible," grunted the hotel man. His tone was thoughtful. "Have ye seen the deed, lad?"

Oliver shook his head. "No—but I've seen the two men he claims witnessed the transaction and I'm positive the pair of them are lying— that they're Sandell's paid tools. Sandell had me draw up a sworn statement for them to sign"— the lawyer scowled—"something—they were poor actors, and years too young—made me suspicious. I refused to accept their statements; Sandell blew up . . . actually threatened me."

"So ye're leaving San Luis fer good, eh?" murmured Pop. He eyed the young man shrewdly. "Sandell would likely put ye in the way of making plenty of money; if ye'd work along with him, I'm thinkin'."

"Plenty," answered Oliver gloomily. "Don't care for that kind of money—and don't like helping him victimize that young girl."

"She's a real gal, is Miss Shirley," Pop declared. He smiled, gave the other a sly look. "So is the pretty Cota lass, if ye ask me."

Oliver reddened. "I'll tell you something, Pop," he confided; "I think Carmel Cota is the loveliest girl I've ever known, even if she hasn't been particularly cordial to me." He smiled ruefully. "I don't blame her. Sandell's attorney wouldn't be

226

popular with the Box B ranch." He shrugged his shoulders. "Just the same I'm going out there this afternoon to see Miss Benson . . . tell her what I know of Sandell's crooked schemes—"

"Did ye tell Mort Sandell ye was goin' out to see the gal?" frowned Pop, interrupting him.

"I certainly did," Oliver admitted.

Pop wagged his head worriedly. " 'Twas rash of ye," he muttered. " 'Twas signin' yer death warrant, I'm thinkin', Mr. Scott."

"What do you mean?" The lawyer's voice was startled.

"There's a lot ye don't know," grumbled the hotel man; "Mort Sandell is wuss than a crook. Ye'll niver reach the Box B ranch, Mr. Scott, now thot ye've told Sandell yer intintion ter go there with yer story."

"You mean he'll have me murdered?"

Pop's glance went significantly to the man lounging in the doorway across the street. "Mort Sandell won't let ye run loose, now ye know about his plans—the railroad coming to San Luis, Mr. Scott. Do ye carry a gun?" he asked after a pause.

Oliver shook his head, frowned.

"There's one in the office desk ye can have," Pop said, "and if ye're set on going out to the Box B I'd wait till after dark if I was you. Jake Weems'll have a good horse waiting fer ye down in the willows back of the hotel. And once ye get there and have told the gal what's on yer mind, I'm advising ye to keep on riding till ye get to Mesa where ye can catch the train fer some place a long ways from here. Ye'll be a marked man, Mr. Scott, now ye've fallen out with Mort Sandell."

"I'm not afraid of Sandell," declared Oliver, rising from his chair. "Thanks for the gun, though; and if you'll have Jake Weems saddle me a horse I'll start immediately for the ranch." There was a determined look in the young lawyer's pleasant eyes. "If Miss Benson can use me in any way at all I'll stay here in San Luis and help her fight Sandell to the finish." He strode into the lobby.

The old man waited a few minutes, saw Chico Lopez saunter down the street and disappear behind the swing doors of the Red Front saloon. "Maybe I'm wrong," he muttered, "but I'm thinkin' the snaky-eyed varmint has had his orders about young Scott." He rose stiffly and limped into the lobby.

Chico Lopez paused inside the swing doors of the Red Front. It was the slack hour for business and with the exception of a lone cowboy holding maudlin conversation with the bored, drowsy man behind the bar, the place was deserted. Chico's indolence had dropped from him. Throwing the drink dispenser a brief nod he went swiftly to the door at the end of the bar and knocked gently.

"Gotta see the boss in a hurry," he whispered to Frenchy when the latter thrust out his sleek dark head.

The saloon man nodded, motioned for Chico to enter.

Sandell was sitting at his desk in the secret conference room. Near him were Vin Sarge and Bat Brimms, the latter with an arm in a sling. The banker eyed Chico expectantly.

"Scott is figgerin' to slope," said the marshal, answering the unspoken question; "been talkin' awful excited with that old jasper across the street—"

Sandell scowled. He had been a fool to take the young lawyer into his confidence. He had sized the young man up wrong—believed he would jump at the chance to make money. Well, all was not lost yet, if something happened to prevent Scott from carrying his story to the Benson girl as he had threatened.

"Where's Pecos—and Red Hansen?" he snapped.

"Pecos is watching things down at the stables," Chico informed him; "no chance for Scott to slope and us not know"—the marshal's smile was sinister—"Red's already staked out in Apache Pass—case Scott gits that far from town—"

"Red is too dumb," frowned Sandell; "can't take chances. Scott mustn't reach the ranch. He knows too much." He looked at Brimms. "How's your shoulder, Bat? Think you can ride with Pecos, on this Scott job?"

"Sure I can ride with Pecos—and throw plenty hot lead, too," grinned the little gunman.

Sandell nodded. "All right, Chico; you and Bat and Pecos stick to Scott's trail"—the banker's smile was malevolent—"and make sure his trail ends somewhere near Apache Pass—"

Vin Sarge's deep voice interrupted him. "Reckon the boys might as well ride on to the Bar 7—after they gets done with the Scott hombre," he suggested. "We'll need 'em for the Circle Dot job."

Chico Lopez gave him a startled look. "What you mean?" he wanted to know.

"Vin's got word that a Circle Dot trail herd is heading this way for the Box B," explained Sandell. He eyed his town marshal curiously. "What of it, Chico? Do you know something about the Circle Dot outfit?"

"I'm from the Cimarron country myself," Chico told him, "fact is, boss, I used to ride for the Circle Dot outfit—"

The others stared at him, and an angry red flushed over Sandell's face.

"Then you know Clay Brant?" The banker eyed his hired killer suspiciously.

"Sure I know him," admitted the man. He shrugged his shoulders. "Too bad for him if we meet up ag'in," he added with an oath.

"Maybe you're his spy," Sandell said softly.

"You're crazy," retorted Chico Lopez indignantly. "What's it all about—that you're so scared of Clay Brant?" He eyed their intent faces sullenly. "Mebbe I can put you wise to somethin' about Brant if you'll open up."

Vin Sarge gave Sandell a surprised look. "Ain't you told Chico nothin' 'bout the Brant hombre?" he wanted to know.

"Been too busy with this mortgage tangle," grumbled the banker sourly; "anyway, sort of got the idea from the letter his lawyer wrote me that Clay Brant was still in Cimarron—"

Chico grinned at them. "Brant ain't in Cimarron," he said, "he's somewheres round these parts—"

Sandell stared at him, his face suddenly pale. "Are you sure, Chico? You—you mean you've seen him?"

Chico nodded. "He was with them two ol' HM fellers I've heerd you talk about," he informed his attentive listeners. With some reluctance the marshal gave them a doctored version of his encounter with the HM partners.

"Was comin' across the desert, headin' for this town, when some jasper tried to bushwhack me. Hally an' McGee found me layin' half dead at Poison Springs"—Chico grinned—"the two ol' longhorns seemed to be expectin' me. Thought I was Clay Brant, so I let on I was, jest to figger out their play, and then Brant turned up and spilled the beans for me."

"How come Brant turned you loose when he caught you wearin' his name?" queried Sarge curiously.

"Reckon he figgered I'd do what he told me— clear outer the country." Chico shrugged his lean shoulders. "Suited me to stick around, so I got me a job with your Bar 7 outfit, Sarge—and then yuh gets me this job as town marshal." He grinned at the circle of deeply interested faces. "And that's all I know," he finished.

Sandell nodded. "All right, Chico. You and Brimms go make your plans with Pecos about that Scott business. Be just too bad if he gets away from you."

"You ain't answered me about them Circle Dot cows," reminded the marshal. "Who told you the Circle Dot's sending a big trail herd down this way, Sarge?"

"Texas Jack," answered the Bar 7 foreman. "He's a new man I took on a week or two ago— when I sent you in town to be marshal, Chico. You ain't met up with him."

"Texas Jack!" sneered the former Circle Dot rider. "Some hombre's sure pullin' your leg, Vin!"

"What you mean?" flared the big rustler.

"Texas Jack was strung up by Clay Brant's Cimarron vigilantes same night they hung ol' Sig Gillis."

A savage oath from the Bar 7 man interrupted him.

"That true, Chico? You mean Texas Jack ain't alive?" Sarge sprang from his chair, glared at the marshal, lowered head thrust forward like an enraged bull.

"I was there," muttered the half-breed; "saw Texas Jack kickin' at the end of a rope with my own eyes—"

"What does this Clay Brant look like?" again fiercely interrupted the Bar 7 foreman.

"Tall, more'n six foot—dark reddish hair—gray eyes; and a sort of quiet, icy way with him, fast as lightning with his guns—"

Sarge whirled on Sandell. "It's him!" he said in a choking voice; "that Texas Jack feller we put on our payroll is Clay Brant! *We've been tricked!*" He eyed their attentive faces. "Fellers," he added solemnly, "there's plenty rope reaching for our necks—'less we fix Mister Brant o' Cimarron so he'll never trick us no more—"

Brimms scowled at his bandaged arm, stinging reminder of the night in the Red Front, when he had stopped Clay Brant's bullet. Two other men were still under the doctor's care for wounds caused by bullets from the same gun. "I'll say we was tricked!" he muttered. Mirth suddenly seized the little gunman as he recalled the humiliating treatment accorded Pecos and Red Hansen.

"Sure was funny, the way them two rannihans

was hog-tied to their chairs," he gasped; "sure looked like a coupla ol' turtles, staggerin' round with them chairs roped to their hides—"

Frenchy Larue stared with glittering eyes at the long knife that suddenly slid into his hand. He, too, had a score to settle with Clay Brant.

And big Vin Sarge was recalling with growing unease that somewhere in the vicinity of Painted Valley was the dreaded leader of the vigilantes who had so completely wiped out Sig Gillis and his fellow desperadoes. The same thought was like a gnawing worm in the mind of Mort Sandell. Clay Brant was running loose in their midst! Clay Brant—the Nemesis of lawless men! And at his back—those two canny old wolf hounds from the Spanish Sinks!

CHAPTER XVI
A MESSAGE FROM SAM

The morning's rest in the little pasture at the foot of the Porcupine had put the big buckskin horse in fine fettle for the three-hour trip across the desert. He traveled easily, a tireless running walk that ate up the miles; and the afternoon sun was still above the western rim when finally Clay swung from his saddle in the lengthening shadows of the giant pinnacle known as Indian Head, the scene of his first meeting with his grandfather's old friends, Sam Hally and Seth McGee. To his disappointment neither of the veteran HM cowmen were at the rendezvous.

He drew closer into the darker shadow of a crevice in the side of the big butte, keen eyes warily scanning the rugged terrain, hands resting lightly on gun butts. The failure of Sam, or Seth, to meet him as agreed, might indicate some lurking enemy, waiting for his own arrival— might mean that death or disaster had overtaken Shirley Benson's two staunch old defenders. For several minutes Clay scrutinized every boulder, every bush within gun range, where some concealed would-be assassin might be lying in wait. Certain signs finally reassured him—a ground squirrel busily foraging, a pair of big hawks winging leisurely to their nest in the lofty crags of the butte, his own presence unnoticed—told him that no humans save himself were invading their domain. He made and lit a cigarette—the buckskin needed a breathing spell after the stiff climb from the torrid floor of the desert.

For several minutes he stared thoughtfully across the vast expanse of cactus and mesquite lying at his feet. Only some unexpected circumstance would have kept Sam and Seth from the rendezvous. One of them, at least, would have been waiting for him, or they would have sent a message. A troubled look crept into Clay's gray eyes as he gazed at the lavender and blue shadows creeping up the steep ridges of the distant desert hills. Those creeping shadows told him it was close on six o'clock, a good hour later than the appointed time of meeting; even if his friends for some reason had not waited, they would have left a message. The thought aroused him. Grinding the unfinished cigarette under bootheel he commenced a careful search. They would know how to leave him a sign, those two wily old Indian fighters. It would be a sign noticeable only to eyes looking for it—something insignificant—yet something he would recognize as coming from them.

Patiently he studied the stony ground, scrutinized boulders and pebbles. At least one rider had been at Indian Head that day, he quickly saw from the freshly scarred hoof marks. Leading from where the horse had been standing were the faint imprints of bootheels, imprints that might have been left by the high heeled boots of any cowboy, but which Clay suddenly knew were imprints left either by Sam Hally or his partner. He knew this because of the two partly-smoked cigarettes lying in one of the impressions and so placed as to form an arrow head, and pointing toward a large flat boulder crowded against the side of the butte. It was hardly possible that those cigarette butts had fallen there by chance.

A half dozen strides took Clay to the big boulder. What to look for he had no idea and it was only after several moments of painstaking search that he espied the empty rifle-shell lying innocently in the crevice between the boulder and the granite side of the butte. He drew the shiny bit of brass eagerly into his fingers, eyed it with a contented smile. Sam and Seth both still clung to their old-fashioned Sharps buffalo rifles; and the empty shell was from a Sharps.

He tapped it against the side of the boulder, dribbled out a tiny stream of fine gravel. A moment's work with a match extracted a wad of cigarette papers Sam Hally had used for his brief message.

Clay read the blunt-penciled lines with knitted

brows. Apparently there was trouble at the ranch, he gathered, or threatened trouble; and Sam felt it unwise to leave and he would expect Clay at the Box B after dark. Felipe would be waiting at the side entrance to his vegetable garden.

Clay glanced at the sun dipping toward the lofty crest of the San Luis Rey hills. Three hours, he calculated would get him to the ranch about an hour after dark, with the moon lifting at his back. The long detour would make it impossible for him to return to the Bar 7 camp on the Perdido by dawn, as he had planned. No telling what might happen if Vin Sarge turned up at the camp and found that neither Droon or himself were at their posts. Curly Smith would be certain to send word of Droon's mysterious fall to death from the Devil's pitchfork. His own disappearance would arouse the Bar 7 foreman's suspicions. The fact that he had sent Droon to keep tab on him at the camp was proof that Sarge had his doubts regarding the man he knew as Texas Jack.

Brows knitted in a frown he again read Sam's laconic message; and suddenly, the thought of danger threatening the Box B took on a new significance, filled him with a curious, unexplainable dread—a fierce desire to be riding swiftly to the aid of the young bright-haired mistress of the Box B. Danger threatening the ranch meant that danger was threatening Shirley Benson!

Face set in grim lines, Clay ran to the buckskin

horse and in another moment was tearing across the mesa, following the same trail he had ridden with Sam and Seth the day of the first visit to the Valley of the Kings.

Common-sense quickly forced him to draw rein; the distance was too great, the trail too rough, for a pace faster than the buckskin's usual tireless running walk.

Somewhat to his surprise, Shirley Benson was suddenly tenaciously in his thoughts; their first meeting in the ancient garden by the little bridge, the second meeting in the old ranch-house kitchen. The picture of her came to him vividly—a gallant little figure in a simple white linen dress, a gleaming helmet of bright fair hair, and eyes—her eyes eluded him—save that they were indescribably lovely, amazingly frank and fearless—and proud; Shirley Benson, with the simple straightforward manners of good breeding. For some reason he was unable to fathom, the crowding brief memories of her quickened Clay's pulse, brought a bewildered look to his eyes. He had not thought that the summoning of her picture could so stir him; nor had he even suspected that such details had taken root in his memory.

He pushed the buckskin to a faster stride, his expression sober, perplexed—troubled, as he recalled the last time he had seen Shirley Benson. The friendliness had fled from those lovely eyes that night in the upstairs hallway of the Daly House. She had thought him a recreant, a desperado—a liar. He regretted, now, that he had not listened to old Sam's wise counsel—regretted bitterly that his own insistence for secrecy had made his role of scoundrel a reality in the mind of the young mistress of the Box B ranch. Shirley could have no other thought of him. Sam, and the others, would have kept their promise of secrecy only too well.

The trail left the sunset glow of the mesa and plunged abruptly into the gloom of the deep gorge. Clay hurled his horse recklessly down the winding precipitous descent; and the gloom of the gorge was no darker than his own unhappy thoughts.

CHAPTER XVII
NEWS FOR SHIRLEY

Oliver Scott glanced uneasily over his shoulder at the three horsemen leisurely following him. Pop Daly's warning was still fresh in his mind. Pop had been confident that Mort Sandell would make an attempt to prevent his reaching the Box B ranch. It seemed incredible that the smooth-spoken banker would stoop to a cold-blooded murder. He pushed his horse to a faster stride. A brief look told him that the mysterious riders had quickened their own pace to match his. The young lawyer's uneasiness grew; there was sinister purpose in the way they had clung to his trail, always maintaining the same distance, as though waiting for him to reach some pre-arranged spot on the lonely road before closing in on him. It came to him that the place they would choose would be in the deep and narrow gorge of Apache Pass—an ideal place for a killing—with the swift waters of the creek ready to seize and hide his lifeless body.

He slackened speed, reluctant, now, to hasten the moment of his doom; and debated his chances to out-race his pursuers. His horse was speedy— he had Pop's assurance that Jake Weems would give him the fastest animal in the stables—and yet, something—the fact that his pursuers made no attempt to overtake him, even though he was no less than a quarter of a mile from the mouth of the pass—warned him not to make a rash attempt to outride them. It was obvious they were confident that he could not escape.

The answer came to Oliver like a sickening blow in the pit of his stomach. He was riding into an ambush. Somewhere along the lonely road, probably in the gloom of the narrow gorge, a fourth man lay in wait. Sandell would have arranged the trap, knowing his intention to ride to the ranch. The men trailing him were to make certain he could not escape.

Again he glanced over his shoulder. The three had drawn nearer, but were making no apparent effort to overtake him. The tallest of the trio, wearing the high-crowned Mexican sombrero, would be the cold-eyed Chico Lopez, Oliver surmised. A cold prickle ran down his spine. Stealthily he drew Pop Daly's big six-gun from his pocket.

The feel of the weapon in his hand steadied him; he rode on more resolutely, refraining from backward looks; his immediate danger was somewhere in front of him—a snake, lying in ambush by the side of the trail, waiting to launch its venomous lightning death thrust. It was possible he would have the chance to kill the snake before the snake could strike—just barely possible.

He drew nearer the mouth of the pass, eyes warily searching bush and boulder for the assassin's likely place of concealment. His animal suddenly pricked up its ears, nickered softly; and Oliver saw a horseman emerge from the high-walled mouth of the lower canyon. Apparently startled by the horse's unexpected call, a sandy-haired, savage-eyed face popped up quickly from behind a big boulder some thirty feet away.

Oliver sank in his spurs in a desperate attempt to flee past the ambusher. The man straightened up, gun spitting flame.

Oliver reeled in his saddle, his own gun roaring as the maddened horse fled past; he had a vague picture of his attacker crumbling face down—the sound of drumming hoofs behind him—the crashing report of a rifle from the lower canyon trail as consciousness left him.

The lengthening shadows of twilight lay across the trail when he opened his eyes. He ached from head to foot and his left shoulder seemed curiously numb, until he tried to move, and then the pain turned him faint for a moment. A voice spoke to him softly, reassuringly.

"Don't try to move, yet. You took a bad spill from your bronc—caught a couple of bullets—"

Oliver closed his eyes, relaxed against the knee of the speaker.

"Lucky I came along," went on the voice. "You drilled that feller that was layin' for you square between the eyes, but those other three hombres sure would have fixed you in another minute if I hadn't horned in on their play. One of 'em got away," added the voice regretfully. "Reckon he took some lead along with him at that."

Oliver opened his eyes; from where he lay supported against the knee of his rescuer, he now saw a man sprawled face down in the dust of the trail. Another man sat on a rock near the dead man, an arm dangling limply, blood oozing from under his leather chaps—a man he dimly recognized as Chico Lopez. He looked up at the face bending over him, a vaguely familiar face.

"I seem—to know you," he said faintly; "can't—can't remember—now."

"Save your strength," advised the stranger. "You'll soon be all right again."

Oliver struggled for coherent speech; there was something he must say to this man—in the event of the worst—something about the Box B ranch. Yes—something Shirley Benson must know.

Summoning all his waning strength he opened his eyes again.

"I was riding to the Box B ranch," he whispered, "I have important information for Miss Benson . . . Sandell—is plotting—to—to—" The young lawyer's voice faded; he relapsed into unconsciousness.

Clay Brant stood up. His first reaction had not been in Scott's favor. He knew that the lawyer was a confidant of Morton Sandell—his attorney. The fact that Sandell's gunmen had tried to kill him was proof that Scott had evidently defied Shirley's enemy, was proof of his own honesty. Sandell plotted his death because Oliver had refused to obey his orders, and was on his way to the ranch to expose him.

Clay's gaze went to Chico Lopez. Bad as the half-breed might be, he was not lacking in fortitude. Clay knew the man must be suffering excruciating agonies, yet no sound passed his tightly-set lips; sullen, silent, he sat on the rock, coolly making a cigarette with the fingers of his one good hand.

Clay went over to him and offered a lighted match for the smoke.

"*Gracias*," muttered the man; he drew in a mouthful of smoke, hard black eyes defiantly returning Clay's pitying look.

"Too bad you didn't take my advice and clear out, Chico," muttered the young cattleman. "Too bad you left the Circle Dot for this sort of thing. Your dad was a good man . . . was with my grandfather when he started the Circle Dot. You were born on the old ranch. Why did you turn crooked, feller."

"*Quien sabe*," mumbled the half-breed.

Clay looked at the dead man sprawled across the trail. Pecos, he saw, would never again ride out to do murder; nor would his friend, Red

Hansen, lying in a huddled heap by the boulder where he had lain in wait for the man whose wildly-flung bullet had terminated his vicious career.

"Who was the hombre that got away, Chico?" he queried.

"Brimms," grunted the outlaw.

"Can you fork a saddle, feller?" Clay wanted to know.

"Sure." Chico eyed him uneasily. "What you aim to do with me?"

"Take you to a place I know. Not letting you run round loose any more, Chico."

"Just as soon go with you as go back to San Luis, way things have turned out," muttered the half-breed.

"Sandell's back of this play, ain't he Chico?"

"I didn't say he was," answered the man, suddenly wary again. He resumed his sullen silence, watched indifferently while Clay lifted the senseless Oliver to his saddle and mounted behind. At a gesture from the cattleman he climbed awkwardly to his own horse; and so Clay continued his interrupted journey to the Box B ranch.

It was a slow procession; Chico riding in front, Clay following, one arm supporting Oliver's limp form in the saddle, gun ready in his free hand for any dash for liberty on the part of the prisoner. But Chico was too sick a man to even meditate a break for freedom; it was all he could do to cling to his own saddle.

The moon was lifting by the time they were over the Pass and following the easy trail that looped down into the Valley of the Kings. There was a broader wagon road, but Clay desired the better concealment of the old trail. Sam had hinted at threatened trouble, which might mean anything—spies, danger from a raid, although he doubted the latter. He had kept a close watch at the Bar 7—read the signs as well as he might considering Vin Sarge was too shrewd to talk of his plans in front of an untried though supposedly notorious desperado. Clay smiled grimly. By this time it was possible that the Bar 7 foreman had heard the news of Wes Droon's mysterious fall to death from the towering cliffs of the Painted Valley.

The ranch-house lights glimmered faintly in the distance, twinkled like tiny stars through the restless foliage of the trees. Moonlight wove delicate tapestries with threads of silver and ebony. The Valley of the Kings! something tugged at Clay's heart, a mist clouded his eyes; *El Valle de los Reyes*! Home of the old Box B ranch— the ranch Bill Brant and Ed Benson had carved from the heart of a wilderness; valiant against all foes, drought and famine, the painted warrior, the more subtle, dangerous chicanery of cheap politicians. *El Valle de los Reyes*! Now coveted by the scheming Morton Sandell. A certain verse came to Clay's mind as the big buckskin went slowly with his double burden down the trail that reached like a silver ribbon toward the winking, beckoning lights of the ranch-house; a verse that he had not read in years, about a king, named Ahab, who had coveted the property of another man and hirelings were sent to destroy him so that Ahab might possess what he desired.

The cold gleam of distant Polaris high in the heavens was no colder than the steel in Clay's eyes. Ed Benson, and others, had been slain, so that Morton Sandell might possess the coveted Valley of the Kings. If Chico Lopez had dared a backward glance at that moment, he would have immediately relinquished any thought of attempting an escape.

The twinkling points of light steadied, loomed like soft yellow moons through the trees. Clay spoke softly to the man on the horse in front of him. Chico obediently swung to the right, followed the picket fence winding between a double row of moon-misted pepper trees, to the pale white of the spear-pronged gate, where old Felipe kept eternal watch over his garden.

The two horses came to a halt at a muttered word from Clay. He slid from the tired buckskin, caught the limp lawyer's form in his arms and lowered him to the cropped Bermuda grass; Chico was slumped over saddle horn, he saw; he caught the half-breed in his arms, vaguely aware that the man was making an effort to speak.

Felipe was already at the gate, lean brown fingers shaking with fright as he strove to unfasten the chains. "Senor!" he quavered in Spanish, "More killings—more dead ones! Ah, *Dios*! It was so they brought Don Eduardo— through this very gate—the night he was slain! A curse has befallen this *rancho*!"

"Less talk, old man!" rasped Clay impatiently. "Open the gate, Felipe, open quickly!" He laid Chico's now limp body on the grass and gathered the senseless Oliver Scott into his arms.

Booted feet ran heavily, but swiftly up the path and Sam Hally's huge frame loomed from out of the shadows; some yards behind hurried his shorter, less fleet partner. The former's huge hand spun the frightened *mozo* from the gate. "My gosh!" he gasped "what you got there, Clay?" He jerked the gate open.

"No time to talk," muttered the young cattle- man. "You bring the other man, Sam. It's Chico Lopez." He brushed past the two startled old HM men and hurried up the path with his burden. "Seth! You hot foot it to the kitchen and tell 'em we'll want plenty bandages . . . hot water . . . everything they've got in the house for gun wounds!"

The little man was already in full stride, booted feet pistoning the soft earth. Clay followed swiftly and close behind towered the giant Sam, the unconscious Chico Lopez in his big arms.

Felipe gazed after them until they were lost in the shadows.

"*Dios!*" he muttered. "Always dead ones coming through my gate!" Shaking his white head sadly, the old *mozo* led the two weary horses into his garden and replaced the gate chains with trembling hands.

The medicine closet in the big ranch-house kitchen was well stocked, and Clay and his friends skilled in the treatment of gun wounds. In a few minutes Oliver Scott was lying in a big old-fashioned bed, the bullet hole in his shoulder dressed and bandaged, the bruises sustained from his heavy fall properly treated. He was still unconscious and unaware that Carmel Cota sat by the bedside, one of his limp hands clasped tenderly between soft little palms, her dark eyes grave and anxious. Clay smiled at her from the bedroom door.

"He's your patient now, Miss Cota," he said softly as he withdrew.

Carmel's calm gaze followed him for a moment. It was most puzzling, the dramatic reappearance of the man who had so basely betrayed Shirley's confidence; this man everybody said was a notorious outlaw. Carmel stared thoughtfully at her patient's white face. There was something mysterious about it all, she reflected; something that Sam Hally had not fully explained. It was bold of the man to dare show his face at the ranch—a wanted fugitive, a price on his head—a hireling of Shirley's wicked enemies. And yet it was fine of him, too, to risk his life to save the life of another. It was possible that Sam and Seth might attempt to take him prisoner at the point of their guns. Carmel hoped they would not be so heartless, her gaze anxiously intent on the pale face lying so still against the pillow. It was a pity, she thought unhappily, that Oliver Scott was a friend of Morton Sandell; he had such beautiful curly hair, almost the color of yellow gold; and such deep blue eyes. . . . She had always liked Oliver Scott, she knew he liked her . . . a woman always knows when a man likes her—a lot. Carmel's thoughts went to Shirley. It was fortunate that Shirley was not in the house when the two wounded men were brought in, that she was down at the "rose garden." It would have been dreadful if she had come face-to-face with this Texas Jack creature. Carmel had a shrewd suspicion that Shirley had rather cared for the man she had known as Bill Clay. She had acted very queerly ever since that terrifying night in the Daly House when Bill Clay had been exposed as a wicked desperado. Carmel's melancholy musings came to an abrupt ending. Her patient's eyes were open, were looking up into her face with the bewildered expression of one who cannot believe what his eyes tell him. She smiled gently, cautioned with uplifted finger.

"You must not talk."

He proceeded to disobey her. "It's—it's *you!*" His voice was scarcely above a whisper.

"I'm your nurse; you must obey me," insisted Carmel sternly. Her smile was not stern.

He seemed content, closed his eyes for a moment. Suddenly he was looking at her again, his expression oddly troubled, imploring. "I *must* talk," he said weakly; "it's important news for—for Miss Benson . . . She must know—at once."

Carmel's dark head bent close to his. "All right," she told him gently, "tell me, Mr. Scott—Oliver—"

"I'm—I'm through with Sandell," Oliver went on, after an astonished, incredulous pause; "he's a crook . . . he wants the ranch because the railroad is coming through San Luis—"

Carmel's face was very close to his, now, and she put her hand on his lips, silenced him. "No more talk, for the present," she ordered in a curiously breathless voice. "You've said enough—and Shirley will be made very, very happy by your news"—her lips were close to his, her voice hardly audible—"and I'm very happy, too, but not for the same reason—quite—Oliver—" Her lips brushed his lightly, the caress of a petal falling from a rose. "I always was sure you were what I wanted you to be," she finished in the same hushed, breathless tone. "And now you must be very good and obey your nurse—and rest."

Oliver smiled contentedly up at the vivid lovely face; his eyes closed, and when, a few moments later he peacefully slept, the smile remained to wipe out the pain that had been there.

Carmel, gently disengaged her hand and stood for a moment, smiling down radiantly at her sleeping patient, a hand pressed to her heart, then sped on swift noiseless feet from the room. She had news, *big news,* for Shirley!

CHAPTER XVIII
A MAN DIES

Mixed emotions struggled for supremacy in the bright black eyes of the good Senora Maria Cota—dismay, annoyance, pity; the last, winning by a mile as her gaze returned to the long limp length of Chico Lopez lying on the well-scrubbed ancient adobe bricks of her kitchen floor. "No!" she declared vehemently, "let him remain—the poor *muchacho*! If he is to die, he shall die on a clean floor, not in a vermin-ridden *cuartel*!" Maria spoke in the mother tongue she loved, knowing it was familiar to her small audience.

Her sympathy for Chico Lopez seemed to make little or no impression on the two grim-faced men who had just completed an expert job of bandaging the young outlaw's wounds. Sam Hally shrugged his big shoulders.

"Wimmen is too soft-hearted," he grumbled.

"Such talk!" scoffed the old housekeeper. "No female born carries a heart more gentle than your own, Senor Hally."

The big cowman reddened. "Have it your own way, Senora Cota," he retorted with an embarrassed chuckle. "Sure is your kitchen floor; as for talk of me being soft in the heart—all I can say is you've a heap to learn about Sam Hally of the HM ranch." He glared at his partner. "Who you grinnin' at, mister?"

"Was only thinkin' of that there stone-cold heart you wear under your vest," cackled Seth, one-time Box B top-hand and fighting man. "Kick 'em in the pants . . . throw 'em out on their necks . . . shoot 'em in the back and feed 'em to the coyotes—that's Sam Hally."

"Doggone your onery hide," exploded the big cowman indignantly; "for a red cent I'd turn you across my knee and larrup you plenty—"

"Well!" interrupted Maria impatiently, "don't stand there like a pair of old roosters making believe you're going to scratch each other's eyes out. We must not leave this poor boy to die on my kitchen floor!"

"You just done got through saying he could," protested Seth a bit crossly. "You won't let Sam and me haul the *hombre* over to the ranch *cuartel* and now you're beefin' 'cause we let the onery cuss lay here on the floor. My idee would be to string him up."

"The Senor Brant shall decide," reproved Maria as a door opened.

Clay came in quickly from the patio bedroom where he had left Oliver Scott to the care of Carmel. He halted abruptly at the sight of Chico Lopez still lying on the floor.

"Why let him lie there?" he asked quickly. "Is

he dead? Is Chico dead, Sam?" Clay eyed the old man worriedly.

It was Seth who answered, voice hard, belligerent, "We've fixed him up good as any doc could do. We wasn't lettin' a coyote like him die too easy, so we've got him all saved for trial. Plenty good trees outside," he added significantly.

"That's out," Clay said curtly. Again his glance challenged Sam Hally.

The latter cleared his throat nervously. "Chico's a right bad sort of hombre, Clay," he gruffed; "mebbe there's a heap of sense in Seth's talk of plenty trees . . . dang you Miguel! What you aim to do with the knife?" Sam's voice was suddenly an enraged bellow; he leaped toward the big chair in which was huddled Maria's old husband—"Dang you, give me that there knife!" He wrenched the wicked blade from the ancient *vaquero*'s bony brown hand, growled angrily.

"Enemies of the *rancho* must die," muttered the old *vaquero*. His sunken eyes glowed like hot coals. "I am old—*si*—old like the *rancho* trees—but not too old to fight for the *rancho*, Senor Hally! The man must die!" Miguel leaned forward, bony fingers clutching the blackened oak arms of his chair and stared with blazing eyes at the recumbent form of Chico Lopez. Maria ran to her husband, sank to her knees by his side.

"No! no! Miguel, *mio*! Such talk is wicked! I

understand, but it is not for you or for me, to say this man must die! It is in the hands of the Senor Brant—in the mercy of the good God!"

For a moment the aged *vaquero* resisted the quieting caress of Maria's arms; then suddenly he relaxed into the depths of the big chair. "I came to *El Valle de Los Reyes* with our senors," he muttered; "it was my hand that forged the first Box B iron—so many years ago, Maria *mia*—I brought you here from Mexico, years later. . . . I, already so old—you so young—so beautiful! And it is here on the *rancho* we raised our children." Miguel's voice came in a sort of croak, "The *rancho* must never die—as our senors have died—as I—soon must die—"

"The *rancho* shall not die, Miguel, old friend of Bill Brant and Ed Benson," reassured Clay in soft Spanish; "rest in peace, Miguel Cota! The *rancho* shall continue to reign in *El Valle de Los Reyes*. You have the word of one who is of Bill Brant's blood and name."

"*Si*, Senor," muttered the old Mexican, his eyes closed, "you speak with the tongue of him I served—and loved—" Miguel's voice was suddenly still. And they saw that he was asleep; indeed—truly asleep. Maria's head lowered over the arm of his chair. She wept, softly.

It was the dour little Seth McGee who first spoke, the tone of his voice strangely gentle, hesitant.

"Death!" he soliloquized in a solemn whisper; "my Gawd—I've seen death more'n a score times these fifty years, since I was nigh a growed man, and now I'm certain there ain't no such thing as death for a hombre that's loyal and true and honest and brave—like old Miguel; here"— Seth broke off, glared at his big partner—"dang you!" he choked. "Who are *you* grinnin' at, you dang ol' longhorn—"

For answer, Sam Hally reached out long arms, drew his life-long friend into an affectionate bear-like hug.

"I'm grinnin' at you, you runty lil' maverick," he said huskily.

They watched, wordless, while Clay bent over Chico Lopez and gathered him into his arms. Clay read the unspoken question in their eyes.

"I must find a bed for him in this house," he said in a low voice; "Chico was born on the Circle Dot . . . we used to play together . . . his father was Bill Brant's friend—and Bill Brant's friends are my friends—"

The two old HM men nodded solemnly: Maria Cota rose to her feet, said simply, "Your grandfather's friends are my friends, too, Senor." She gestured for him to follow her. "Come—we shall make the poor *muchacho* comfortable— there is always a bed for a friend, no matter what he has done. We can only do our best for him and leave the rest to the mercy of the good God—"

Maria threw a wet-eyed glance at the silent figure in the big chair, uttered a little gasping cry and went swiftly out to the wide patio corridor. Clay followed with his burden.

Sam and Seth eyed each other oddly; and Sam said, very softly, "Bill Brant would do the same, huh, feller?"

"The same," agreed his partner solemnly.

They clasped horny palms.

CHAPTER XIX
MOONLIGHT—AND A KISS

Clay made his way under the old oak trees that separated the ranch-house from the maze of corrals. His brief talk with Sam Hally had convinced him of the need for haste. The Circle Dot trail herd was less than two days away; Juan Cota and all available Box B riders, were already on their way to meet the big herd at Cottonwood Crossing, which was one reason why the two HM partners had been unable to keep the rendezvous at Indian Head. Sam had considered it unwise to leave the women without protection, especially as Seth had caught a prowler near the house the previous night. The man had been locked up in the ranch *cuartel*, but so far had refused to explain his presence. One of Sandell's spies, without doubt.

The early arrival of the Circle Dot cows made it imperative for Clay to locate the Bottle Neck. It was more than possible that by now Vin Sarge was aware of the herd's expected arrival at Cottonwood Crossing and would plan to pull off his raid immediately. Clay had informed the HM men of his plan to use the herd as bait in order to catch the rustlers red-handed. It was certainty that the stolen cows would be rushed to the

Painted Valley. Clay had planned there would be no attempt to fight off the raiders. The combined Box B and Circle Dot crews, together with the HM partners and men from their own outfit, would secretly follow the rustler's trail and trap the entire gang in their hidden rendezvous. There was one flaw in that Clay had not yet located the mysterious Bottle Neck—the secret entrance into the valley. He suspected the place was some sort of deep gorge, or the dry bed of an underground stream. It would be like putting a stopper into a bottle; there could be no escape for the rustlers, with the men of the combined outfits guarding the exit. Sam and Seth had thought well of the plan. The immediate problem confronting Clay was to locate the Bottle Neck in time to set the trap.

Clay's thoughts went to Shirley. He had hoped for a glimpse of her. Sam Hally, in answer to his question, had reluctantly admitted that the girl had been greatly disturbed by his supposed knavery.

"Best for you to keep out of her sight," was the old man's solemn advice; "the gal acts awful mad; she'd likely put a bullet into your hide if she ran into you—and had a gun handy. She's a high-tempered filly, is Miss Shirley."

"Ain't so certain you figger the gal right," was Seth McGee's argument. "Seems to me she's more sort o' hurt—and sad . . . like she's grievin' "—Seth nodded his head sagely—"sort o' like her heart is plumb broke to little bits, Sam."

"Mebbe so, mebbe so, feller"—Sam's voice was dubious—"wimmin is funny critters; never could figger 'em out myself. No telling what's in their minds, for certain."

Clay had chosen to turn the conversation, suddenly self-conscious, and inclined to suspect that his friends were secretly having mild fun with him. They were too solemn—too carefully judicious in their analysis of Shirley's feelings toward him. There had been no time to indulge in a private quest of the girl, nor had he the heart to worry Maria Cota with his own more intimate affairs. Maria had her share of grief to shoulder, what with the sudden demise of old Miguel and the presence of two wounded men in the house. It was in Clay's mind that there would be another death in the house within a few hours. He had small hope that Chico Lopez would survive the night.

He came to the edge of the woods and paused for a lingering last look back at the old ranch-house. Lights gleamed softly at him through the trees. He was strangely reluctant to leave, without once seeing Shirley. Perhaps one of those lighted windows was hers; perhaps she purposely avoided him as one too utterly beyond the pale and had remained cloistered in her room until he should remove his loathsome presence from

262

her house. For a moment he fought an impulse to return—demand to see her. With a shrug of his shoulders he put the thought from him. There was work to be done.

He went on across the moonlit yard, past the deserted corrals that seemed to reach out gaunt hungry arms—dismal ghosts of happier days when their vast enclosures sounded to the clash of horns, the stamp of hoofs. The stable door was wide open, he saw with some surprise.

Vaguely uneasy, Clay hastened his stride. He wanted his big black horse for the long arduous ride ahead. Midnight was ideally suited for the night's hazardous work, fast and tireless, gentle as a kitten and trained from his colt days to obey Clay's commands.

He hurried through the open door, came to an abrupt halt.

Somebody was standing by the bars of Midnight's box stall, a slim figure in white, etched in the misty moonlight against the shining ebon of the big horse—Shirley—one arm flung over the glossy arched neck, an apple in her hand. She turned a startled face, stared at Clay with amazed, disbelieving eyes.

"Oh!" she exclaimed, faintly, then defensively, "I—I was only feeding him an apple—he is fond of apples—"

Midnight's velvety nose muzzled her impatiently; with a nervous little gesture she fed the horse the remaining piece, fascinated gaze fixed upon the tall young man framed in the stable door.

"Yes—he's fond of apples"—Clay's voice was dazed—"he—he seems to like you—"

"He's a—a good horse. I'm very fond of him." Shirley's tone was suddenly disdainful. "I suppose you've come to take him away, when nobody was looking!" Her arm tightened over the arched ebon neck. "Perhaps I won't let you have him, Mister Texas Jack! He's too good for—for you—"

"He's my horse," Clay reminded coldly.

"How dare you come here—show your face on this ranch?" she wanted to know fiercely. "I suppose," she added bitingly, "if I try to prevent you taking him you will knock me down—shoot me with one of your dreadful guns."

"Perhaps you'll let me explain," he began. She interrupted him with an angry gesture.

"I don't care to listen!"

"In that case I might as well be on my way." He went toward the horse, and Shirley, after a moment's indecision, drew aside, watched in silence while he drew the silver-mounted saddle and bridle from the peg and carried them into the stall."

"I don't know why I'm letting you do this," she half wailed. "Oh, I wish I were a man . . . I wish Sam Hally and Seth were here!"

"They're not very far away," he retorted coolly. "Why don't you call them?" He eased the saddle to Midnight's back and drew up the cinch.

"You know why I don't call them," she told him miserably. "I don't want more killings on this place—have you shoot them down, for the sake of a horse."

He finished saddling and led the horse outside; Shirley followed. The big black looked magnificent, she thought, standing there in the moonlight, head held high, one foot lightly pawing the ground; and so did the man, she reluctantly admitted to herself, so tall and straight and resolute of face. His was certainly not the face of a desperado. He was looking at her gravely.

"I'll tell you this much," he said to her, "Sam Hally knows I'm taking Midnight. He knows I'm here—and knows why I came." He gave her an odd smile. "Tell Sam I want him to explain all that he knows; and if I were you I'd lose no time getting back to the house. You're needed there."

"I'm afraid that I don't—don't understand." Shirley's voice was startled, bewildered. "You really mean Sam knows you are here?"

"I don't blame you for all the things you think about me," Clay said. "It's been my fault— you mustn't blame old Sam." He turned to the horse.

"You're getting me all mixed up," confessed the girl. She eyed him uncertainly. "Am I to understand that you are Sam's friend—the Box B's friend—not one of Sandell's gunmen?"

"Sam will explain," he reiterated. "Midnight and I must be moving . . . We've a job of work ahead—and no time to lose—"

Shirley's hand touched his arm, drew him round to face her. "Wait!" Suspense, indignation, made her voice brittle, and a curious relief—a suddenly reborn hope—was in the look she gave him. "You mean, it's been a trick—a trick to keep me in the dark?"

"Sam will explain," he said again.

"Then—you are not Texas Jack?"

"My name is Clay Brant—of Cimarron," he told her reluctantly.

She stared at him, puzzled.

"Clay Brant!" she echoed faintly, "you mean— the Clay Brant—of the Circle Dot ranch—Clay Brant of *the* Cimarron vigilantes—"

He nodded briefly.

Indignation—relief, were in the look she gave him.

"I—I think you've been mean—hateful," she suddenly burst out. "I—I hate you! I never want to see you again!" Tears sparkled on her dark lashes; with a little choking cry she turned, fled across the wide yard toward the ranch-house lights twinkling through the trees. In an instant Clay was in the saddle; at his low word the great stallion soared like some sable monster of the night. In an instant horse and man were by the side of the fleeing girl; she came to a petrified standstill as Midnight slid to a halt. Clay leaned down to her, a reckless, jubilant smile on his face. "I hate you, too—just like this—" His arms went around her, lifted her to him . . . she felt his lips on her lips; the next moment she was standing alone in the middle of the moon-bathed yard, a bit dazed—breathless—strangely without anger, listening to the staccato thunder of the black stallion's flying hoofs vanishing into the distance.

For long moments Shirley stood there, like one under a spell, the soft moonshine touched her bright hair gently stirring to the caress of the night winds. The hoof-beats died away; stillness again held sway in the old ranch yard; only one sound came to her ears—the beating of her own heart. She began to run toward the twinkling lights. There were questions she wanted to ask old Sam Hally; questions that Sam Hally must answer!

Shirley hurried on, her confused thoughts reaching futilely for a solution to the mystery. She had been gone from the house for over an hour; first down in the "rose garden," and finally over at the stable for her evening visit with the big black horse. She had become attached to Midnight, not only for his own intelligent, affectionate self, but because he was a link to something she knew now had been precious to her. It seemed to her impossible that a wicked, ruthless desperado—a Texas Jack—could ever have been the master of so noble an animal. The horse reflected something innately fine, something he could have gained only from one whose heart was clean—one who was above reproach. So many of the Box B horses were such vicious, squealing brutes, made so by the hard-faced pitiless men who broke and rode them. Midnight was different; she had found comfort in talking to him—gained a certain reassurance from him—from his honest, brave, lustrous eyes. Midnight had been trying to tell her the truth, that his master was not a desperado. Her tiny seed of faith had born fruit. Why had Sam kept her in ignorance of the truth? And what had brought the famous Clay Brant down to the Box B ranch in the guise first of a lowly puncher, then as a notorious rustler? The answer seemed easy. Sam had sent for him because of his fame as head of the Cimarron Vigilantes. Shirley was vaguely dissatisfied with the explanation. There was some deeper mystery about Clay Brant, else she would not have been kept in the dark. Clay had not wanted her to know his identity. He had told her that Sam would explain.

Another thought came to the girl as she sped into the patio. Clay had said she was needed at the house. Something serious must have happened during the past hour!

Sam was in the kitchen, huge frame sprawled in a rawhide chair; and squat on his heels, cowboy fashion, his back against the wall, was Seth McGee, wide-brimmed Stetson pulled low to shield his eyes from the light of the big hanging kerosene lamp; he was reflectively whittling thin shavings from a piece of wood and listening to a low-voiced monologue from his partner. Both men glanced round quickly as Shirley entered. Their faces were unusually serious, she saw.

That old Miguel's chair was vacant, conveyed nothing to Shirley's mind. It was past his usual bedtime, and Maria was doubtless attending to him as was her nightly custom. Nevertheless her friends' sober looks sent a quick chill of fear through her. Something *had* happened— something serious!

"What is it?" she demanded a bit breathlessly, "what's wrong? You look so solemn!"

"You've been gone a long time, Shirley." It was Sam who answered in his kind, mild tone. Seth, after a curiously brief glance, resumed his meditative whittling.

"I've been down to the rose garden, doing a little watering," she explained. "It's such a lovely bright moonlight I hated to come in."

Sam nodded. He knew that by the "rose garden" she meant the little ranch cemetery at the foot of the garden. "Things git dry awful fast, this weather," he remarked.

"What's wrong?" she repeated, then, unable to keep her mind from a vastly more interesting matter, "Sam, why have you deceived me about Clay Brant? Why have I been led to believe that he's a notorious rustler? What is his business down here?"

The HM partners exchanged startled glances, and Sam answered cautiously, "You're asking a heap of questions all in a breath, Shirley. I take it you done run into him right recent—"

Shirley nodded, eyed him impatiently.

"What did he say to you?"

"He told me you'd explain—everything?"

Sam deliberated for a moment. "He told you who he really is?" he asked doubtfully.

"He told me he's Clay Brant," the girl assured him; "he said you would explain everything else—about him—"

"Where did you run into Clay?" persisted the old cowman.

Shirley colored. "I—I was in the stable . . . took an apple to that black horse of his," she confessed. "He came in—"

Sam and Seth exchanged sly grins, and the latter said solemnly, "You sure got a tender heart, taking apples to that no-count feller's bronc, thataway, Shirley gal."

"He—he's gone off with Midnight," she informed them. "What is it all about, Sam? He was in a rush . . . said he'd work to do tonight—"

Sam nodded. "Clay's got a right busy night ahead of him," he agreed placidly.

Shirley saw that the old man was evading explanations for the time being, was not certain how much he was supposed to tell her, was striving for time. "Mr. Brant positively said you would explain *everything,*" she reminded. "Speak up, Sam! I want the entire story! What is the mystery about Clay Brant? Of course," she added, smiling oddly, "I know he owns the Circle Dot ranch, which explains a lot about the two thousand cows you and Seth are sending to the Box B range on a fifty-fifty deal with me."

Sam drew a deep breath. "Clay is half owner of the Box B ranch," he said.

She gave him a bewildered look. "It—it's not true—not possible," she managed to gasp. "I'm the owner of the Box B! You know I am, Sam!"

"Clay is the grandson of your dad's old pardner—"

"I don't know what you are talking about!" she declared. "Father never had a partner—that I've ever heard of," she amended, suddenly doubtful.

"It was years ago," he explained, "years before you was born. Bill Brant and Ed Benson was pardners when they first come into the Valley of the Kings. You can ask Maria Cota and"—Sam paused—"and Seth, here," he added hurriedly.

"And Miguel, you *meant* to say," she interrupted shrewdly.

"Sure . . . Miguel—he was along, too," Sam agreed hastily. "Well, it's kind of a long story—"

"Tell me everything," commanded the girl. She perched on the arm of his chair, looked at him expectantly.

"Reckon I'll let Seth tell it," mumbled the big man nervously.

"You're elected to do the talkin', mister," declared his partner with a scowl.

"Well," reluctantly continued Sam, "Bill Brant and Ed Benson was pardners here, equal owners of the Box B and they fell in love with your mother when she was a young gal. It got so one or the other had to get out and leave a clear field; they cut cards to see which one of 'em would go . . . but Paula, she loved Ed Benson the most and she stacked the cards so Ed would win the cut."

Breathless and wide-eyed, Shirley listened to Sam's rather halting account of that momentous night in the Valley of the Kings when Bill Brant rode away, never to return, after signing away his half ownership in the ranch to the victor.

"Bill knew what Paula done," Sam said softly; "he never let on to Ed that she'd stacked the cards. He knew then that he was too old for Paula—old enough to be her daddy. She loved him a lot, but in the way a gal loves her daddy. Bill had a growed son already, him who was Clay's dad."

"Bill Brant must have been a wonderful, wonderful man," murmured Shirley.

"They never come no finer than old Bill," asserted Seth in his high, positive voice.

" 'Cept mebbe, his own grandson," mused Sam. He gave the girl a sharp look. There was no indication in his face to show that what he read in her unguarded eyes pleased him. "It was Paula who told me what she done," he went on; "she felt awful sorry for Bill to lose his share of the ranch 'cause of her. When she found the deed years later in your dad's desk she hid the paper." Sam paused, nodded his head—"don't think your dad ever 'tended to claim Bill's half interest, at that. Reckon that as the years went by he kind of forgot it all . . . forgot he'd had a pardner— figgered in time that he was sole owner, like most folks did round these parts; like Mort Sandell did when he loaned money on them mortgages."

"What happened to the deed," Shirley wanted to know, "not that I really care," she added quickly and coloring under the intent look of the two old cowmen. "I'd never make use of it—put it on record—"

"Your mother give it to me 'afore she died," Sam told her. "She made me promise to do what was right with it—when the right time come. She meant for me to destroy it if it seemed best and right for Clay to have his interest in the old ranch . . . if he should be in need. Clay had plenty so I never saw fit to destroy the paper—knew that old Bill Brant would have wanted Paula's gal to have the ranch all to herself—"

Shirley's arms, suddenly around his neck, interrupted him. "You're a dear. And I'm glad that Mother felt the way she did. It was a cruel thing to happen! Don't you dare put that deed on record. Clay Brant must not be robbed of his birthright!"

"You needn't worry till we've got this Sandell business fixed up," Sam assured her. "As long as that deed ain't on record we've got Mort Sandell up a tree about them mortgages. They ain't worth a hoot to him 'cause they was signed by your pa as full owner; and he never was full owner. The minute that paper is recorded it makes you full owner of the Box B and them mortgages legal and binding."

Shirley's expression was troubled. "Father did borrow the money from Sandell," she pointed out honestly. "Sandell really thought Father was the sole owner—else he would not have advanced so much money."

"Don't you worry none," again reassured the big cowman earnestly. "Clay would pay them mortgages quick as a flash—only for one mighty big reason—" He hesitated, and Seth broke in fiercely.

"Sam means that we figger Mort Sandell is back of all this rustlin' that's put the Box B on

274

the scrap heap, Shirley. He aimed to ruin your dad and the quickest way was to steal his cows. If he hadn't stolen your pa's cows your pa'd have paid the mortgage easy." The old ranch's one-time top-hand rider's black eyes took on a cold light, his voice, a deadly tone. "There's worse'n cow-stealin' at Mort Sandell's door. When Clay was here a hour back he told us Wes Droon has confessed he killed your dad, time of that last raid. Droon won't hang for it, though," he added regretfully.

Sam nodded grimly. "Droon—he's buzzards' meat now. Fell off the Pitchfork in a rough and tumble with Clay," he told Shirley.

The girl shuddered, hid her face in her hands. She had grown very pale, perhaps from the reference to the slaying of her father—perhaps because of the picture of Clay, fighting with her father's assassin on the towering heights of the Devil's Pitchfork. She rose from the arm of Sam's chair, regarded her two old friends with sober eyes.

"I think that I quite understand everything, now," she said steadily. "I feel, too, that you are right; that Clay is right, in your attitudes toward Mr. Sandell. If what you say about him is true, and I'm sure you have reasons for saying what you do about him, then no punishment can be too great for so wicked and vile a monster. I'm going to leave it all in your hands—in Clay's hands from now on," she assured them with a faint smile; "you know better than I what should be—must be done." She turned to the patio door with a weary gesture. Sam's voice stayed her.

"There's something more you must know, Shirley," he said gravely.

The girl's dark-fringed eyes questioned him; and Sam continued in the same grave tone: "A lot of things happened while you was out in the—the garden. Sandell's crowd tried to ambush that there young lawyer, Oliver Scott. Seems like Scott didn't cotton none to Sandell's schemes and told him so to his face. More'n that, Scott told him he was riding out here to the ranch to tell you some important news Sandell let slip—"

"Yes!" she exclaimed feverishly, "go on, Sam"—sudden horror widened Shirley's eyes—"you mean that Oliver Scott has been shot—is dying!" She clenched little fists. "Poor Carmel!" she added brokenly, "why must *she* be dragged into my troubles!"

"He won't die," put in the big cowman hastily. "Clay mixed into the fracas; near Apache Pass it was. Red Hansen and Pecos as used to ride for you was killed, and another hombre you don't know, Chico Lopez was bad shot up. Reckon he'll cash in. Clay brought him along to the ranch, him and young Scott"—Sam's eyes twinkled—"Carmel's got Scott all tucked away in bed now and is playing nurse to him. Reckon he feels right pert by now—"

"Oh," said the girl, relieved; "oh," she repeated; "I'm so glad! I've been hoping so much that things would work out for Carmel and Oliver. I never could believe he was really crooked!" Her tone was suddenly curious. "What was the—the important news he wanted to tell me?"

"It explains a heap of things," chuckled Sam. "Seems the railroad is building into San Luis. Sandell's scheme was to get control of the Valley of the Kings before the news leaked out—needed the water rights for colonizing—planned to cut up the whole range into little farms—"

A wrathful snort from Seth interrupted him, "Cut up the range, huh?" he rasped; "the onery money-grubbin' critter! I'll be doing some cuttin' my own self. I'll cut a rope jest long enough to swing him clean off'n his mangy toes!"

"Such talk ain't fittin' for a gal's ears," reproved his partner.

"Don't you go argufying with me, mister," fumed the irascible Seth. "You know dang well you aim to pull on that there rope."

"Clay went off afore Scott spilled the news, or I should say afore Carmel could think to tell us," continued Sam, ignoring his partner's retort. He hesitated, eyed Shirley from under shaggy white brows. "Carmel was some upset," he finished cautiously.

"She would be," agreed Shirley. "Poor Carmel—"

Sam took a deep breath.

"It weren't Scott that upset her," he went on sorrowfully, " 'twas something else that happened; something that's going to make you feel real bad—"

She gave him a wild look. No wonder Clay had told her she was needed at the house!

"Old Miguel got some excited," plunged Sam. He saw by the look in her eyes that she understood, went to her quickly. "A good hombre, Miguel Cota," he told her gently, "was with us when we first come to the Valley of the Kings—and he was allus a real man. You needn't be sorry, lass . . . you needn't cry—too much—"

"I—I can't help it," sobbed the girl, "I—I—"

She turned blindly to the door, saw Maria through her tears, pausing in the entrance. With a choking little cry she ran to the old housekeeper and took her into her arms.

CHAPTER XX
SHIRLEY RIDES ALONE

The hard glitter had gone from the black eyes of Chico Lopez; they were softly pleading, imploring, decidedly worried, Maria Cota observed with some pity. She bent over the wounded young outlaw attentively, wondering if he wanted to speak—to tell her something.

Maria was not one to shirk the daily round of duty, despite her sudden bereavement. Life, she knew, must go on, as always; and she must continue to do the things she had done for so many years. It was her business to keep the domestic wheels of the Box B ranch turning smoothly. Miss Shirley had other, more serious matters on her young shoulders; and Carmel—well, one could not expect much from Carmel now that she had her lawyer man to nurse back to health and strength. The good God did things in a strange way, sometimes, Maria reflected, but she was certain His way was always the best way. A tender smile warmed her brown old face. Miss Shirley knew now, the truth about Clay Brant; she had never seen such a change in a girl. Despite the crowding anxieties the girl had bloomed overnight. Of course she had wept for

Miguel Cota; but then, life must go on, always on, Maria told herself not unsadly. Her thoughts suddenly fixed upon the wounded man. He was looking at her so imploringly; trying to tell her something.

"What is it, *amigo*?" she questioned gently in Spanish.

His lips formed the words—*Clay Brant*. Maria shook her head. "The Senor Brant is not here at the ranch, *amigo*. The senor has gone into the mountains." She watched the swarthy face attentively; again the lips moved. "The Senor Hally?" she echoed, "you wish to speak to him? *Si* . . . I shall get him—quickly—" She went out of the room; and very soon was back with Sam Hally, and Seth—and Shirley. Wisely, she had brought them all. One never knew what might happen—when a man lay dying and desired to relieve his mind.

"What is it, son?" Sam's tone was kindly, without enmity.

Chico seemed to draw on his waning strength; his voice came distinctly. "I have not lived a good life," he said in Spanish, "I have been like a dog that bites the hand of one who has been a good and kind friend. I am sorry—"

"That's man talk, Chico," approved the big cowman heartily.

"—I bit the hand of a good friend," continued the dying outlaw, "I tried to kill Clay Brant and he forgave me—treated me like a brother—carried me in his arms to this bed and ordered that I should have a chance to live. For his goodness and kindness I must tell him something he does not know. He is in great danger . . . Sandell—the others—have found out that he is Clay Brant and plan to kill him. He does not suspect they know . . . he may walk blindly into a death-trap—" Chico's voice was scarcely a whisper. "Tell him," he gasped, "and tell him that I tried to—to warn him at the gate . . . but my tongue would not move—"

He was suddenly silent, although he still breathed, they saw. Shirley clutched Sam's arm. Her face was pale, her eyes filled with fear.

"He'll—he'll be killed!" she moaned; "Clay will be killed, unless we can do something to warn him . . . He doesn't know, you see—he doesn't know they have found out—"

The faces of the two old HM men were set in grim lines. "Come on, feller," Sam growled tersely; "we're riding Clay's trail—and riding now—" He went swiftly out of the room and was followed by his partner.

Shirley started to run after them, was halted by a whispered word from Maria. "Wait," cautioned the old woman; she gestured at the bed; "the man still lives . . . see . . . he tries to speak. . . . something important—I can tell by his eyes."

Tensely they watched the swarthy face on the

white pillow, watched and waited while the gray lips struggled to form the words Chico wanted to utter. Shirley clung to Maria's hand, suspense, impatience, tearing at her heart. From the corral yard drifted the rapid beat of horses' hoofs; Sam and Seth were riding away on their search for Clay.

Suddenly Chico was speaking again, very slowly, faintly. "I . . . heard you . . . Senorita . . . you cannot warn Clay because you do not know where to find him . . . you do not know where to look for the Bottle Neck." His eyes closed.

Shirley and Maria exchanged dismayed looks. Chico's voice came again, stronger now, as though he were calling upon the last spark of life in him. "I . . . know . . . where the Bottle Neck is . . . Listen—" He raised up from the pillow, spoke quickly, described the trail that led to the rustlers' secret entrance to the Painted Valley.

"*Sabe usted?*" he finished in a faint whisper.

"I could find it in the dark," Shirley assured him. She stooped and clasped his hand. "Thank you, Chico—" She smiled into the wide-open eyes. An answering smile appeared on Chico's face—a look of peace—his head relaxed on the pillow.

"Come," said Maria Cota, quietly, "it is done—for him—" She took the girl out, softly closed the bedroom door.

Outside, in the patio garden, life smiled gaily,

282

sparkled merrily in the golden glow of early dawn; humming birds hovered and darted like tiny winged jewels in perfumed jasmine and honeysuckle; and roses, redolent and fresh with morning dew sent out fragrant incense to the new day. Shirley hurried down the wide old corridor to her own room, oblivious of the beauty and charm of the garden she loved. One thought only was in her mind—could be in her mind. Sam and Seth would not know where to find Clay Brant, they had ridden away on a blind trail; it was left to herself to carry the warning to Clay. She tore off her dress, hurriedly threw on riding clothes and boots.

"Where are you going?" demanded Maria, standing suddenly in the open doorway. Alarm sprang to her eyes as she saw the riding clothes and sensed the girl's purpose.

"I'm going to the Bottle Neck." Shirley's tone forbade argument. Maria could only shake her head, watch in silent dismay as the girl ran across the patio to the yard gate. In a moment she was lost from view. Maria drooped helplessly against the bedroom door, lips moving in a prayer; and presently, she heard the quick beat of hoofs. She hurried to the gate in time to catch a glimpse of the girl spurring away.

"*Madre de Dios*," muttered the old woman unhappily; "it is a wild thing for her to do!" and then, something like pride, admiration, filled

Maria's eyes. "A brave thing, too," she reflected. "Paula's child could do no less."

Comforted by the thought, Maria turned to make her way back to the house. The rattle of wheels halted her; she looked quickly over her shoulder. A buckboard, drawn by two horses on the dead run, was whirling into the yard. Maria stared with startled eyes. What new trouble was this that had come to add to the woes of the old ranch? She flung through the gate, hastened with panting breath and soft pad of slippered feet along the path that led to the corrals, amazement filling her as she saw that the driver was old Pop Daly. Squeezed into the single seat with him were his granddaughter, Nora, and the rotund Dr. Kirk. The latter sprang out, hurried to meet the breathless housekeeper.

"How is he?" he demanded, "how's young Scott? Not dead, I hope!"

"He is not," Maria answered a bit crossly, between gasps for breath. "He has a good doctor with him now," she added; "you can do her some good by giving her a chance to get the sleep she needs."

Dr. Kirk eyed her blankly for an instant, then broke into a chuckle. "Well, well, so little Carmel is playing nurse to the young man, eh?" The doctor chuckled again. "Very good—couldn't be better. Just the same I'll take a look at him." He smiled at Pop's pretty granddaughter. "Nora—it

284

appears you are not really needed, but now you are here we might as well give Carmel a rest. Come along, my dear!" He hastened down the path with his bag.

Nora paused to speak to the old housekeeper. "We heard the news of the shooting late last night," she hurriedly explained. "Don't you worry, Mrs. Cota . . . I'll stay and help as long as you and Carmel need me. A lot of exciting things have happened in town. Grandpa will tell you—" She started to run after the doctor, came to a standstill. "Why—here's Juan!" she exclaimed.

Followed by a half score cowboys the cattle boss dashed into the yard. He swung from his saddle, pleasure and astonishment in the look he gave Pop Daly's granddaughter.

"*Buenas dias*," he saluted. Juan broke off, alarm in his handsome eyes as Maria flung herself into his dusty arms. "*Madre mia!*"

"Juan . . . my son . . . your father . . . last night—" Maria's voice broke in a sob.

"*Madre mia!*" repeated the burly ranch foreman, understanding. He held her to him, looked at Nora with stricken eyes. The girl put a comforting arm around the quietly weeping mother.

"I'll stay with you; I'll do anything to help you, Mrs. Cota," she again assured Maria. "I—I told you I would—" Nora felt Juan's hand close over hers; she clung to it, gave him a look in which was understanding, affection, sympathy—a promise.

Maria Cota dabbed at her eyes, struggled for composure. "There is more to tell you," she said, with a return of her quiet dignity. "Our Senorita has ridden alone into the mountains, the Porcupine, to warn the Senor Clay that his life is in danger. You must follow her at once, Juan— you and your men—"

The cattle boss muttered a stifled exclamation, darted a look at the clustered cowboys silently watching the scene. "Horses!" he bellowed. "Queek! fresh horses! We ride *muy pronto!*"

Pop Daly was climbing stiffly from the buckboard. "Before ye ride there's a bit o' news ye must know," he croaked to Juan. "Sandell's gittin' ready to beat it across the border."

Juan and his mother stared at him incredulously—with growing excitement.

Pop's voice rose to a shrill cackle of triumph, "San Luis'll be a dacent place ag'in—the ould town I started with me two freight waggins the time thim scalp-huntin' Apaches made away with me mules." Pop wagged his white head. " 'Tis the truth," he chuckled, "Brimms' last words to Doc Kirk and mesilf before he wint to hell from lead poisonin'. Vin Sarge and his pack o' killers has quit Sandell . . . they're on the run for their hideout, Brimms said . . . some place called Painted Valley—"

An anguished cry burst from Maria Cota. "My lamb!" she moaned in Spanish, "my little senorita—it is to the Painted Valley she has ridden—to the place called Bottle Neck, the secret entrance. She will ride straight into their wicked hands, my poor senorita!"

Juan's big voice filled the yard. "The horses!" he bellowed again to the *vaqueros*. "The fresh horses . . . We ride for the life of our senorita—"

Jaded cow ponies come to life, reared, plunged, went thundering in a cloud of dust toward the horse corral as spurs drove into sweaty sides. Juan turned to his frightened, weeping mother.

"Come, *Madre mia*," he said gently, in their native tongue, "we shall take you back to the house, Nora—and I."

They moved slowly toward the patio gate, Nora and Juan, the old mother between them, supported by their strong, loving young arms. Pop Daly watched them thoughtfully for a minute, nodded as though entirely content with what his shrewd old eyes told him.

" 'Tis a good husband he'll make for the lass," he muttered as he limped back to the buckboard to attend to his weary team of horses.

CHAPTER XXI
BEFORE THE DAWN

Morton Sandell paced restlessly up and down the length of his luxurious room. He moved with the short jerky steps of one in the relentless grip of an ungovernable fear—a devastating rage that had torn to shreds his last vestige of self-control.

The passing hours had stripped him of his sleekness, his suavity, his mask of geniality; there was no smile on the heavy beefy face, no kindly twinkle in the piggy bloodshot eyes; there was a wildness in his manner, the ferocity of a savage boar at bay.

Chico's assertion that Texas Jack was Clay Brant had appalled them all. The fame of the young Cimarron cattleman as the nemesis of cattle thieves and border bad men was well founded. Clay Brant always followed to the end of the trail; there was no shaking him off. Adding graver menace to his presence in the Valley of the Kings was the fact that he owned a half interest in the Box B ranch—had a personal motive in hunting down and destroying the despoilers of the ranch, the murderers of Shirley Benson's father. Already men had paid with their lives for their part in the crimes. The roll call had mounted with stunning swiftness: Whitey Joe, Tulsa Jones, Pecos, Red Hansen, Bat Brimms, Wes Droon, Chico Lopez. The startling story from Curly Smith's ashen lips of Droon's fall to death from the Devil's Pitchfork had only one interpretation. Sarge had sent Droon to the Perdido, to spy on Texas Jack—and the latter had proved to be Clay Brant. The scene of the death was evidence that Clay had located the rustlers' hidden valley in the Porcupine.

Increasing the dismay of Sandell and his accomplices was the fiasco of the attempt to assassinate Oliver Scott; the latter's escape, the death of the four would-be murderers. The dying Brimms was certain that Chico Lopez had gone down under the deadly guns of Clay Brant.

From the moment of Brimms' return they all knew the game was up. Vin Sarge, Curly Smith, the others, had fled to the Painted Valley, determined to make a desperate attempt to run the stolen cattle across the border. There was one hope for them. Clay would be unaware that Chico Lopez had betrayed his identity; he might unsuspectingly rejoin his late Bar 7 companions for the purpose of gaining further information about the gang—information that would put a rope around Morton Sandell's neck. The banker's teeth showed in a savage grin. Vin Sarge wouldn't waste time adding Brant's name to the death roll; Brant wouldn't last long in that company—not any longer than it took them to empty their guns into him.

Sandell halted his restless pacing as he considered the possibilities of Clay unsuspectingly walking into such a trap. He thrust the notion aside. Brant was too wise. No chance for escape in *that* idea. It was immediate flight—a dash for the border—or the hangman's noose. It was lucky he had cached that fifty thousand in the Painted Valley. Not even Vin Sarge knew he had that money hidden in a cave near the Bottle Neck.

Sandell grinned again. Painted Valley was less than five miles from the border. It would be worth the risk to recover the hidden fifty thousand on his way to the safety he would find in Mexico. Treasury gold notes—easily carried.

He looked at the pair of bags lying on the floor. Another fifty thousand or more in those bags, some of the money in gold. He would have plenty for a fresh start. There were always opportunities for a man with brains—even in Old Mexico.

The large Navajo blanket, draped on the wall behind him, shifted slightly, revealing the glittering eyes of Frenchy Larue. Inch by inch the gaudy drape slid back—the saloon man glided in from the stairs that led down to Sandell's secret office in the rear of the Red Front bar. There was a curious expression in Frenchy's black eyes as he watched the other man, the look of a cat about to pounce upon an unsuspecting rat; trim black mustache lifted, exposed white teeth in a derisive smile.

It may have been the faint swish of the heavy drape, or pure animal instinct, that warned Sandell. Slowly he turned his head, stared with bulging, startled eyes at his visitor.

Frenchy drew nearer, let the drape fall back into place.

"You ver' surprise, eh, my frien'?" he said softly, "you no expec' me tonight—or, I should say, thees morning"—he gestured at the street windows faintly luminous with approaching dawn—"the sun, she soon come?"

Sandell slowly turned and faced him.

"Thought you'd gone with the rest of them, Frenchy," he said in a strangled voice; "thought you'd beat it with Vin—was in on the play to run the cows across the border."

The saloon man's smile was scornful. "No, no," he purred. "I 'ave no care for go weeth the cow . . . too mooch trouble—ze cow." His hard glance rested for a moment on the pair of fat bags. "I 'ave more good plan for me—"

"What do you mean, Frenchy?" Sandell's tone was uneasy; his own glance darted a look at his bags. He attempted to bluster. "I don't like the way you sneaked in. When did you learn about those stairs?"

"I 'ave know ze secret ver' long time," smiled the French-Canadian. "I know somet'ing else, my clever frien' . . . I know you 'ave mooch money in ze bank, which ees why I no go to Painted Valley for ze cow." His glance went again to the bags. "I 'ave watch you all night," he went on smoothly; "I see you in ze bank a leetle while ago—see you get ze money—"

"Planning to rob me, is that it, Frenchy?"

The saloon man laughed mockingly.

"What ees stolen once can be stolen twice, eh?" He shrugged his shoulders and with the movement his long-bladed knife slid into the palm of his hand. "I take ze money you 'ave in ze bag," he said in his purring voice; "I am in beeg 'urry—before ze sun come I mus' be long way from here—on ze way to my own lan'." He smiled wolfishly. "Do not try prevent me, my frien'; it will be ver' bad for you—"

Sandell's face was the color of dirty tallow. He knew the deadly work French Larue could do with that glittering blade; he knew he would have small chance to reach for the little derringer in his side pocket before the knife would be in his throat.

"You—you crook!" he croaked, "you—devil! You're nothing but a plain thief!"

"That ees nize talk—from you, my frien'." The saloon man's laugh was amused. He balanced the knife in his palm significantly and the smile left his face. "Stand back!" he suddenly snarled, "stand back—way back—by ze wall—"

Sandell obeyed sullenly; the movement for a moment concealed the right-hand pocket of his coat; his fingers closed over the derringer.

Cupidity, his eagerness to get the bags and be on his way, his utter contempt for one whom he regarded as an arrant coward, rendered Frenchy Larue careless for a fatal instant. As he stooped toward the bags the little gun in his victim's pocket exploded; Frenchy pitched forward on his face, lay shuddering across the treasure bags. Sandell whipped the smoking derringer from his pocket and stepping close, deliberately sent a second bullet through the dying man's head.

The murderer staggered back, smoking gun clenched in his hand, hate, triumph, distorting his face. Suddenly he began to tremble; the last few moments had left him undone; he stared wildly at the gun in his shaking hand, an insane light in his eyes, an ugly twisted smile on his lips. It was not the first time he had made use of the little derringer. He had told Frenchy so, one night not so long ago, the night Clay Brant had first come to town. And now Frenchy knew that he had spoken the truth—the *truth!*

With an oath Sandell let the weapon slip from his trembling fingers and staggered to the desk. There was a bottle of whisky in a drawer; a big drink would straighten him up—stop the ague that was shaking him like a leaf. He jerked out the drawer, drank long and deeply from the bottle, drank until he gasped and choked.

The trembling fit left him; color flowed back into his face.

Presently he put on his expensive wide-brimmed Stetson, returned the fallen derringer to his pocket and coolly pulled the dead man from the bags. He picked them up, one in each hand, and went softly down the stairs to the street.

The town still slumbered, he saw with satisfaction. Before the dawn was red above the horizon he would be far on his way to the Painted Valley. He went quickly into the alley, where his horse was waiting.

CHAPTER XXII
THE BOTTLE NECK

Clay glanced appraisingly at the sun. It was all of ten o'clock he realized uneasily, and the secret of the Bottle Neck still a baffling mystery. For hours he had combed the maze of canyons and gullies for the hidden entrance to the Painted Valley.

He reined the stallion and swung down; Midnight needed a few minutes breathing spell and his own legs a little rest from the saddle. Horse and man had been on the go since the crack of dawn, after a brief camp in the Burro flats where there was good grass and water for the horse. Clay had managed to get a couple of hours sleep and eat the sandwiches he had provided from the kitchen larder.

He made and lit a cigarette, moody gaze studying his rugged surroundings. Somewhere in this labyrinth of hills was the portal to the little valley he had viewed from the heights of the Devil's Pitchfork.

His gaze followed the course of the creek, observed that the stream emerged from the mouth of a narrow gorge about a mile directly northwest. It seemed a waste of time to explore

295

there. The canyon ran in the wrong direction, would take him miles from the valley, which he knew lay to the east.

Clay's eyes were suddenly thoughtful. He was using the wrong method to solve the riddle of the Bottle Neck. There would be no difficulty in finding the way into the Painted Valley if the approach were obvious. He must abandon the probable and try the improbable. The little gorge from which tumbled the waters of the creek *was an improbability.*

Clay snubbed his cigarette and hurried to the horse.

He reached the mouth of the canyon, or gorge, and found that the stream ran directly under the sheer cliffs on his side of the creek.

He returned to the shallows and forded to the opposite bank.

His hunch was right.

Clay reined the black horse and stared with elated eyes at the trail sweeping from the mouth of the canyon and bending sharply to the left around the bluffs, away from the creek.

He pushed on. No matter that the gorge ran due northwest away from the valley, he knew there would be an explanation.

The high hills closed in on him. The sun must reach its zenith before its rays could penetrate the narrow high-walled canyon; he rode in gloom, in silence save for the roar of the rushing brawly stream on the right, the sharp click of Midnight's iron hoofs against the stones.

The cliffs drew apart, forming a tiny oblong meadow; the stream widened and ceased its noisy rush. Clay's interested eyes studied the scene. The improbable road had brought him to his goal.

Another narrow gorge, little more than a high-walled gully, branched into the main canyon from the right. The strip of oblong meadow was the bottle—the steep-walled narrow gully, the neck of the bottle.

He forded the creek a second time and rode toward the gully. It was really a chasm, splitting through the mountain ridge, an ancient mountain bed of a torrent that once had emptied into the Painted Valley, fed by the waters of a lake no longer existent, that now was a bit of pretty meadow land in the heart of the hills.

Midnight took the descent in a swinging stride, and suddenly they were through the Bottle Neck and in the bright sunlight—in the Painted Valley.

Save for the browsing cattle, a faint wisp of smoke from the log house, there was no sign of life. Clay was not surprised. The cook was probably the only man left in the valley. Vin Sarge would have taken every available man for the raid at Cottonwood Crossing. By now the stolen cattle would be well on their way to the rustlers' stronghold.

Smiling grimly, Clay turned the black's head

back to the Bottle Neck. He had a rendezvous with Sam Hally and the boys of their combined outfits. They would soon have Vin Sarge and his ruffians like rats in a trap. He little dreamed that swiftly-moving events had entirely altered the picture.

The first suspicion of disrupted plans came with startling, almost fatal abruptness. Midnight's nervously pricking ears gave the first inkling of danger. He knew the meaning of those uneasy ears, and sent the black soaring to the cover of a dense clump of elders.

He could hear them plainly, now, the clatter of shod hoofs, the jingle of spurs, men's voices; and presently they swung into view around the bluffs, eight horsemen, riding two abreast, with Vin Sarge and Curly Smith heading the column.

They surged past at a rapid gait, scowling-eyed, hard-faced men, and vanished into the gloom of the gorge.

Clay drew a long breath, conscious of a cold prickly feeling. Death had hovered unpleasantly close for a moment.

He rode on his way, puzzling over the unexpected encounter.

Only Sam and Seth were waiting at the appointed place in the Burro flats, sitting dejectedly on the trunk of a fallen tree. Clay wondered at the vast relief in their faces.

He swung from his saddle.

"What's happened?" he asked curtly.

"Plenty," growled Sam. He gave Clay a laconic account of the early morning events at the ranch. "Soon as Chico told us the gang had you spotted for Clay Brant we hopped our saddles and lit out to find you," he finished. "We're sure glad to see you, son."

"What about the trail herd?" Clay wanted to know.

"Don't know nothing about the cows," Seth McGee grumbled "Our bronc's legs is all wore out chasing you round these hills since sun-up," he grinned. "Only done it 'cause Shirley went plumb crazy when Chico told us Sandell's outfit knew who you was."

His big partner nodded solemn confirmation.

"Never saw a gal so plumb hysterical as Shirley was when she figgered you was due for a dose of lead poisoning," he drawled.

Clay reddened, hastened to bring the conversation back to immediate problems.

"I've got some dope on the trail herd, even if you fellers haven't," he said; "there's been no raid. Something has happened to upset their plans."

Sam nodded.

"Mebbe the trail herd wasn't at Cottonwood Crossing like we figgered. Might be a day or two late," he surmised.

"I ran into Vin Sarge and his outfit," Clay went

on, "heading for the Bottle Neck, less than an hour ago."

He told them briefly of his own morning's work—his narrow escape from the outlaws.

Seth McGee's hard black eyes glittered; he got up from the log and started briskly for his horse.

"Where do you think you're going?" called the surprised Clay.

Sam chuckled softly. His partner's reactions were an old story with him.

"I'm hitting the trail for that there Bottle Neck," answered the little cowman. "Sure aim to put a cork in that there bottle—" He patted a low-slung .45.

"Too big a job for one man," demurred Clay.

"There's three of us," the dour Seth reminded thinly.

"We'll need more lead than our guns can throw," insisted the young man. "No sense making hash out of the job. One of us must head back for the ranch and get Juan's outfit."

"You're elected to carry the message, mister," observed Seth's partner gravely.

"You're plumb crazy!" retorted the little HM man indignantly. "I'm ridin' with Clay to the Bottle Neck."

Clay decided the argument.

"We'll all ride to the little gorge I told you about," he said. "If you two go alone you'd waste hours trying to find the place. When we get to the gorge we can toss a coin to see which one of us rides to the ranch. The other two go on to the Bottle Neck and do the best they can to be a cork. Reckon two of us can keep 'em bottled up until the boys come."

The two partners nodded grim assent.

Horses shuffling along at a fast running-walk, the three men rode in silence up the rough trail.

It was Seth who first broke into speech.

"Allus was unlucky tossing coins," he muttered glumly.

"Mebbe your luck'll turn this time," bantered his big partner, "mebbe you'll win the toss and git to ride to the ranch—" he grinned.

"Dang you!" shrilled the enraged Seth, "that's just what I *don't* want to do!"

Steadily, swiftly, they flowed up the twisting trail; and as they rode, Clay's thoughts returned again and again to the girl who his two companions asserted was worried because she thought his life was in peril. A smile softened the grim set of his lips.

They came to the creek and splashed across the shallows to the left bank.

Clay reined his horse.

"Might as well decide here which one of us goes to the ranch," he said. He gestured upstream. "There's the gorge leading to the Bottle Neck. You couldn't miss the trail now." He fished in his pocket for a coin.

Sam spoke softly.

"Not so fast, Clay. There's a bunch of riders coming round that bluff yonder. What do you make of 'em?"

Clay reached quickly for his glasses.

"Juan Cota!" he exclaimed, "Juan—and his outfit. Wonder what's he doing out here?"

The three horses leaped forward to the touch of spurs.

The two groups came together at the mouth of the canyon. The Box B outfit's jaded, sweat-lathered horses told of a furious ride. Juan threw Clay an anguished look.

"Ah, Senor!" he exclaimed wildly, "have you seen her? Have you seen our little Senorita?"

Clay went suddenly pale.

"Seen who?" he demanded roughly.

"Shirley," the foreman's voice was husky, "Chico told her the way to the Bottle Neck; she thought to find you—warn you. The trail herd has not reached the Cottonwood Crossing so we returned to the ranch and find the Senorita gone."

They looked at him with growing dismay.

"Are you sure the gal came up this trail, Juan?"

It was Sam who asked the question. Clay seemed paralyzed.

The Box B foreman nodded vehemently.

"We followed as soon as we heard the news! She must be in front of us, or we would have met her—overtaken her! *Dios*! It is terrible!"

There was a startled snort from the black stallion as Clay's spurs sank in; he reared, pawed the air, went plunging into the gloom of the gorge.

"Come on, you rannihans!" shrilled Seth, "pour your leather—"

His own horse leaped to the gouge of spurs, the lash of swinging quirt.

The others strung out behind him—lofty cliffs flung back the thunder of drumming hoofs.

CHAPTER XIII
MIDNIGHT LOOKS THE OTHER WAY

Shirley's one shred of comfort was the thought of Clay Brant. Her own folly had placed her in jeopardy. She might have known that Clay was too clever to walk into any trap. What the outcome would be she dare not even contemplate. She forced herself to think only of Clay Brant; harm would not touch her while he lived. She clung to the thought.

Her face pale, the girl sat limply on an up-ended box by the cabin door, listening mutely while the men wrangled over her fate. She was sure that Morton Sandell was quite insane. There was a terrifying wildness in his bloodshot eyes. Chills ran down her spine every time he glanced at her. It was plain that Vin Sarge himself thought something was wrong with the man.

"You're crazy as a loon," the big rustler grumbled in his deep voice; "bringin' the gal into the valley was loco play." He scowled at Shirley. "Sandell says he nabbed you snoopin' round the Bottle Neck. What was you snoopin' round the Bottle Neck for, Miss Benson?"

"Perhaps I was looking for my stolen cattle," she retorted coolly.

Sarge glared at the other man.

"See what you done!" he growled angrily. "Like as not we'll have Clay Brant and his crowd down on us afore we can get the cows away." The rustler's glance went uneasily to the bawling herd being hurried toward the Bottle Neck, urged on by the shrill yips of the anxious riders.

"You've no brains!" yelped Sandell, "we've got an ace card in this girl, you fool! Brant nor anybody'll dare do a thing while we've got her."

"Fool your own self," growled Sarge. "The game's up! I don't aim to buck that Brant hombre. All I'm thinkin' of right now is to git south of the border with a whole skin and take the cows with me. Less than five miles to the border," he added. "You're plumb loco if you don't make dust coverin' them five miles awful fast."

"We can use her for a lure—for bait." Sandell's smile was cunning, "We can send word we'll exchange the girl for Brant. He's just the sort of young fool to hop into our pan—to save a girl—"

Shirley was on her feet, fists clenched, eyes flashing.

"You—you coward!" she stormed; "you'll do no such thing. I won't let you!"

"You have nothing to say about it, my dear." He leered at her, chuckled insanely.

Shirley sank back on the box, closed her eyes.

She felt horribly dizzy, seemed to be in a whirl. She hoped she was not going to faint. Vin Sarge's rough tones beat at her ears dully.

"You're loco," she heard the big man say contemptuously. "I may be a lot of things, includin' cow-thief and train-bandit, but I ain't your kind of skunk. I ain't a kidnaper and I don't use gals in my work."

The bawls of the cattle, the shrill cries of the urging rustlers, drew nearer. The herd was approaching the Bottle Neck.

Sarge watched the straggling lines of cattle for a moment.

"I'm done talkin'," he announced. "You can do what you've a mind to, Mort, but me and the boys is on our way to the border." His glance went to the cook, watching the scene from the open door of the cabin, a grin on his unshaven face. "Git your chuck fixed up, feller. We'll be out of here inside half an hour—"

Shirley came to her feet again.

"Please!" she gasped, "please don't leave me alone with this mad man . . . please take me with you . . . you can have the cows . . . I'll give them to you—only don't leave me with—him—" She clutched his shirt sleeve frantically.

The big rustler shook her off impatiently.

"Ain't putting my neck in a noose for no gal," he gruffly refused; "your own fault for snoopin' round where you'd no bus'ness." He swung quickly to his saddle and spurred away.

She started to run after him; Sandell's arm blocked her.

"Sit down!"

The threat in his voice, the wild gleam in the red-rimmed piggy eyes, terrified Shirley. She obeyed, stared at him with mounting horror.

Sandell had come upon her so suddenly in the Bottle Neck; there had been no opportunity to elude him.

Noises came from the cabin, the rattle of pots on the stove. Another sound came to the girl's ears. The quick beat of galloping hoofs rising above the deep diapason notes from the massing lines of cattle.

She looked at Sandell, saw that he had not caught the sound. He was eyeing her with a queer smile, a speculative smile.

"You saw those two bags I hid in the Bottle Neck?" he asked suddenly.

Shirley nodded.

"I wish I'd told Sarge about them," she said fiercely. "I forgot—"

"There is fifty thousand in those bags," he informed her. He smiled cunningly. "Wasn't going to let Sarge know I had that money."

Shirley shrugged her shoulders indifferently, ears straining for the sound of those galloping hoofs.

"I've another fifty thousand—hid in that little

cave, my dear," continued Sandell, still eyeing her with his curious, speculative smile.

She ignored him, kept her face averted so that he would not see the mounting terror in her eyes.

His insane laugh came again, sent prickles of horror through her. The man was mad—a maniac. Shirley closed her eyes, fought to keep herself calm. She did not want to faint now. . . .

Again she thought she heard that crescendo beat of distant hoofs.

"Clay! Clay! . . . I'm here—*here!*"

She sent out the message desperately . . . Sent it out on the wings of faith.

"When Sarge and his scoundrels are gone, we'll ride on our way, too, my dear."

Sandell's voice was thick, his utterance jerky.

"Only a few miles to Mexico," he chuckled, "less than five miles, Sarge said. Lots of things we can do in Mexico, eh, my dear?"

His mood changed, he was suddenly ugly, menacing.

"You little vixen, you caused all my trouble—brought me to ruin—and now you'll pay!"

Insane rage twisted his face into a mask of ferocity; he took a step toward her.

"You'll pay," he repeated thickly. "If I can't have the Valley of the Kings, I'll have its pretty mistress—"

Shirley scarcely heard him; she was listening tensely to something else—the staccato thunder of galloping hoofs echoing from the granite walls of the Bottle Neck.

The shrill cries of the rustlers changed to alarmed shouts. She could see them scattering to boulders and bushes, the herd forgotten. She sprang to her feet.

Sandell's ears now caught the tumult. He turned, stared stupidly.

The roar of hoofs drumming down the Bottle Neck came in gusty waves of sound. Shirley was unaware that she was suddenly screaming Clay's name.

Sandell leaped at her.

"Shut up!" he shouted savagely, "shut up!"

He dragged her to the cabin door. She fought him desperately, was helpless in his maddened grip. The cook ran out, a hairy, unkempt Swede.

"Hey!" he gabbled, "w'at you do?"

Sandell ignored him, dragged the struggling girl into the kitchen. The cook followed them, seized the madman's arm.

"Hey!" he repeated, "you leave her loose, you—"

Sandell turned on him, hurled him violently against the stove; there was a sickening thud of skull against iron as the stove overturned, spilling out red coals—flaming bits of fuel. The cook lay where he had fallen.

Shirley realized with horror that the man was dead.

The insane murderer glared around the kitchen, seeking some means of securing his frightened victim. His glance fell upon the storeroom door. Muttering incoherently he dragged the girl across the floor and pushed her into the room.

"I'll be back for you, soon," he promised excitedly; "must get my money from the Bottle Neck . . . Brant's in the Bottle Neck . . . he'll find it . . . Brant's clever—a devil . . . must hide my money where he won't find it." He grinned at her foolishly, pulled the door shut with a slam, turned the key, and ran out without a glance at the dead man lying close to the fallen stove.

Flames were already licking along the grease-soaked planks.

He hurried to his horse tied to a tree. A gun cracked as he hastily climbed into the saddle— the echoing distant report of a rifle. He looked across the valley—saw the Bottle Neck was spouting horsemen.

They came out with astonishing speed—like bullets from the mouth of a gun. Puffs of smoke clouded up from boulders and bushes where the rustlers had taken concealment. The oncoming riders scattered, sought cover where they could find it.

Sandell lashed his horse with his quirt, went tearing down the valley toward the Bottle Neck. One thought was in his disordered mind—his money! He must remove his money before Brant could find it.

Smoke curled from the cabin window, billowed through the open door as the flames hungrily fed upon the grease-soaked planks, took hold of the dry resinous log walls.

Guns crackled in the distance, rising sharply above the bellows of the excited herd milling not far from the mouth of the Bottle Neck. Clay's plan to merely hold the entrance to the valley and force the outlaws to surrender had gone to smash. Like Sandell he too had but one thought in his mind. Shirley was in peril—a captive of these desperadoes. Otherwise he would not have risked lives in so reckless a charge against the guns of Vin Sarge and his men. Already two of the Box B riders were down, their horses shot from under them.

Clay left the battle in the capable hands of Sam and Seth and spurred toward the cabin. A bullet whined viciously past his head. Again Vin Sarge fired and almost instantly followed the deep roar of Seth McGee's big Sharps' buffalo gun. Clay saw the rustler chief stagger from behind a bush and collapse like a bag of meal.

The burst of gunfire from the Box B contingent kept the remaining outlaws too busy to think further of Clay. Sam and Seth, seasoned veterans of range warfare, were using all their tricks to give him a chance to reach the log house.

A lone horseman rode furiously down the valley, circling around the restless milling cattle.

From his attire Clay saw that the rider was not a cowboy. The man was too far away for recognition. But Clay knew he could be none other than Morton Sandell, apparently making a desperate attempt to escape through the unguarded Bottle Neck. For an instant he was tempted to give chase. Something else he saw checked the impulse . . . Smoke was pouring from the windows and doors of the log house.

His face paled.

Fire! And Shirley, perhaps a prisoner there bound—helpless!

Clay's raking spurs sent the black horse hurtling like a thunderbolt up the valley.

Shirley was completely a prisoner in the dark little storeroom. The one small window set in the thick log walls had been tightly boarded up, and the lock on the heavy door was too strong for her to force. The sinister sound of the flames, the smoke, drove her frantic with terror and despair. She knew by the faint crackling of gunfire that a battle was being fought down in the valley.

The thought of being burned alive appalled her.

Already the inner walls were too hot to touch. She shuddered away to the outer logs, crouched under the window she could not open.

The smoke was stifling. She pressed closer to the log wall, suddenly spied a tiny chink. She put her lips to the opening, sucked in a mouthful of air, only to gasp and choke. There was no fresh, clean air, only smoke, everywhere.

The gunfire was lessening. She pressed an ear to the chink, suddenly heard the thudding beat of hoofs nearing the cabin.

Shirley began to scream. And again the name she called was Clay's name.

The pounding hoofs came close, suddenly ceased. She heard Clay's voice shouting that he was coming—shouting for her to hold on—that he was *coming to her!*

One wall was almost completely in flames as Clay rode up. His heart sang, leaped again as the girl's frantic call reached him. Almost before Midnight slid to a halt he was out of the saddle and running to the door.

One glance inside told him that she was not in the kitchen—was behind the locked door of the storeroom. His distraught glance saw the cook's ax by the woodpile. He seized it and rushed inside.

Agonizing moments . . . smoke . . . flames . . . blistering heat . . . the door open at last . . . Shirley in his arms . . . the fresh reviving air!

Brief moments—*big* moments!

Shirley was completely happy, the horror of the past hours forever blotted from memory. The man she loved had fought and conquered the death that had reached so terribly for her. And Clay was completely happy. He knew that the girl he loved better than life, loved him. Clinging arms, the look in her eyes as he bore her to safety, had told him as plainly as tongue ever could.

He put her down, drew her gently into his arms.

The black horse had followed them down to the creek. He took one interested look and discreetly sauntered on toward an inviting bunch of grass. Midnight was a gallant gentleman.

CHAPTER XXIV
TRAMPLING HOOVES

The restless milling of the gathered herd was increasing. The hurried round-up had created a nervous tension in no way soothed by the roar of rifles and six-guns. The cattle instinctively knew they had been gathered for a drive; the sight of Sandell riding at top speed into the Bottle Neck was a signal to follow. They were accustomed to follow a horseman when on the trail. Slowly the big herd got under way ... The movement grew to a brisk walk, a trot, then suddenly the thunderous explosion of the stampede as a stray rifle bullet slashed the flank of a big steer. Tails up, the massed thousands boiled down on the Bottle Neck.

Sandell had just dismounted near his cache when the roar of the stampede stunned his ears. Before he understood what had happened, his horse was in startled flight.

Still Sandell failed to realize his danger. He might have taken refuge in the little cave where he had cached his treasure; instead he ran in futile pursuit of the runaway horse.

A sea of horns suddenly appeared in the mouth of the Bottle Neck, a foaming tide of white faces, the earth trembled with the thunder of their coming.

Too late, Sandell realized the death avalanching upon him.

He ran, screaming, up the narrow passage of the Bottle Neck.

CHAPTER XXV
THE DAY'S WORK DONE

Roan horse and bay, jogged along sedately, spur chains jingled, saddle-leathers squeaked. Lights and shadows of eventide on the mountains—two old men contentedly homeward bound.

Seth McGee broke the silence.

"Seems like we been gone from the ranch a awful long time, Sam. Sure will be good to be back in the Sinks ag'in."

"Sure will, Seth," rumbled his big partner, "sure will, feller. Ain't no place like home," he added with conviction.

Instinctively their eyes sought the towering crags of old El Toro, guardian peak of the Spanish Sinks.

"Looks awful pretty, Sam," muttered Seth, "sort of like a sunset crown he puts on—all rose and pink—and, you know what I mean, same color as the flowers on that tree in Shirley's garden—"

"Lilac," Sam informed him.

He nodded appreciatively.

"Yes, feller, sure is pretty—that old mountain."

They rode on, each busy with his thoughts. Seth spoke again.

"Reckon cow-stealing sure has gone plumb out of style in this country for a spell, Sam."

The big HM man nodded.

"Plumb out of style," he agreed contentedly.

As if by mutual consent they reined their horses and gazed back at the wide valley they were leaving behind them.

"The Valley of the Kings," old Sam Hally murmured softly. "Been a heap of years since we first rode down between them hills, Seth."

Silence held them while memories leaped down the long lane to the day when Bill Brant had given the name of *El Valle de los Reyes* to the home of the new Box B ranch.

Sam suddenly heaved a deep sigh, fumbled in a pocket and drew out a folded age-yellowed paper.

"What you aim to do with that old deed of Bill Brant's?" queried his partner curiously.

For answer Sam solemnly tore the paper into tiny pieces.

"Ain't no sense keeping it anymore," he said significantly.

"Shirley's asked me to the wedding," Seth announced pridefully.

"Clay promised to come and git our scalps if we don't show up at his wedding!" chuckled Sam.

"We done promised Carmel, and Nora, to be at their weddings, too," reminded his partner. He scowled in mock dismay. "Seems like we're due to wear the legs off'n our broncs going to weddings."

They gazed in silence down into the wide valley. The lowing of cattle pleasantly touched their ears. Two riders came into view, a man on a big black horse, a girl on a slim chestnut. They were riding very slowly, very close to each other.

"The Valley of the Kings," old Sam repeated softly.

"And two hearts that rule as one," surprisingly added dour little Seth McGee.

Their hands lifted in silent homage.

Roan horse and bay, jogged along sedately, spur chains jingled, saddle-leathers squeaked. Lights and shadows of eventide on the mountains—two old men contentedly homeward bound.

Center Point Large Print
600 Brooks Road / PO Box 1
Thorndike, ME 04986-0001 USA

(207) 568-3717

US & Canada:
1 800 929-9108
www.centerpointlargeprint.com